Also by Ana Huang

KINGS OF SIN SERIES

A SERIES OF INTERCONNECTED STANDALONES

King of Wrath

King of Pride

King of Greed

King of Sloth

TWISTED SERIES

A SERIES OF INTERCONNECTED STANDALONES

Twisted Love

Twisted Games

Twisted Hate

Twisted Lies

IF LOVE SERIES

If We Ever Meet Again (DUET BOOK 1)

If the Sun Never Sets (DUET BOOK 2)

If Love Had a Price (STANDALONE)

If We Were Perfect (STANDALONE)

if we ever meet again

ANA HUANG

Bloom books

Sourcebooks and the colophon are registered trademarks of
Sourcebooks. Bloom Books is a trademark of Sourcebooks.

Published by Bloom Books, an imprint of Sourcebooks
P.O. Box 4410, Naperville, Illinois 60567-4410
(630) 961-3900
sourcebooks.com

Originally self-published in 2020 by Ana Huang.

Cataloging-in-Publication data is on file with the Library of Congress.

Printed and bound in the United States of America.
WOZ 10 9 8 7 6 5 4 3 2 1

Playlist

"The Hardest Thing"—98 Degrees
"Chances"—Backstreet Boys
"Free"—Broods
"Skyfall"—Adele
"Crush"—3Gs
"Ocean Eyes"—Billie Eilish
"Like You'll Never See Me Again"—Alicia Keys
"Impossible"—Shontelle
"Moral of the Story"—Ashe
"I Never Told You"—Colbie Caillat
"Here's to the Night"—Eve 6
"Glad You Came"—The Wanted
"The Time (Dirty Bit)"—Black Eyed Peas
"See You Again"—Wiz Khalifa featuring Charlie Puth
"Don't Forget About Us"—Mariah Carey
"If We Ever Meet Again"—Timbaland featuring Katy Perry

Author's Note

This is book one in a duet. It's a full-length novel with no sudden cliff-hangers, but Blake and Farrah's story continues in book two, *If the Sun Never Sets*. HEA guaranteed in book two.

PROLOGUE

THIS WOULD KILL HIM.

It didn't matter how much he prepared; these next thirty minutes were going to rip his heart out and pulverize it.

It was inevitable.

"We haven't talked in a while." She sounded equal parts accusing and uncertain.

He didn't blame her. If he were in her shoes, he would've given up on himself a long time ago. She hadn't, which made him love her even more, but her loyalty made this conversation all the harder.

He rested his forearms on his knees and clasped his hands together. He focused on the grain of the wood floors beneath his feet until it swirled in front of his eyes.

"I've been busy."

"With?"

"Classes. Bar plans. That sort of thing."

"You'll have to do better than that."

His head snapped up at the sharpness in her voice. Looking at her turned out to be a mistake.

His chest squeezed at the sight of her face and the hurt swimming in those beautiful brown eyes. It'd been two weeks since they were last alone together, but it may as well have been two lifetimes.

His dread mixed with a strange exhilaration at being alone with her again, and it took all of his willpower not to sweep her up in his arms and never let go.

"Tell me the truth." Her voice softened. "You can trust me."

It would be so easy to pretend everything was fine. To give her the reassurances she wanted to hear and go back to the way things were.

He did trust her—but the truth would shatter her.

So he did the only thing he could do: he lied.

"I'm sorry." He wiped the emotion from his voice and funneled it into the pit of despair swirling in his stomach. Could she hear it? The panicked *thump-thump-thump* of his heart beating against his rib cage, screaming at him to stop? "I didn't want to do it like this, but I don't think we should see each other anymore."

Farrah's face paled. His heart beat louder.

"What?"

He swallowed hard. "It was fun while it lasted, but the year is almost over and I—I'm not interested anymore. I'm sorry."

Liar.

"You're lying."

He flinched. She knew him well. Too well.

"I'm not." He tried to sound nonchalant when all he wanted to do was fall to his knees and beg her not to leave him.

"You are. You said you loved me."

"I lied."

He couldn't look her in the eyes.

Her sharp inhale twisted his heart into a painful knot.

"You're full of shit." Her voice quavered. "Look at you, you're shaking."

He clenched his hands into fists and forced his body to still. "Farrah." *This was it.* His breath came out in short, shallow bursts. "I got back with my ex-girlfriend over the holidays. I didn't know how to tell you. I love her, and I made a mistake here, with us. But I'm trying to fix it."

Her sob ripped through the air. Tears stung his eyes, but he blinked them back.

"I'm sorry." Such a stupid, inadequate thing to say. He didn't know why he said it.

"Stop saying that!"

He flinched at the venom in her voice. She clutched her necklace with one hand, betrayal swirling in her eyes.

"It was all a lie then, this past year."

He dropped his gaze again.

"Why? Why did you pretend you cared? Was it some sick joke? You wanted to see whether I'd be gullible enough to fall for you? Well, congratu-fucking-lations. You won. Blake Ryan, the champion. Your father was right. You shouldn't have quit. No one plays the game better than you."

So this was what dying felt like. The pain, frozen inside like a lump of jagged black ice. The regret over words he couldn't say and promises he couldn't keep. The loneliness as he slid into dark, starless oblivion with no one left to save him.

"I'm sor—"

"If you say, 'I'm sorry,' one more time, I'll go to the kitchen, come back, and cut your balls off with a rusty knife. In fact, I may do that anyway. You're a fucking asshole. *I'm* sorry I wasted all this time on you, and I'm sorrier for your girlfriend. She deserves better."

God, he didn't want her to leave hating him. He wanted, more than anything, to tell her it was all a joke and that he was messing with her. He wanted to grab her and breathe in that orange-blossom-and-vanilla scent that drove him crazy, to confess how head over heels he was for her and to kiss her until they ran out of breath.

But he couldn't. The first part would be a lie, and the second... well, that was something he could never do again.

Farrah walked to the door. She paused in the doorway to look back at him. He expected her to hurl more venom at him—he deserved it. But she didn't. Instead, she turned away and closed the door behind her with a soft click that echoed in the silence like a gunshot.

His shoulders sagged. All the energy drained out of him.

It was over. There was no going back.

It was the right thing to do, and yet...

He squeezed his eyes shut, trying to block out the pain. He couldn't get the image of her face out of his mind, the one that said she thought so little of him she didn't want to waste any more energy yelling at him.

Because of her, he believed in love. The kind of knock-you-down, once-in-a-lifetime love he used to dismiss as a fantasy concocted by Hollywood to sell movies. It wasn't a fantasy. It was real. He felt it to his core.

If only they'd met sooner or under different circumstances...

He'd always been a practical person, and there was no use dwelling on what-ifs. Duty bound him to someone else, and sooner or later, Farrah would move on and meet a guy who could give her everything she deserved. Someone she would love, marry, and have kids with...

The last intact piece of his heart shattered at the thought. The shards pricked at his self-control until he could no longer hold back the tears. Huge silent sobs wracked his body for the first time since he was seven, when he'd fallen out of a tree and broken his leg. Only this time, the pain was a million times worse.

All their moments together flashed through his mind, and the boy who'd once sworn he would never cry over a girl...cried.

He cried because he'd hurt her.

He cried because it kept his mind off the desperate loneliness that weighed on his soul the moment she left.

Most of all, he cried for what they had, what they lost, and what they could never be.

CHAPTER 1

Eight months ago

"ONE CLASSIC MILK TEA AND ONE HONEY OOLONG milk tea with tapioca. Regular sugar, regular ice."

Farrah Lin slid a twenty yuan note across the counter toward the cashier, who smiled in recognition. Four days in Shanghai and Farrah was already a regular at the bubble tea joint by campus. She chose not to dwell on what that meant for her wallet and her waistline.

While the staff prepared her order, Farrah examined the menu. She knew *nai cha* (milk tea) and *xi gua* (watermelon). She recognized a few other Chinese characters but not enough to form a coherent phrase.

"Here you go." The cashier handed Farrah her drinks. "See you tomorrow!"

Farrah blushed. "Thanks."

Note to self: ask Olivia to make tomorrow's run.

Farrah stepped out of the tiny shop and walked back to

campus. The sun began its descent and bathed the city in a warm golden glow. Bicyclists and motorcyclists zipped by, battling with cars for space on the narrow side street. The delicious smells wafting from the restaurants Farrah passed mixed with the far-less-pleasant scents of garbage and construction dust. Street vendors called out to passersby, hawking everything from hats and scarves to books and DVDs.

Farrah made the mistake of making eye contact with one such vendor.

"*Mei nu!*" *Beautiful girl.* It'd be flattering if Farrah didn't know the hard sell that accompanied such a greeting. "Come, come." The elderly vendor beckoned her over. "Where are you from?" she asked in Mandarin.

Farrah hesitated before answering. "America." *Mei guo.* She dragged out the last syllable, unsure whether the admission would hurt or help.

"Ah, America. ABC," the vendor said knowingly. ABC: American-Born Chinese. Farrah had heard that a lot lately. "I have some great books in English." The vendor brandished a copy of *Eat, Pray, Love.* "Only twenty kuai!"

"Thanks, but I'm not interested."

"How about this one?" The woman picked out a Dan Brown novel. "I'll give you a deal. Three books for fifty kuai!"

Farrah didn't need new books, and fifty kuai (around $7 U.S.) seemed pricey for cheap reprints of old novels. But the vendor seemed like a nice old lady, and Farrah didn't have the energy to bargain with her.

She skimmed the English options and went straight for the romance: Jane Austen, Nicholas Sparks, JoJo Moyes.

Okay, Sparks and Moyes write love stories, not romance, but still.

Given the drought in Farrah's dating life, she'd settle for any kind of romantic relationship, even one that ended tragically. Well, maybe not with death, but with a breakup or something. Anything that proved the crazy, head-over-heels love you found in books and movies existed in real life.

After a disappointing freshman year filled with mediocre dates and fumbling stops at third base, Farrah was ready to give up on reality and live in fantasyland full-time.

"I'll take these." She set her drinks on the ground so she could pick up *Pride and Prejudice* (her personal favorite), *The Notebook*, and *Me Before You*. She'd read all of them already, but what the heck, a reread never hurt anybody.

Farrah paid the vendor, who beamed and gushed her thanks before turning her attention to the next passerby.

"*Mei nu!*" The vendor flagged down a young woman in a cobalt dress. "Come, come."

Farrah looped her shopping bag around her wrist and picked up her drinks while the young woman fended off the vendor's aggressive sales pitch. She speed-walked back to campus, taking care not to make eye contact with any more vendors lest she got suckered into buying something else she didn't need.

Farrah stopped at the crosswalk. Instead of crossing when the pedestrian light flashed green, she waited until a group of teenagers stepped off the curb before following them into the jungle that was Shanghai traffic.

Rule #1 of surviving in China: cross when locals cross. There's safety in numbers.

By the time Farrah arrived at Shanghai Foreign Studies University, her study abroad program's host campus, she'd already finished her drink. She tossed the empty container into a nearby trash can and pushed open the door to FEA's lobby.

FEA, a.k.a. Foreign Education Academy, occupied one of the oldest buildings at SFSU. Not only did the four-story building lack an elevator, but the interior design left much to be desired. The lobby had potential—marble floors, tons of natural light streaming in through large windows facing the courtyard—but the furniture was straight out of the '80s (and not in the cool retro kind of way).

A cracked brown leather couch lined the wall beneath the windows alongside mismatched chairs and tables. A spindly magazine stand sagged beneath the weight of dozens of back issues of *Time Out Shanghai*. Faded Chinese landscape paintings hung on the wall, adding to the musty feel.

As usual, Farrah couldn't help mentally redecorating the space. As she took the stairs to the third floor, she swapped out the current furniture for a cushioned wicker set with glass-topped tables, which would visually expand the lobby. Out went the old watercolors and in came the panels of Asian-inspired art—perhaps some up-close representations of the lotus flower or plum blossoms with modern Chinese calligraphy. There could be a wall of bookshelves for—

"Ow!" Farrah had been so absorbed in her design daydream, she slammed into the wall. Her hand shot to her forehead as pain ricocheted through her brain. Fortunately, she couldn't feel a bump.

Olivia's bubble tea also remained intact, thank god. She was scary when she didn't get her sugar fix.

The wall moved. "Are you okay?" it asked.

A walking, talking wall. She must've hit her head harder than she thought.

Farrah peeked out from beneath her hand and found herself staring into a pair of crystal-blue eyes. She recognized those eyes. They'd stared back at her from the cover of *Sports Illustrated* last year, along with the accompanying high cheekbones and cocky grin.

Now, they examined her with a mix of amusement and concern.

"You're not a wall," she blurted.

"No, I'm not." The not-a-wall cocked an eyebrow. A hint of a smile played over his lips. "I've been called a lot of things in my life, but that's a new one."

Farrah fought the flush of embarrassment spreading across her face. Of all the people she could've run into, she had to run into Blake Ryan.

Even though she wasn't a sports fan, she knew who he was. Everyone did. A hotshot football player from Texas who caused a national uproar when he quit the team at the beginning of the year. Besides the *Sports Illustrated* cover, Farrah remembered Blake from an ESPN documentary about the most talented college athletes in the country. Farrah's roommate last year forced her to watch it because she was obsessed with the point guard on California Coast University's basketball team, and she needed someone she could gush to.

It'd been the most boring seventy-five minutes of Farrah's life, but at least there'd been plenty of eye candy, none of whom were dishier than the Texan standing in front of her.

Six feet two inches of tanned skin and chiseled muscle, topped with golden hair, glacial-blue eyes, and cheekbones that could cut ice. He wasn't Farrah's type, but she had to admit the boy was fire. Blake looked the way she'd pictured Apollo looking when she learned about Greek mythology in seventh grade.

"Well, you're really hard." The words slipped out before Farrah could catch them.

I did not just say that out loud.

The flush traveled from her face to the rest of her body. No matter how hard she prayed, the floor didn't open up and swallow her whole, that bastard.

Blake's other eyebrow shot up.

"I mean, your *chest* is really hard. Nothing else. Although I'm sure it could be hard if it wanted to be."

Kill me.

The hint of amusement blossomed into a full-fledged grin, revealing twin dimples that should have been classified as lethal weapons.

"It sure can," Blake drawled. "Especially when I'm around someone as beautiful as you."

Farrah's mortification screeched to a halt. "Oh, *please.* Do they actually work for you?"

"Excuse me?"

"Your cheesy pickup lines. Do they actually work for you?"

"I've never had any complaints. Besides, look at me." Blake gestured at himself. "I don't need pickup lines."

"Wow." Farrah shook her head. *Typical jock.* "It must be difficult walking around with such a big head."

"Babe, that's not the only part of me that's big."

Farrah couldn't help it; her eyes dropped to the region below Blake's belt. An image of what hid behind the denim flashed through her mind's eye. Her mouth went dry.

"I'm talking about my chest, of course." Blake shook with laughter.

Farrah's gaze snapped up to his face. "I knew that." The mortification crept back up her neck.

"Sure. Since you've already undressed me with your eyes, we should—"

"I did *not* undress you—"

"Properly introduce ourselves." He held out his hand. "I'm Blake."

She knew who he was, and they both knew it. Farrah played along because (1) her mother raised her to be a polite human being, and (2) while she knew his name, there was every chance he didn't know hers. They'd met briefly at orientation dinner the first night, but there were seventy students in FEA. Farrah herself couldn't remember the names of half the people she'd met. "I'm Farrah."

She slid the handle of her plastic bag onto her other wrist so she could grasp his hand. His palms were warm and rough against hers. When they made contact, a tiny unexpected shock sizzled through her veins.

"Farrah from California."

She couldn't have been more surprised if he started reciting *The Iliad* in ancient Greek. "You remember."

"How could I forget?" Blake's gaze swept over her face and lingered on her mouth.

Farrah's heart rate kicked up a notch. He was the opposite of her ideal romantic hero—tall, dark, and handsome, with a side of sensitive, cultured, and well-read—but there was no denying Blake's sex appeal. It dripped from him like honey from a hive.

"So we didn't need to introduce ourselves."

"No." He stepped closer without releasing her hand. "But I wanted an excuse to touch you."

No, Blake wasn't her type, but any girl in the world would melt under the heat of his gaze. Farrah hated to admit it, but she was no exception.

She'd be damned if she showed it, though.

While she struggled to come up with a witty rejoinder, Blake lowered his head to whisper in her ear. "Still think my pickup lines are cheesy?"

Farrah yanked her hand out of his and ignored his laughter. The deep, velvety sound rolled through the empty stairwell, filling it with its richness.

"As a matter of fact, I do," she said with as much dignity as she could muster. "You're not as hot as you think you are." *Lies.* "There are plenty of guys as good-looking as you."

"Aha! So you think I'm good-looking."

Dammit. "Only from a physical point of view."

"Er, that's what good-looking means."

"I have more important things to do than stand here and argue with you. So if—"

"Like read depressing-ass novels?" Blake nodded at the bag in her hands. The cover of *The Notebook* showed clear as day through the thin red plastic.

"I don't expect you to understand, but this is a great love story," Farrah huffed.

"Hey, whatever floats your boat. I don't have anything against love stories. Plus, if you're looking for something to do besides argue with me, I have a few ideas." Suggestiveness dripped from his voice. "You, me, my room—a great love story."

Farrah snorted. "Not even in your dreams. You're not my type."

"I'm everyone's type."

Farrah didn't bother to dignify his arrogance with a response. She brushed past him and stalked up the stairs. "I hope you and your ego have a good night," she tossed over her shoulder.

"My ego and I always have a good night. By the way," Blake called after her. "I hate seeing you go, but I love watching you leave."

Farrah pressed her lips together, struggling not to smile at his intentionally clichéd line.

Blake Ryan may have a better sense of humor than she expected, but he wasn't leading-man material.

Not for her.

Not even close.

CHAPTER 2

BLAKE WAS STILL GRINNING WHEN HE STEPPED INTO his room and switched on the lights. The expression on Farrah's face when he asked if she thought his pickup lines were cheesy?

Priceless.

She was in FEA, which meant she was off-limits. That didn't mean he couldn't flirt with her.

He had to keep life interesting somehow.

Blake tossed his keys onto his desk and surveyed his tiny kingdom. Technically, it was his and Luke's tiny kingdom, at least until orientation week ended and Luke moved into his homestay.

But Luke wasn't here, which meant Blake had all one hundred and fifty square feet to himself.

Compared to his off-campus spread at Texas Southeastern, this place was a dump. The dark wood floors creaked. The cinder-block walls resembled those in a jail cell. The twin beds may as well have been made for ten-year-olds. But the FEA dorm had one thing his TSU apartment didn't: freedom.

For that luxury, Blake would give up all the plasma TVs and king-size beds in the world.

He flopped down on his bed and closed his eyes, luxuriating in the silence. No stares. No whispers. Nothing but the quiet peace of a small room in a big city halfway across the world from home. For the first time since February, he felt as though he could breathe.

The musical tones of Blake's custom phone alarm interrupted his bliss. Cleo had downloaded it when they started dating last summer. He woke up before dawn every day for football conditioning camp, and she hated the sound of the default alarm at 4:30 a.m.

He should change it back.

Blake cracked one eye open. It was 7:30 p.m., which meant it was six thirty in the morning in Austin. Time to call home.

He rolled over onto his stomach and flipped open his laptop. He stared at the Skype icon, thinking of excuses why he needed to cut the conversation short before hitting the call button.

To his relief, Joy was the one who answered his call.

"About time, loser." Joy popped a potato chip in her mouth. "You're late."

"Remind me again, was it you who wrote *How to Win Friends and Influence People?*" Blake tapped a finger on his chin. "Oh, wait. In order for you to do that you'd have to, you know, be literate. My bad."

"Ha. Looks like Shanghai hasn't improved your terrible sense of humor." Joy cocked her head. "You look terrible. Is that a *pimple* I see on your chin?"

No way. He didn't get pimples.

Nevertheless, Blake rubbed a hand over his jaw to check for unwanted intruders. Nothing except for the scratch of his five o'clock shadow. "Bullshit."

"Yes, but I made you worry." Joy cackled. "You are so vain."

"I'll hang up on you right now."

"Do it."

"I will."

"Fine."

"Fine."

They glared at each other.

Joy caved first. She grinned. "I miss you, big bro."

"I miss you too." Blake's sister was a pain in the ass, but she was also one of his best friends and he loved her. Most of the time.

Some of the time.

"How's Shanghai?"

"Great, for the most part. A bit noisy and polluted, but..." Blake shrugged. "You can't have it all."

He was happy to be in Shanghai—to be anywhere except Texas, really—but, truth be told, he found China strange and overwhelming. The food was weird, people stared at him wherever he went, and there was a lot of everything everywhere, all the time.

Noise. Lights. Cars. For a boy who grew up in the quiet suburbs of Texas, Blake felt like someone had plucked him out of a fishbowl and dropped him in the middle of a highway during rush hour.

Not that he'd ever tell his family that. They gave him enough shit about his decisions as it was.

Besides, he'd arrived less than a week ago. He had plenty of time to get acclimated to Asia.

"You ready for TSU?" he asked.

"Of course. I've been preparing all summer. Besides, I've visited you on campus enough to know what it's like." After a stint at the local community college, Joy was transferring to TSU for her sophomore year. "Cleo's been amazing. She gave me the lowdown on everything I need to know—which classes I should take, bars I should go to, boys I should meet."

Wariness settled in Blake's stomach. "I didn't realize you two were spending so much time together."

"Um, she's practically my sister." Joy gave him a pointed look. "She'd be my *actual* sister—well, sister-in-law—one day if you hadn't fucked things up."

Here we go again. "Don't start."

"I'm not starting anything."

"Good."

"All I'm saying is, Cleo is the best girlfriend you could've asked for—"

Blake groaned. "For God's sake, we've been through this."

"—and you *broke up with her*." Joy shook her head. "What were you thinking?"

"I was thinking it's my love life and none of your business." This was one of those times Blake did *not* love his sister. She'd been on his case about Cleo all summer. He thought she'd be over it by now.

Apparently not.

"Mom and Dad are pissed."

"Tell me something I don't know." Between quitting football and breaking up with Cleo, Blake hadn't exactly endeared himself to his parents this year.

"Joy? Is that your brother on the line?"

Joy smirked. "Speak of the devil."

"Who are you calling the devil?" Blake's mom scolded playfully. She poked her face in front of the screen. "Hi, dear."

"Hi, Mom."

"Are you eating enough? You look skinnier."

Joy snickered. "That's my cue. I'll let you talk to Mom." She stood up. "Don't be a stranger, danger."

"That makes no sense."

"Whatever. Byeee!"

Blake's mom wasted no time getting down to business. "How's the food in China? Is that why you're not eating? Oh, Blake, you should've studied abroad in Europe."

"I have been eating, and the food is fine." It took some getting used to, was all. Turned out General Tso's chicken was not a thing here, as Blake discovered when he tried to order it last night. "Don't worry."

Helen Ryan pinned her son with a glare. "I'm your mother. It's my job to worry, especially when you're spending a year in some strange country across the world."

"Technically, any country except the U.S. is 'strange,'" Blake quipped. He was the first in his family to travel outside the U.S. and Western Europe, so he understood their concern, but they acted like he was studying in a war zone instead of a major international city.

"You know what I mean." Helen twisted her bracelet around her wrist. "I'm sure the people are lovely, but couldn't you have gone somewhere more...familiar? London, for example. They speak English there. It might not be too late to switch programs for the spring."

"Going somewhere unfamiliar is the point." Not to mention Shanghai was way farther from home than London. "Besides, Chinese is a useful language to learn."

"I suppose you're right." Helen sighed. "I'm worried about you, Blake. You've been acting strange all year."

"I have a few things I need to figure out." Like what the hell he was going to do with his life now that football was out of the picture. "I'll be fine, I promise."

"All right." His mom didn't appear convinced, but she dropped the issue. "Do you want to talk to your father? He's around here somewhere." She turned toward the living room. "Joe!"

"No!" Blake cleared his throat. "I mean, another time. I have an orientation thing soon."

"This late at night?"

"Uh, yeah. We're going to a...night market," Blake fudged.

"Oh, ok." Helen looked disappointed. "Have fun. I'll talk to you soon. I love you."

"I love you too, Mom."

Blake signed off. That was a close call. He didn't need to speak with his father when Joe Ryan's voice already echoed in his head like a bad dream.

Are you STUPID? Did you get hit too hard in the head during the game...? Can't quit football; it's the only thing you're good at... Quitters are losers...

A dull ache blossomed behind Blake's temple. The mere thought of his father drove him crazy.

A loud slam caused him to jump. Blake thought the sound was an alarming escalation of his headache until he saw his roommate in the doorway.

"Sorry." Luke Peterson grimaced. Standing at six foot two and north of two hundred and fifty pounds, he looked every inch the rugby player he was. "Had a few too many drinks."

"It's cool." Blake eyed his roommate's flushed face and short brown hair, which stuck up all over the place. "Where did you have drinks? A wind tunnel?"

"Har-har." Luke smoothed a self-conscious hand over his hair. "I was pregaming the pregame in Courtney's room. They're at Gino's now, but I forgot my wallet."

Gino's, a dive bar near campus, was fast becoming FEA's favorite pregame spot. The food was crappy, but the drinks were cheap, which was all a college student could ask for.

Blake didn't care about the food or drinks, really. He went to bars for the energy and solidarity. There, strangers could bond over the simplest things, from a mutual love for a song to a goal scored by their favorite team on TV. Everyone was welcome, regardless of whether they were there to hang out, hook up, or drown their sorrows.

"Perfect timing." Blake stood up and pulled his sweatshirt over his head. It got crazy hot in Gino's. "I was about to head over there myself."

Forget his father. He wasn't going to let the old man ruin his time in Shanghai.

The great thing about being more than seven thousand miles from home? You can do whatever the hell you want.

CHAPTER 3

"WE HAVE TO DECIDE." OLIVIA TANG FISHED A PEN OUT of her purse and scribbled on a cocktail napkin. "I'll make pro-con lists. The holiday is coming up, and if we don't book soon, everything will be full."

"The holiday is in more than a month," Sammy Yu pointed out. "We have time."

"This is China. Do you know how many people will be traveling then? A *lot*," Olivia said before anyone could answer. "I'd prefer to get our ducks in a row before we're stuck camping in the woods instead of sunbathing on a beach."

"Camping sounds good to me," Sammy said. Olivia frowned. "Or we could go sunbathing. Sunbathing sounds good too."

Farrah, Courtney Taylor, and Kris Carrera exchanged amused glances. Despite Olivia's denials, it was obvious Sammy had a thing for her. Farrah didn't know why Olivia bothered denying it. Sammy was good-looking, sweet, funny, and a math major at Harvey Mudd, one of the most elite liberal arts colleges in the country. He was every girl's (and every Asian mother's) dream.

"No need for pro-con lists when we can just vote." Courtney

placed her hand on Olivia's cocktail napkin, forcing the other girl to stop writing.

"I enjoy making lists."

"I know, sweetie, but we're at a bar." Courtney swept her arm around Gino's. "Let's knock this out so we can enjoy it. Show of hands if you want to go to Thailand."

Farrah, Sammy, and Leo Agnelli raised their hands. After a longing look at her lists, Olivia raised her hand too.

"Japan?"

Kris.

"Philippines?"

Courtney and Nardo Crescas.

Nardo looked at Kris. "You don't want to go to the Philippines? Your family is from there."

"Exactly. I go every year." Kris yawned. "No, thanks."

"Luke mentioned earlier he wants to go to the Philippines too, so we'll chalk that up to three. Either way, Thailand wins. We'll book our tickets tomorrow." Courtney clapped. "Yay! Now let's do something fun to celebrate."

"Wait. We haven't decided where in Thailand we want to go," Olivia protested.

"Liv." Farrah wrapped an arm around her friend's shoulder. "We'll figure it out tomorrow."

Olivia sighed. "Fine. But if we end up in a roach motel because everything else sells out, don't say I didn't warn you."

"I won't." Farrah didn't care if they ended up sleeping in a car on the side of the road. All that mattered was she going to visit Thailand.

Four days in FEA and the semester was already more interesting than her entire freshman year at California Coast University.

Farrah's stomach fluttered with excitement. Between the trips, the people, and all the inspo she was going to get for this year's national student interior design competition, Shanghai was shaping up to be the best decision she'd ever made.

Having a great group of friends helped. Farrah met Olivia at the airport while waiting for the FEA shuttle to campus. Olivia struck up a friendship with Kris and Courtney, who introduced them to the boys (Courtney collected friends the way Mardi Gras partygoers collect beads), and the rest was history.

"Speaking of Luke, where is he?" Leo looked around for their missing friend. "He went to get his wallet ages ago."

Farrah tried to ignore the second, more worrying flutter in her stomach, the one that happened every time Leo spoke. And every time she looked at him. Or thought about him.

Unlike Blake, Leo was one hundred percent her type. Finally, a boy who made her heart jump when he entered the room! A boy with curly dark hair and a knowing smile, who spoke five languages and could quote classic authors at the drop of a hat.

Too bad said boy was taken.

"I'm sure he'll be here soon." Courtney snuggled into Leo's side.

You could say a lot of things about Courtney, but you couldn't say she didn't move fast. Farrah didn't even get a chance to introduce herself the first night before Leo and Courtney started making out in the corner of 808.

They weren't dating per se, but they were hooking up with each other exclusively. In college, that was basically the same as dating.

Farrah sipped her drink and scanned the bar to avoid looking at the couple. Gino's was like an American college bar on steroids. Throngs of students, local and international, crowded around tables heaped high with burgers, fries, and alcohol. The latest Top 40 hits from the States blasted through ceiling-mounted speakers, muffling the cheers from the two beer pong tables in the back. Graffiti from past patrons covered every wall and crept onto the ceiling.

Farrah zeroed in on the messages closest to their table. *Be nice to your cabdriver*, someone advised in black marker, *or they'll leave you in the middle of nowhere*. Above that was a random phone number, and above that, a simple hashtag: *#ballsballsballs*.

Gotta love bar graffiti.

Olivia leaned toward Farrah. "You ok?" she whispered. She was the only one who knew about Farrah's crush.

"Yes," Farrah lied. Courtney was her friend, Leo was Courtney's (sort of), and that was that. Besides, Farrah wasn't a stranger to unrequited love. She had a habit of falling for guys she couldn't have, even when she didn't know they were taken yet. "I'm over it."

Olivia appeared unconvinced.

"What are you talking about?" Sammy poked his head over Olivia's shoulder. "Tell me."

"The mind-your-business gene." Olivia smiled despite her words. It was hard not to smile around Sammy.

"C'mon, I won't tell. I can keep a secret." Sammy wiggled his eyebrows. "Is it something naughty?"

"You wish." Farrah threw a fry at him. "Is sex the only thing guys think about?"

"No. Sometimes we think about food." Sammy caught the fry and tossed it in his mouth.

Olivia jabbed her elbow into his side. He tickled her in response, causing her to squeal and nearly fall off the bench from laughter.

Farrah hid her grin behind her glass.

"Oh, look. There's the Uncouth One himself, bearing gifts." Kris raised her eyebrows. "Including one Blake Ryan. How thoughtful."

Farrah's head whipped around.

Luke bore down on them with a fishbowl cocktail in each hand and Blake in tow.

"Talking shit again, Kris?" Luke set the drinks on the table.

"You couldn't possibly have heard me over the noise."

"I didn't need to. You're always talking shit."

Courtney laughed. "He has a point."

"Whose side are you on?" Kris harrumphed.

"Yours, of course." Courtney patted Kris's hand. "You are my sorority sister."

Besides Sammy and Nardo, who were best friends and classmates at Harvey Mudd, Kris and Courtney were the only ones in FEA who'd known each other before the program started.

"Twice in one night." Blake winked at Farrah. "I'm beginning to think you're stalking me."

"I was here first."

"That's what they all say." Blake handed Farrah a bottle of beer. "Drink?"

"I don't like beer."

"C'mon, live a little. Get outside your comfort zone."

"Drinking beer is hardly living." Nevertheless, Farrah swiped the Tsingtao from him. His hand brushed hers, and another electric current sizzled over her skin.

She popped open the cap and took a swig, grimacing at the taste.

Blake laughed at her expression. "You really don't like beer."

"It tastes like urine."

"How do you know what urine tastes like?"

Farrah took another swig. "I can't talk to you. You're exhausting."

"That's ok. There are other things we can do besides talk. Can't guarantee they'll be less exhausting, though."

Blake sat across from her. Even in a plain black V-neck tee

and jeans, he looked like he just stepped off the cover of *GQ*. The shirt showed off his broad shoulders and muscular arms, and his skin glowed golden in the bar's dim lighting.

Blake caught her staring and flashed a cocky grin. "Like what you see?" he mouthed.

"I've seen better," she mouthed back. She had—in the sculpture sections of Italy's art museums.

Blake smirked with the confidence of someone who knew he was the hottest guy in the room.

Luke said something to him. When Blake turned his head to reply, Olivia grabbed Farrah's arm. "What was that?"

"What was what?"

"That." She gestured at Blake. "I almost melted from the sexual tension."

"Ha! You've been drinking too much." Farrah had never heard anything more absurd. "There was no sexual tension."

"Oh, honey. Yes, there was. Why deny it? Blake is hot." Olivia lowered her voice. "He'll help you get over you-know-who."

For the first time in her life, Farrah was thankful for the red flush that took over her face every time she drank alcohol. It concealed the heated embarrassment on her cheeks.

"He's not my type."

"Don't be ridiculous. He's every girl's type."

Farrah sighed. She was tired of hearing that.

"Guys, look what Luke brought." Courtney waved a deck of cards in the air. "What do you say? Y'all up for a game of Kings?"

"Hell yeah! I'm the king of Kings." Luke pounded his chest. "Bring it on."

"Your resemblance to a gorilla is remarkable," Kris observed.

"Bite me."

"You wish."

"Children, settle down." Courtney shuffled the cards and

spread them face down around the bottle of *baijiu* they smuggled in. It'd been sitting there unopened for the past hour. The staff didn't seem to care, but no one in the group had the guts to open it. *Baijiu*, which ranged from eighty to one hundred twenty proof, was the Chinese equivalent of moonshine. It was no joke.

"Normal rules, yeah? Ace is waterfall, two you, three me, four floor..." Courtney ran through the instructions in one breath.

"I agree except for one thing." Blake spoke up. "Ace is hot seat. Whoever draws it has to answer one question from every other player. *Honestly.*"

"Oooh." A grin spread across Courtney's face. "I like that. I like that a lot."

Farrah narrowed her eyes. Blake *would* be the type to barge in and change the rules.

The game heated up. Everyone took turns pulling a card, each of which came with a predetermined rule. For the first few rounds, Farrah pulled innocuous cards such as a ten (categories) and a five (all guys drink).

Her luck ran out in the fifth round.

After Olivia pulled a three (me, which meant she had to drink), it was Farrah's turn. She examined the remaining cards. Her hand hovered over the one closest to her before she changed her mind and plucked a card from the other side. She flipped it over.

An ace. The first of the night.

The table erupted into cheers.

Farrah groaned. "I hate you guys."

"No one forced you to choose that card. It was fate," Sammy teased.

"Yeah, yeah." Farrah resigned herself to her so-called fate. She spread her arms. "I'm ready. Have at it."

They did. Her friends peppered her with rapid-fire questions. As expected, most were sexual but harmless.

Ever have a threesome? *Nope.*

Weirdest hookup spot? *Lifeguard stand at the beach (depending on how you interpret the word "hookup").*

Celebrity fantasy? *Ian Somerhalder or Henry Cavill. Or both.* Farrah added that last part as a joke, though it earned her a few speculative glances from the guys.

Men. So predictable.

Blake asked the next question. "If you could hook up with one person in the program, who would it be?"

Farrah froze. Everyone stared at her expectantly as she worked to keep her face expressionless and her gaze from flicking in Leo's direction. She was convinced any movement on her part would give it away. She thought about making something up, but she didn't want someone thinking she had a crush on them when she didn't.

Lie or take the shot? On the one hand, the smell of *baijiu* alone made her want to vomit. On the other...

Fuck it.

Farrah picked up the *baijiu*, poured the clear liquid into an empty shot glass, and knocked it back straight, holding her breath so she didn't have to inhale its fuel-like odor.

Her friends burst into a spontaneous round of applause. Blake was the only one who didn't clap. Instead, he watched her drink with a knowing smirk.

Farrah grimaced as the cheap, fiery liquid burned its way down her throat. Why the hell did Chinese people like *baijiu* so much? It smelled and tasted like rubbing alcohol.

Olivia handed her a glass of water, which she downed in five seconds. She wiped her mouth with the back of her hand and took a deep breath. The urge to vomit subsided, but the alcohol's brutal aftertaste lingered.

"You are a champ." Sammy reached around Olivia to pat her on the back.

"You that desperate to hide something from us?" Leo joked.

Farrah played it cool with a shrug and a smile. "No follow-up questions," she reminded him. She avoided his gaze.

Leo held up his hands in surrender. "Ok. Here's an easy one. What's your number?"

A.k.a. the number of people she'd slept with.

She paused before answering. "Zero."

Olivia knew this, so she didn't blink an eye, but the rest of the table stared at Farrah like she'd grown another head.

"You're shitting me," Luke said.

"Nope." Farrah lifted her chin with equal parts embarrassment and defiance. A nineteen-year-old virgin from LA was a novelty these days, but she wasn't a prude. She had experience on all the bases. She'd just never hit a home run.

"And there's nothing wrong with that," Olivia said loyally.

"Of course not." Farrah couldn't tell whether Leo was impressed, amused, or bemused. "You're ready when you're ready. Don't let anyone convince you otherwise."

Farrah forced a smile. She chose not to mention that, if she had her way, she'd have lost her virginity already. Last year, she came this close to giving it up to Garrett Reiss, the hot junior in her Visual Communication class. After their third date, they made it all the way to his dorm room and to the pivotal moment before Garrett realized he was out of condoms. Before their next date could happen, she caught him playing tonsil hockey with another girl at the movies, and that was that.

Farrah didn't want or need to wait for marriage or true love (although there was nothing wrong with that), but a girl had to have some standards. Sadly, every time she got close to doing the deed with someone who seemed to meet those standards, something came along and ruined it—wrong place, wrong time, no protection, guy turned out to be an asshole. The list went on.

At this point, Farrah was never going to have sex. She could picture her headstone engraving already: HERE LIES FARRAH LIN, WORLD'S OLDEST VIRGIN, WHO TRIED TO GIVE IT AWAY BUT COULDN'T. MAY SHE REST IN PEACE.

"So how far have you gone?" Nardo looked intrigued. "Second? Third? Or—" He paused. "Wait. Have you gone past first?"

Luke snorted out a laugh that morphed into a cough when Courtney shot him a dirty look.

"Of course I have," Farrah snapped. "I'm a virgin, not a nun."

"Let's move on. We've broken the no-follow-up-questions rule enough tonight." Blake pulled a jack. "Never Have I Ever."

Farrah exhaled in relief as everyone refocused on the game. She wasn't ashamed of her lack of sexual experience, but she didn't want to be grilled about it all night, either.

Farrah looked across the table and caught Blake's eye. He gave her a discreet wink.

Huh.

Maybe Blake Ryan wasn't so bad after all.

CHAPTER 4

IF BLAKE'S OLD TEAMMATES COULD SEE HIM NOW, they'd laugh their asses off.

Blake Ryan, studying on a Friday night instead of hitting the town? Unheard of.

While he'd been one of the few football players at TSU who chose a "serious" major (business administration) and took academics seriously, he'd never stayed in on Friday nights. Back then, he had appearances to keep up.

But Blake wasn't a football player anymore, and he was in Shanghai, not Texas. Not to mention, FEA's curriculum was hard as shit. Four-hour language classes four days a week, on top of daily homework and vocabulary lessons, weekly written/oral exams, and two elective classes conducted all in Mandarin. The teachers, or *laoshis*, were patient with Blake, who spoke zero Mandarin coming into this program, but he still had no clue what was going on half the time.

He tapped his pencil against the table. "*Dui bu qi. Dui. Bu. Qi,*" he muttered, trying to imprint the characters in his mind. *Sorry* in Mandarin. He could pronounce it fine; writing it out was another matter.

Blake covered the characters in his textbook with one hand and attempted to write them based on memory. He got through the first two and guessed the third. A quick check told him it wasn't close.

"Dammit." His mom was right. He should've studied abroad in an English-speaking country like England or Australia.

But no, he had to choose China, home to one of the hardest fucking languages in the world.

Blake slammed his textbook shut and rubbed his eyes. His vision was blurry after hours of staring at the lines, curves, and squiggles that made up the Chinese written system. Meanwhile, the clock's deafening tick echoed in the otherwise empty library, taunting him. Reminding him he'd been at it for two hours and still couldn't get the easiest vocabulary words right.

"I need a break."

Now he was talking to himself. Fan-fucking-tastic.

Blake blamed Daniel Craig for his predicament. If Shanghai hadn't looked so dope in that *Skyfall* scene, which he watched right before he submitted his study abroad application with his city choice, he wouldn't be here. He'd be in Sydney, hooking up with surfer babes and living his best life on the beach. Australia was even farther from home than China. It would've been perfect.

Stupid Bond fight sequence.

Blake stood to stretch his limbs. He rolled his neck and shrugged out his shoulders. Nothing better than movement after hours of sitting.

The library door opened. Farrah walked in with what looked like a sketch pad and a stack of magazines tucked under her arm.

Now there was trouble. Farrah was beautiful, and Blake got a kick out of riling her up, but she was off-limits. Not only was she in FEA—which meant he had to see her every day if things between them went south—but she was a virgin.

Blake slept with a virgin once, in high school. Granted, he didn't know Lorna was a virgin until after the fact, and when he declined to make things exclusive between them, she took a key to his beloved Chevy until it resembled Freddy Krueger's face.

Fun times.

Then Lorna's father found out Blake slept with his precious daughter and tracked him down after football practice with a shotgun in hand. Luckily, Blake's coach saw them and called the police before Blake found himself eating dirt six feet beneath the ground. The police let the man off with a stern warning, since he technically hadn't tried to shoot Blake (yet), but Blake still filed a restraining order against the girl's entire damn family.

Even funner times.

Lorna transferred schools soon after, and Blake swore never to hook up with a virgin again. That didn't mean he couldn't flirt with Farrah, though. Flirting was harmless.

He retook his seat, laced his hands behind his head, and kicked his feet up on the table with an insouciant smile.

Farrah arched an eyebrow at his unorthodox position. Instead of commenting, she sat at the table next to him and opened one of her magazines.

Blake stretched his arms over his head in a way that showed off his abs—one of his best assets. Along with everything else on his body.

It ain't cocky if it's true.

To his annoyance, Farrah didn't look up. She continued to read, serene as a monk.

Blake swung his feet to the floor. He walked over to her table, plunked his ass in the chair opposite hers, and rested his chin in his hands.

The clock ticked. The AC hummed. The pages rustled as she turned them.

Finally, Farrah slammed her magazine shut with a huff. "Can I help you?"

Blake grinned. Success!

"Now is that the proper way to greet someone?" he drawled. Austinites didn't have strong accents, but he could lay it on thick when he wanted to. "Didn't your mama teach you manners?"

"She did. That's why I left you and your vanity in peace. It would've been rude to interrupt."

Blake placed a hand over his chest. "Vain? Me? You break my heart."

"I doubt anyone could break your heart." Farrah fluttered her lashes. "If they do, the proofs from your solo photo shoot earlier will ease the pain."

His body vibrated with laughter. "You know, I'm down-to-earth once you get to know me."

"Is that your favorite thing about yourself?"

"Favorite, as in one? I can't pick just one." He frowned. "Oh. I see."

"Uh-huh. Now that we've established the obvious fact of your vanity, can you be quiet? I'm trying to work."

"So am I."

"You are not working."

"I *was* working until you came in and interrupted me."

"I didn't say anything when I came in!"

"You distracted me with your radiant presence. It was like a goddess descended from the heavens. How can I focus on something as mundane as Chinese vocabulary when faced with such an extraordinary vision?"

Farrah's mouth twitched once, twice, until she caved and doubled over with laughter.

A grin stretched across Blake's face. There was something magical about seeing someone so composed let loose and knowing he was the one who made her laugh like that.

"I don't know what to do with you." She wiped tears from her eyes.

"I can suggest a few things." Blake pictured Farrah climbing into his lap and straddling him. Taking his shirt off. Taking her shirt off. Gripping his hair and moaning while he feasted on those sure-to-be-delectable breasts of hers.

Hey, he was a guy. He couldn't help himself.

Except this guy now needed a cold shower.

Blake discreetly adjusted himself under the table. He liked having a dick. He and Junior got along great. But sometimes the friend downstairs popped up at the most inconvenient moments.

"Anyway, you're reading…*Vogue*?" Blake squinted at the magazine cover. "I can't imagine that's part of the syllabus."

"First of all, this is *Vogue China*, which means I'm practicing my Chinese reading skills. Second of all, it's not for FEA. It's…" Farrah hesitated. "Never mind."

Blake's intrigue radar blipped. "You can't leave me hanging like that. What's it for?"

Farrah sighed. "Every year, the National Interior Design Association hosts a student competition. The winner gets an all-expenses-paid summer internship at the NIDA member firm of their choice. It's one of *the* most prestigious honors in the industry."

"Sounds fancy." Blake didn't know a single thing about design, but he wished he did. Not because he wanted to be a designer, but because of the way Farrah's eyes lit up when she talked about it. He wanted to know what made her so passionate about the subject. Maybe it'd help him figure out what the hell he wanted to do with his life. "I don't get the *Vogue* part though."

"It's for inspiration." Farrah fiddled with the pages. "We have to submit a portfolio with different design concepts, and I'm stuck on what I want to do for the last one."

"But it's a fashion magazine." Blake had heard his sister gush about the overpriced items in *Vogue* since they were teenagers.

"Design inspiration can come from anywhere—fashion, travel, food, nature." A dreamy look took over Farrah's face. "There was a feature about the actress Marion Lagarde's house in France. She designed her bedroom after her favorite Chanel couture gown. It's fabulous."

A smile tugged at Blake's lips. "I'll take your word for it."

"So you see, it's important for me to have peace and quiet. I need to work on my portfolio," Farrah said pointedly.

"Ok."

"Ok."

Farrah reopened her magazine, and they fell into silence.

A minute later, Blake's stomach growled.

She glared at him.

"What? I can't control the noises my stomach makes." Blake forgot he'd skipped dinner. No wonder his body was rebelling. He grabbed his laptop from the other table. "What do you want to eat?"

"I'm not the one who's hungry."

"Come on, you need fuel for your imagination. You said food can inspire design."

Farrah exhaled sharply. "I'm not going to get any work done tonight, am I?"

Dimples creased his cheeks. "There's Thai, Indian...oh shit, McDonald's has twenty-four-hour delivery here."

"We did not come all the way to Shanghai to eat McDonald's."

After some bickering, they settled on Malaysian. Forty-five minutes later, the delivery guy arrived with two bags of steaming hot takeout. Blake met him downstairs and brought the food up to the library, where he and Farrah wasted no time digging into the feast. Beef rendang for him, Hainanese chicken for her, plus chicken satay, roti canai, and sambal fried okra to share. Oh, and mango sticky rice for dessert, because it ain't a full meal without dessert.

"Where are your girls?" Blake lifted a forkful of beef to his mouth. The rich flavors of lemongrass, ginger, cinnamon, and other spices he couldn't name exploded on his tongue. *Damn.* Rendang looked like shit (literally), but it tasted like heaven.

Blake liked simple foods. Tacos, pizza, and burgers were enough to satisfy him, but after two weeks in China he was developing an appreciation for international cuisines.

He drew the line at chicken feet, fish eyes, and yak penis, though. He wasn't brave enough to attempt those yet.

"Out." Farrah ripped off a piece of roti canai and dipped the flatbread in curry sauce.

"Why aren't you with them? I thought the four of you were joined at the hip." Blake didn't understand why girls traveled in packs like wolves, even to the bathroom. *Especially* to the bathroom. What did they do in there, throw a party?

"My throat hurts so I sat tonight out. Better safe than sorry."

"If you'd said something earlier, we could've ordered some chicken noodle soup."

A small smile touched Farrah's lips. "I'm good. Thanks."

Their gazes lingered on each other. Farrah's eyes resembled pools of melted chocolate. Beautiful, delicious melted chocolate.

Blake's heart did a weird skip.

Farrah looked away. "What about you? Why are you holed up in the library on a Friday night?"

He didn't bother lying. "Homework."

"That's it?"

"That's it."

"I did not figure you for the studious type."

Her tone rankled him. Blake was used to people thinking he was a stupid jock. He usually shrugged it off—who was the one with a 3.8 GPA, bitches?—but Farrah's assumption stung.

"Why not?"

Farrah appeared taken aback by his cool tone. "I don't know. I guess it's because you're a football player and the athletes at my school aren't exactly familiar with the library."

"I'm not an athlete at your school, and I don't play football anymore."

"You're right. I'm sorry." She bit her lip. "I shouldn't have assumed."

Blake's ire melted at the chastised look on her face. "It's fine. I'm used to it." He shoved another forkful of beef into his mouth. He chewed and swallowed before adding, "I wasn't getting much done anyway. Foreign languages are not my strong suit."

"What do you have problems with? Grammar? Pronunciation?"

"Everything, but mostly the characters. I can't get them right." How the hell was he supposed to learn a language with no Roman alphabet? There were thousands of Chinese characters, and they all looked the same.

"They're hard," Farrah acknowledged. "I have problems with them myself, but mnemonics can help. Here, give me your textbook. Did you learn radicals yet?"

"Yeah." Depending on how one defined *learn*. Classes started so early, Blake found it hard to stay awake.

"If you memorize them, they can be really helpful. Take *kou*, for example. You see how it sort of looks like a mouth? It's part of most characters whose meanings have to do with the mouth, like *jiao*, to call, or *chi*, to eat." Farrah wrote the words out. She went through a few other examples before moving on to the next radical.

Blake followed along, trying his best not to stare at *her* mouth. Farrah's lips looked like they were made for—

Don't go there, buddy. She's a virgin. She's probably never even given a blow job before.

He refocused on the lesson at hand. To his surprise, the characters made more sense. Not a lot, but more. It was a start.

Every once in a while, Blake broke up the monotony with random stories from his childhood and questions about Farrah's life back home. He told her about the time he donned a bear mask and scared the hell out of Joy during a family camping trip at Big Bend and how Joy tricked him with fake adoption papers in retaliation. That was messed up. To this day, a tiny part of Blake wondered if he was adopted.

Farrah told him about "borrowing" her mother's lipsticks and using them as crayons on her family's freshly painted walls.

Blake smiled at the mental image. A budding creative at age six. Farrah really did have her life figured out.

By the time they finished the first chapter, it was close to one in the morning. The food was long gone, and Blake's eyes were bleary from staring at the text.

"We should call it a night," he said. His brain wanted him to stay, but his body screamed for sleep. "Thank you for helping me with this." He gestured at his notes.

"No problem. Consider it my apology for thinking you're, you know."

"A dumb jock?"

Farrah blushed. "Well, yeah. You're different from what I imagined."

"I *am* awesome," Blake agreed. He scooped the empty food containers into a bag.

"I didn't say that."

"You were thinking it."

She helped him gather up the used utensils and napkins. "Now, the arrogance part, I got right."

"I'm blessed with an abundance of confidence. Besides, I *know* you think I'm awesome."

"Oh, really? How?"

Blake pointed at the clock. "You spent the whole night with me."

Farrah's mouth opened and closed like a goldfish's.

After Blake stopped laughing and dodged a swat from a red-faced Farrah, they disposed of the trash and collected their belongings. He turned off the library lights and followed Farrah into the stairwell.

He paused on the third-floor landing outside the girls' hall. In the distance, a car door slammed, and laughter filtered through the stairwell window.

"Good night." Farrah's gaze tipped up to his. The moonlight reflected in her eyes, and Blake's heart did that weird skipping thing again.

"Good night."

She was so close. If he moved forward a few inches...

No. Nuh-uh. Don't even think about it, buddy. One kiss is not worth ruining your year over. Even if it'd be a helluva kiss.

Blake cleared his throat and stepped backward, breaking the spell. "I'll see you later."

"Yes." Farrah, too, stepped back, widening the gap between them. "See you later."

CHAPTER 5

"THIS IS HELL." KRIS SURVEYED THE HAPPIEST PLACE ON earth the way Anna Wintour would survey an outfit from Walmart. In her $500 jeans and Chanel top, she couldn't have looked more out of place amongst the hordes of screaming children and frazzled parents.

Nearby, a little boy held an ice cream cone in one hand and picked his nose with the other while his parents tried to calm his sister, who cried so hard her face turned scarlet.

Kris shuddered and slipped on her sunglasses like they could protect her from reality.

"Cheer up, Kris. We're at Disneyland!" Courtney sang. "The most magical place on earth.

"Magical, my ass. The only *magical* thing about this place is how many terrible outfits they've crammed into one park. It's like an outdoor convention for the poorly dressed."

Farrah turned her head so Kris couldn't see her laugh. Kris was one of her closest friends in FEA, but she lived in her own little world sometimes.

Farrah's gaze landed on Blake, who chatted with Luke and

Sammy off to the side. Blake was friends with Luke, who was friends with Courtney, which meant Blake was a de facto member of their group.

Farrah was still trying to figure him out. Sometimes, she glimpsed something deeper beneath his cocky playboy persona—a vulnerability that flickered over his face when he thought no one was looking. Then, with the wink of an eye and a smile, it was gone.

Blake's gaze met hers. "What's so funny?"

"Nothing." Farrah's residual smile faded when Blake walked over and slung an arm across her shoulders. The gesture made her heart flutter in a way she did not like. At all.

"What are you doing?"

"Keeping you warm. You look cold."

"It's seventy-five degrees." Farrah shrugged Blake's arm off her shoulder. To her surprise, goose bumps rippled over her skin. After the warmth of Blake's embrace, the park felt like a tundra.

Damn him.

She ignored Blake's chuckle and scooted closer to Olivia.

"I've mapped out the most efficient route for us." Olivia snapped open a map of the park. "We'll start at the farthest section and work our way clockwise back to the entrance. First, we'll go to Fantasyland, then Treasure Cove and Adventure Isle. We'll cut through the Gardens of Imagination and make our way to Pixar Toy Story Land and Tomorrowland on the other side."

Luke grimaced. "You scare me."

"I think it's nice to have someone organized plan things for us," Sammy said.

He and Olivia locked eyes. Olivia blushed and busied herself refolding the map.

Farrah and Courtney nudged each other at the same time. Olivia could deny it all she wanted, but the attraction between her and Sammy was mutual, and everyone knew it. They already had bets on when the two would get together.

Farrah gave them another week, tops.

As the group battled their way through the crowd toward Fantasyland, Nardo looked almost as displeased as Kris. "We could've gone somewhere more authentic for the Mid-Autumn Festival," he grumbled. "This place is so Westernized."

"It's Disney. It *is* Western. And according to the internet, it's one of the best places to celebrate the festival." Courtney leveled Nardo with a stern look. "That'll be the last complaint for today. If anyone wants to be a Debbie Downer, do it on your own time."

"The internet is stupid," Nardo mumbled.

Courtney narrowed her eyes. "What was that?"

"Nothing."

Olivia may have mapped out the best route, but sadly, her efficiency didn't extend to the lines, which snaked in front of every ride and restroom like never-ending spokes of misery.

By lunchtime, Farrah's feet were numb from standing.

"Thank god," she said as they entered the restaurant Olivia had chosen for lunch. It resembled the set of one of those Chinese palace dramas Farrah's mom loved watching. Each dining room featured a different theme. The one they ended up in had glowing fish suspended from the ceiling alongside traditional red paper lanterns. Farrah couldn't figure out the theme. Under the East China Sea? Chinese Little Mermaid? The fish were a little tacky, but hey, this was Disney. They could do whatever the hell they wanted.

Since it was a quick-service restaurant, Farrah volunteered to look after the bags while her friends ordered at the counter. It gave her more time to sit.

To Farrah's chagrin, Blake also stayed behind.

"Well, well. You and me, alone again." Dimples creased his cheeks. "What are the odds?"

"We literally came here together, Blake."

He pouted. "Your indifference to my charms is starting to bruise my ego. Come on, throw a guy a bone."

Farrah's lips twitched. "Your ego could use some bruising, and your charms have no effect on me. Sorry."

That wasn't *totally* true, but he didn't need to know that.

"Why? Do you have a boyfriend?"

"No."

"Are you in love with someone else?"

Farrah hesitated.

Blake's eyes widened. "You are."

"I'm not!"

"Who is it? I won't tell."

She didn't know what it was. The heat? The hunger? The exhaustion? Whatever it was, it caused Farrah to lose her usual control over her reactions. Her eyes flicked toward Leo, who was paying for his food while the rest of the group mulled over their choices.

Farrah caught herself and averted her gaze.

Too late.

Blake's jaw dropped. "Holy shit. You're in love with Leo."

"I am *not* in love with him." Farrah fought to keep her expression neutral even as panic raced through her.

"You are."

"I'm not."

"You are."

"I'm—oh, forget it," she fumed. "You're insufferable."

Farrah had thought he might not be so bad after their conversation in the library last week. Clearly, that was a mistake brought on by copious amounts of delicious food and a dash of late-night exhaustion.

Blake Ryan was the worst.

"I saw the way you looked at him just now. Contrary to what some people think"—the way he said *some* indicated he was talking about Farrah—"I'm not stupid. You want to bang him."

She glared at him. "Do you have to be so crude?"

"Tell me I'm wrong."

"I'm not talking about this with you."

"You already are." Blake's dimples flashed again. "I can give you pointers from a guy's perspective. People would pay for my advice. It's that good."

"No, thanks. Leo is taken, remember? He's with someone named, oh, Courtney?"

"Ah, that is a complication."

"It's not a complication; it's a dealbreaker."

"So you *are* in love with him."

Farrah realized too late Blake was baiting her into a trap. The smugness on his face indicated he knew she knew what he was up to.

"Fine," she said. "I may have a *tiny* crush on him, but I'm not in love with him. And I'll never do anything about it."

"Girl code. I respect that." Blake nodded.

Farrah thought that was the end of it until Blake leaned closer, his eyes swirling with curiosity and something else she couldn't identify. "So what's the draw? Is it the nice-sensitive-guy façade?"

"It's not a façade. I know it's difficult for you to understand but nice, sensitive guys exist."

"They're one in a billion. Most guys use the whole sensitivity schtick to get into a girl's pants. Trust me. I'm a guy, and I know how the male species operates."

"Oh, for fuck's sake."

"Exactly!"

"This conversation is over." Farrah scrolled through her phone, not because she was looking for anything but because she didn't want to talk about Leo anymore.

Blake was wrong. He may be a player, but not every guy in the world was like him.

"It doesn't matter. Like you said, he's with Courtney, so I guess you're doomed to pine after someone you can't have unless..."

Don't look up. Don't look up.

Farrah looked up.

Dammit. She needed better self-control. "Unless what?"

Blake leaned back and laced his fingers behind his head. "You get the hots for someone else."

He wasn't the first person to suggest that solution. Olivia had been trying to get Farrah to hook up with another guy in FEA for weeks, but when Farrah had a crush, she had tunnel vision. Most of the time, anyway.

She chose not to think about the way her stomach fluttered every time Blake smiled—a real smile, not the smirk he was giving her now.

"Don't tell me you're offering yourself up for the position."

He looked offended. "I'm not, but there's no need to sound so disgusted. I have feelings."

Farrah arched a skeptical brow.

Blake kept the pretense up for about ten more seconds before he broke into a wide smile.

There it was again—that stupid stomach flutter. She should get that checked out.

"Kidding. I don't have feelings."

Farrah couldn't help but laugh. Blake's grin widened.

He was so cocky, she hadn't thought him capable of self-deprecation, but it was nice to see he didn't take himself too seriously.

The group returned with the food. Farrah had told Olivia to order for her, and her faith in her friend was well-placed. The Shanghainese pork belly rice was fantastic. They also bought a bunch of dishes to share, including crab meat spring rolls, shao mai (Chinese dumplings), chicken teriyaki skewers, and a quarter roasted duck. Dessert comprised of an assortment of mooncakes, in a nod to the Mid-Autumn Festival.

The festival was a time for moon worship (in the olden days) and family reunions (in modern days), but honestly, it was all about the mooncakes.

Farrah savored the taste of her Disney-themed green tea mooncake. *Yum.*

To Farrah's relief, Blake didn't bring up Leo again for the rest of the day, probably because Olivia and Courtney had them running around like crazy people so they could fit everything in before the park closed.

Despite her exhaustion, Farrah had a blast. It had been ages since she'd visited Disneyland. She was a child swept up in the magic again, especially at night when the park lit up like a sea of fallen stars.

Even Kris warmed to the experience. By the time they left, she'd spent hundreds of dollars on overpriced souvenirs. Farrah didn't know why Kris bought so much stuff. It wasn't like she'd ever be caught dead wearing Minnie Mouse earrings.

Whatever. Farrah was too tired to read much into it.

She collapsed into her seat on the metro. They had a long way to go before they reached SFSU, but Farrah didn't mind. It gave her feet more time to recuperate.

"Today was a good day." Olivia yawned and rested her head on Farrah's shoulder. On Farrah's other side, Courtney and Kris were already fast asleep.

Farrah looked across the aisle to where the guys were

watching a video on Sammy's phone. Blake was laughing so hard, he had tears in his eyes. It was the most genuine smile she'd seen from him yet.

"Yeah." Farrah rubbed Olivia's arm. "Today was a good day."

CHAPTER 6

BLAKE ROLLED OUT OF BED AT EIGHT. HE COULDN'T remember the last time he woke up this late, but Disneyland had taken him out. He'd forgotten how tiring amusement parks were.

Fortunately, it didn't take him long to get ready, and he was out the door by eight fifteen.

Blake's stomach rumbled with anticipation. The jianbing from the street vendor behind campus was the highlight of his mornings. He'd passed by the stand multiple times his first two weeks here, tempted by the smell but wary of buying street food, before he caved. It was the right decision. Those savory, crisp-fried crepes were some of the best things he'd ever tasted.

Blake was so busy fantasizing about the jianbing, he didn't notice the girl walking in front of him until they were in the courtyard.

Long dark hair. Slim, curvy figure. Posture Emily Post would be proud of.

Well, he'd be damned. "Farrah!"

Farrah stopped. When she turned, she wore an exasperated look on her face. "Hi."

"You're up early."

"I could say the same for you."

"I usually get up earlier, but we had a late night." Blake smiled, remembering how adorable Farrah looked when she was sleepy.

Wait. Adorable? Where the hell did that *come from?*

Girls his age weren't adorable. They were beautiful (relatives) or sexy (nonrelatives). *Adorable* did not figure into the equation.

Not that Farrah wasn't beautiful or sexy, but—

Dude. Stop while you're ahead.

Blake cleared his throat. The hunger must be getting to him. "So where are you off to?"

Farrah wore an orange dress that was far too nice for a quick breakfast run. She held a milk tea in one hand and had a sketchbook tucked beneath her other arm.

"I'm going to explore a little."

"Without your girls?"

"They're sleeping. Well, Olivia isn't, but she's working on internship applications." Farrah paused. Sipped her drink. Then, "Do you want to join me?"

Blake nearly fell over at the invitation. He wasn't sure Farrah even liked him, and now she was inviting him to hang out with her.

He shouldn't. He was hungry as hell and he had a date with the gym. He hated going there after 10:00 a.m., when it filled up with guys who were more interested in gym selfies than working out. Besides, Blake didn't like the way his body reacted around Farrah. It was different than the typical sexual attraction—though that was certainly there—and it freaked him out.

"You don't have to," Farrah said. "If you have other plans—"

"I'd love to." *I hope I don't regret this.* "As long as we make a quick detour for breakfast."

"Making demands already," she teased. "Why am I not surprised?"

Blake led the way to the back gate. He'd walked this path so many times, he could do it with his eyes closed.

"Breakfast is a reasonable request. More reasonable than bubble tea at eight thirty in the morning."

Farrah clutched her drink to her chest as they approached the jianbing stand. "Don't judge. This doesn't have boba, so it's technically not bubble tea. Even if it *was*, bubble tea is appropriate at all hours of the day."

"Fine. But we're also getting you a proper breakfast." Blake turned to the vendor, whose eyes brightened with recognition. *"Liang ge jidan, wei la."* Two eggs, mildly spicy." No need to specify the jianbing part—that was a given.

He wasn't fluent in Chinese yet, but he was fluent in the language that counts: food.

Blake paid the vendor and handed Farrah one of the jianbings. "This will change your life."

She rolled her eyes. "I'm Chinese. I've had *jian*—oh my god."

"Told ya." They walked to the metro. "Is it good or is it good?"

"It's amazing." Farrah took another bite and hummed in bliss.

Blake's body reacted viscerally to the sound.

I need to get laid.

The last time he had sex was...holy fuck, in July, right before he broke up with Cleo. Two whole months. It was his longest dry spell since he lost his virginity to the most popular girl in the senior class when he was fifteen.

Shauna Smith. She'd been something. And she earned her title as head cheerleader in more ways than one.

"I can't believe I've never had this before." Farrah tossed her empty wrapper and milk tea container in the trash. "I usually go to Cinnamon for breakfast. Kris insists."

"This is better than café food, and cheaper too." Blake tapped his metro card on the reader. "Don't say I never bought you anything."

Her silvery laugh sent another wave of awareness rippling through his body.

Correction: I really need to get laid.

"So where are we going?"

"Have you heard of M50?"

"Sort of." Blake had never heard of M50 in his life.

"It's Shanghai's contemporary art district. There's a ton of galleries—and design inspo." Farrah waved her sketchbook in the air.

"For the competition."

She looked surprised. "You remember."

"Of course." Blake couldn't forget the way Farrah's eyes lit up when she talked about the competition. She was studying interior design because she loved it, not because everyone said she should. Her passion was refreshing...and depressing. Blake had never felt that way about football or anything else in his life, really.

He knew what he didn't want to do. Now he had to figure out what he *did* want to do.

After ten minutes in M50, Blake scratched *artist* off his potential careers list. As a neighborhood, M50 was cool. It featured old warehouses and factory-buildings-turned-galleries for every type of art Blake could imagine and some he couldn't.

There were confounding multimedia neon and LED light installations and a terrifying exhibit of monstrous spider sculptures. There was also a weird-ass garden where everything—trees, grass, flowers—was made of knitted yarn.

Blake appreciated the creativity, but...he didn't get it. He understood paintings. That was art. Boring art, but art. He did *not* understand the point of knitting a tree (seriously, what the fuck?) or why someone would pay thousands of dollars for a twisted piece of metal.

Rich people needed to find better ways to spend their money.

Farrah, on the other hand, was so busy examining the exhibits and scribbling notes, she'd stopped speaking to him once they started gallery hopping. He didn't mind; watching her work was way more interesting than any of the exhibits on display.

Soon, Blake could identify her every microexpression: the way her brow furrowed when she was thinking hard, the way she tilted her head an inch to the left when she was confused, the way her eyebrows shot up and her mouth parted in excitement when she came across a revelation—he knew it was a revelation because she'd open that notepad of hers and scribble like crazy.

Perhaps he should be an anthropologist, though Blake suspected his interest in studying people was limited to Farrah. He'd never been this engrossed by anyone else before.

By the time they wrapped up their self-guided tour, it was almost three. Blake's stomach growled with anger—they'd blitzed through the galleries without stopping for food.

Blake and Farrah settled for the first café they could find. The airy industrial space doubled as a gallery and studio, and customers drifted through the loft, admiring the art displays with their coffees in hand.

Despite the bustling crowds, they snagged a table in the seating area upstairs. Their meal comprised of coffee, paninis, brownies, and cheesecake.

Healthy? No. Delicious? Hell yeah.

"Thanks for coming with me today." Farrah sipped her drink. "Sorry if I ignored you. When I get in the zone, I tune out everything else."

"It's ok." Blake wasn't used to being ignored, but it was nice being able to do his own thing without other people breathing down his neck. At TSU, he couldn't take a shit without others talking about it.

That was the great thing about FEA. People left him alone. He received a lot of stares and questions the first week or two—why did he quit football? Was he ever going to play again? Why was he in Shanghai?—but soon, everyone was too caught up in their own lives to pay him much mind. The questions tapered off, and Blake felt like a regular student for the first time in a long time.

"Did you like the art?"

"Umm-hmm." Blake wolfed down half his panini to avoid answering her question.

"Sorry, I don't speak caveman." Farrah's eyes sparkled with amusement.

Blake swallowed his food and tried to think of something nice to say. "It was cool. The yarn garden was, uh, interesting."

Farrah burst into laughter, and Blake's skin tingled with pleasure.

"You hated it. You were falling asleep in the yarn exhibit."

So she'd noticed. A grin tugged at Blake's lips. "You can't blame me. It was like being inside a giant blanket."

Another laugh, another tingle of pleasure.

Farrah leaned forward. "Can I tell you a secret? I thought that was weird too."

Blake clutched his chest. "Is it possible? Do we...have something in common?"

"I guess we do." Farrah's eyes flickered with something he didn't dare name, and his heart slammed against his rib cage in response.

The noise and the people surrounding them fell away. All Blake could focus on was the girl sitting across from him—her eyes, her scent, her lips. She smelled like orange blossoms and vanilla, and she was so damn close. If he leaned forward juuuust a few inches, their mouths would touch.

His throat dried at the thought. It was a bad idea. She was a virgin. She was in FEA. But dammit, he wanted to know what Farrah tasted like and whether her lips were as soft as they looked.

The flare of awareness in her eyes told him the attraction wasn't one-sided. Her lips parted. His pulse beat double time. Should he—

Then she blinked, and the moment was gone.

They leaned back.

"We should go—"

"It's getting late—"

Blake and Farrah laughed, their awkwardness mingling to cover up something neither wanted to acknowledge.

"We should head back," Farrah said. "I need to work on my portfolio. I got some good ideas today."

"Yeah, and I, uh, need to go to the gym." Blake winced the instant the words left his mouth. They did not help the meathead image most people had of him. He lived by the philosophy, "Other people's prejudices aren't my problem," but he cared what Farrah thought of him.

He didn't dare ask himself why.

Fortunately, Farrah didn't say anything. They left the café and wound their way through the maze of galleries to the main street, where it took her less than two minutes to hail a taxi.

"Sometimes I can't believe I'm here." Farrah gazed out the window as building after building whizzed by. "I've seen so many photos of Shanghai that when I look at it in person, I feel like I'm in the middle of a postcard and I'm not actually *here*." She shook her head. "Sorry, that doesn't make sense."

"No, I know what you mean." Blake stared at the skyline. The jungle of high-rise chrome and glass looked like a scene from a science-fiction movie.

He, Blake Ryan, was in Shanghai. He'd been so busy with classes and settling in that it didn't hit him until this moment.

He'd up and left Texas to spend a year in a country where he didn't know the language, didn't know the customs, and didn't know anyone when he first arrived. Until now, he'd never been farther east than New York.

Blake wasn't sure how he felt about it yet. He enjoyed the *freedom* of being far from home, but China took some adjusting to. He wasn't a fan of the squat toilets, the pollution, or how fucking hard Mandarin was. He had to communicate with hand gestures ninety percent of the time outside FEA, unless there was someone there to translate for him.

Of course, there were pros to go alongside the cons. The architecture, the cheap prices, (some of) the street foods. Shanghai remained foreign to him, but it also made Blake feel connected to something bigger than himself and the world he'd always known. And sometimes, when he stared out the window at the towering spires of the Shanghai skyline, he thought he might love it enough to never go back.

"I've never been in love." Farrah's non sequitur jolted Blake from his thoughts. She wore a far-off expression, like she was dreaming of something she knew would happen but hasn't happened yet. "I think I could fall in love here."

Her wistful tone made his heart ache in the strangest way. "Aren't you already in love?"

Blake's jaw tightened when he remembered the way Farrah looked at Leo yesterday. He had no reason to be jealous, but the green-eyed monster reared its head at the oddest times.

"Leo's a crush. I want big crazy, stupid love. The kind that's worthy of Hollywood." Farrah sighed. "I just want to know what that feels like."

Blake eased backward and sank deeper into his seat. "That's the con."

"Excuse me?"

"There is no romance like that in real life. Books and movies hype up the idea of a grand love and The One to make money."

The peaceful atmosphere in the cab shattered. Farrah's jaw dropped. "Wow. That is so cynical."

"It's not cynical. It's the truth." Blake wasn't anti-love, but it was overrated. Look at him and Cleo. Childhood friends turned lovers, with plenty of bumps and obstacles along the way. Their story was *made* for the movies, and look how that turned out. Everyone said they were meant to be together, and he did love her, but he didn't love her the way Hollywood said he should.

Hollywood romance was a load of crap.

Farrah crossed her arms over her chest. "I'm guessing you've never been in love."

"I have." What he and Cleo had was love, right? "It's not all it's cracked up to be."

She turned her head and stared out the window again. "I'm sorry. That's really sad." For once, her tone was devoid of sarcasm.

Blake followed her lead and gazed out the window closest to him. The view wasn't nearly as nice on this side. It was all old apartment buildings and concrete and smog.

"I'll survive."

CHAPTER 7

"HAVE A SAFE FLIGHT TOMORROW." FARRAH'S MOM'S voice crackled over the line. "Message me when you land."

"I will." Farrah stuffed another bikini into the crevice of her bulging suitcase. Six swimsuits for one week should be enough, right? "Do you want anything special from Thailand?"

"No. I'm trying minimalism," Cheryl Lau decided. She'd kept her maiden name even after she married Farrah's dad, which turned out to be a fortuitous choice, given how that relationship turned out. "I'm doing a big spring cleaning this weekend."

"Mom, it's October."

"You know what I mean." Farrah could practically hear her mom waving a dismissive hand in the air. "Anyway, I have to go. I'm going ballroom dancing tonight at Blue Coast."

"Ok. Have fun. Talk to you later."

"Talk to you later. Remember, message me!"

Farrah hung up and tossed the phone on the bed, where it landed with a thump next to Olivia.

"You and your mom are so cute." Olivia sounded envious.

"All my mom ever asks me is what my grades are and whether I've heard back from my internship yet."

Farrah cocked her head. "When *do* you hear about your internship?"

"Four to six weeks." Olivia jiggled her foot. "They review applications on a rolling basis."

"You'll get it." Farrah squeezed in one last bikini—just to be safe—and flipped down the lid. "Help?"

Olivia hopped off Farrah's bed and sat on the suitcase while Farrah struggled to zip it up.

"It's one of the most prestigious internships in finance," Olivia said. "CB Lippmann accepts ten interns every summer. Ten! Do you know how many people apply? Ten *thousand*. That's a 0.001 percent acceptance rate."

"I doubt ten thousand people apply every year." Farrah tugged on the zipper, praying it wouldn't break. Sweat broke out on her forehead. Forget the gym. Packing was a whole workout unto itself.

"Fine, that may be an exaggeration, but there are at *least* a thousand applicants. That's still an infinitesimal acceptance rate."

"You are the smartest, most hardworking person I know. If you don't get it, the game's rigged."

"Babe, this is Wall Street. Of course the game's rigged."

The zipper gave way without warning. The unexpected force knocked Farrah on her ass. "Shit!"

Olivia burst into laughter. She stood up and grabbed Farrah's hand, hauling her off the floor.

"I was waiting for that to happen."

"Thanks a lot." Farrah pushed her carry-on into a standing position. *Oof.* "This is probably over the weight limit."

Olivia nudged the case with her foot. It didn't budge. "It's definitely over the weight limit."

"I hope the airline doesn't check." It was a risk, but Farrah sure as hell wasn't going to repack. It was close to midnight, and their flight left at eight tomorrow morning.

"Speaking of summer internships, how's your portfolio going? It's due in January, right?"

Olivia reclaimed her seat on Farrah's bed. Farrah had replaced the lumpy white comforter with a pretty pink one she'd found at a local market. Added pink, white, and gray velvet throw pillows, a framed sketch on the wall, and two tiny succulents on the nightstand, and the place looked a lot more inviting.

Her roommate, Janice, kept the original bedding and didn't decorate at all. Looking at the two sides of their room was like looking at a before-and-after picture.

Farrah itched to do *something* about Janice's bare walls, but (a) Janice was never there for her to bring it up, and (b) she didn't want to overstep her boundaries.

She'd have to make do with a half-decorated room.

"Yeah. I'm making progress." Farrah was close to completing her second design, a restaurant inspired by the stark contemporary lines and splashes of bright color she'd seen at M50. She'd need to tweak it, but at least she knew what she was doing. She had *no idea* what to do for the third design.

"Must be all the gallery hopping last weekend," Olivia quipped. "Alone time is good for the soul."

Farrah coughed. "Right. Alone time."

She hadn't told her friends about her excursion with Blake. It wasn't like they went on a date. It wasn't worth bringing up.

Her discomfort didn't go unnoticed.

Olivia narrowed her eyes. "What are you hiding?"

"Nothing." Farrah swiped her sketchbook from her desk. "Hey, wanna look at my designs and tell me what you think?"

"Yes, after you tell me what you're hiding. Oh my god, did

you meet someone last weekend?" Olivia clutched Farrah's arm, her eyes wide with excitement. "Are you having a secret affair?"

"Don't be ridiculous. I'm with you guys *all the time*. The logistics wouldn't work."

"You weren't with us Sunday."

Farrah sighed. Once Olivia got an idea in her head, she was like a pit bull with a bone. "Fine. If you must know, I ran into Blake on my way out and, on the *spur of the moment*—meaning it *wasn't planned*—I asked him to join me. We went to a few galleries and came back. The end."

Olivia's grip tightened. "You're having a secret affair with Blake Ryan!"

"I am not!" Farrah wrenched her arm away and shook it out. "Jesus, you cut off my circulation."

"Don't change the subject. You spent an entire day with Blake and didn't tell us about it. Why?" Olivia wiggled her eyebrows. "What naughty things did you get up to?"

"None. You read too many erotica novels."

For someone so status driven, Olivia was surprisingly open about her less-than-highbrow reading habits.

"They're great inspiration. Sammy has no complaints."

Farrah wrinkled her nose. "Ew. TMI."

Waaaay too much information.

As she'd expected, Olivia had caved and hooked up with Sammy at 808 earlier that week. They'd gone on their first date the next night and were fast becoming one of FEA's most nauseatingly cute couples.

Farrah was thrilled (the hundred kuai she received for winning the group's bet on when Olivia and Sammy would get together was a bonus), but their relationship also reminded her of the utter lack of romance in her own life.

"Once again, changing the subject. I know he's not your

'type'"—Olivia placed the word in air quotes—"but maybe that's a good thing. Leo's your type, but he's taken. Are you still into him?"

"Who, Blake?"

"Leo!"

"Uh." Farrah pictured Leo's curly dark hair and easy smile. As usual, her stomach fluttered at the mental image, though the sensation was more muted than usual. "I'm getting over it."

"That means you're not over it, which means you need to get over it, because we have a whole school year ahead of us. You're young, hot, and single in Shanghai. You can have any guy you want except, you know, Leo. As your friend, I'm obligated to make sure you don't spend your time here moping over unrequited love."

"Come on. I have other things going on in my life."

"Yeah, but you still think about him all the time. Tell me I'm wrong."

Farrah fiddled with the binder rings on her sketchbook.

"That's what I thought. Now, you know what they say. The best way to get over someone is to get under someone else. In this case, that 'someone else' is a Greek-god lookalike whose name rhymes with Jake Bryan."

"Not going to happen."

Olivia let out an exasperated huff. "I don't understand why you're being so stubborn. The boy is HOT. Capital *H*, capital *O*, capital *T*. Have you *seen* his abs?"

"No." Farrah raised her eyebrows. "Have you?"

Olivia's cheeks colored. "I may have snuck a *tiny* peek when I saw him coming out of the shower on my way to Sammy's room."

Farrah's eyebrows arched higher.

"Stop. I went to return Sammy's pen. Anyway, that's not the point. The point is, Blake is the perfect person to help you get over Leo."

"He's cute, but he's so—" Farrah searched for the right word. "Cocky."

"Mmm. I bet he is."

"Olivia!" It was Farrah's turn to flush red.

Olivia laughed. "Look, you said you're not waiting for The One to lose your virginity to. It's probably better that way. Less pressure. And since we're in Shanghai, what better way to lose your virginity *and* get over Leo than by hooking up with a hot guy who knows what he's doing? Because trust me, Blake looks like he knows what he's doing."

On paper, it made sense. Farrah was physically attracted to Blake. She even enjoyed hanging out with him (most of the time).

But Blake thought romance was a con, which was the most blasphemous thing Farrah could think of.

Then again, it didn't matter what he thought of love if it was going to be a hookup, right?

Ugh. Her head hurt.

Olivia placed her hand on Farrah's arm. "Remember, we're studying abroad. What happens in Shanghai stays in Shanghai."

Did it? Farrah wasn't so sure.

Yet later that night, after Olivia left and moonlight streamed through the curtains like a river of silver silk, Farrah found herself mulling over Olivia's words. She thought about them over and over until she drifted asleep to dreams of Texas and crystal-blue eyes.

CHAPTER 8

BLAKE WAS LONELY.

It was a real bitch, considering he'd spent years wishing for more alone time.

He'd chosen to stay behind for National Day while his friends lived it up in Thailand, but he was starting to regret his decision.

At first, having the dorm to himself was great. Blake walked through the halls half-naked and blasted his music as loud as he liked. He didn't have to study or do homework. He did whatever he wanted whenever he wanted.

The high lasted two or three days before Blake started missing FEA's noise and bustle. He missed bantering with Farrah. He even missed Luke's dumb texts. Sure, he enjoyed exploring Shanghai, but it would have been nice to, you know, have someone join him.

He couldn't even talk to his family or friends back home. Besides the Austin–Shanghai time difference, his mom and sister were busy with school as an art teacher and student, respectively. Landon was busy prepping to take over his mother's empire. He didn't want to call Cleo and open a can of worms, and he would rather poke his eyes out than speak with his dad.

After his morning jog at World Expo Park, Blake went to Nanjing Road instead of returning to the dorm. He needed to be around people.

He got off at the People's Square station and walked to East Nanjing. The famous pedestrian street bustled with activity. He wanted people; he got people. They streamed by in a relentless, never-ending wave of humanity.

Shanghai was the most populous city in the most populous country in the world, and it never let you forget it.

Blake wandered aimlessly, unsure what he was searching for. He passed by couples, families, and tourists gawking at the spectacle. Huge signs and video advertisements loomed overhead, screaming for attention.

A few days ago, these things made him feel alive. Free. No one knew him here. He could do and be whoever he wanted. But now...

Blake stopped. The man behind him cursed and walked around him, knocking into Blake's shoulder as he did so. A harried-looking young mother ran past with three children. Her gaze flicked over Blake before she turned her attention to the child trying to scrape a piece of old gum off the sidewalk. A group of teenagers huddled over a phone and laughed at something on-screen.

Blake saw them but didn't see them. He could only focus on the image in his mind's eye, of himself standing in the middle of Shanghai's busiest street, surrounded by people who didn't know and didn't care who he was.

One ant among thousands.

A stranger in a strange land.

Loneliness settled like a rock in the pit of his stomach.

For the first time in his life, Blake was homesick.

He resumed his walk down Nanjing Road and kept his eyes peeled for something, anything that reminded him of home. He bypassed McDonald's—he wasn't *that* desperate—and made a left onto an adjacent street. Ten minutes later, he stumbled onto a sports bar named The End Zone.

Not the most creative name, but it sounded comfortingly American.

"Hey." The bartender smiled when Blake walked in. She resembled a young Angelina Jolie, and her name tag indicated she was called Mina.

"Hey." Blake parked himself at the bar and ordered a cup of coffee and the signature breakfast plate—eggs, bacon, home fries, toast.

The place was empty this early in the morning, and there were no interesting games on TV, so Blake settled for flirting with Mina, who seemed all too happy to flirt back. In the space of ten minutes, Blake learned she grew up in Phoenix, graduated from Arizona State with a degree in public relations, and took a gap year to travel and visit her brother in Shanghai.

Blake was shocked to learn Mina's brother owned The End Zone. From what she told him, her brother was only a few years older than her, and she was twenty-two, twenty-three tops.

"How'd he end up here?" Blake broke off a piece of bacon and popped it in his mouth. It tasted like home.

The bells above the door jangled as another customer walked in.

"He hated school and dropped out his junior year to back-pack around Asia. He loved Shanghai so much, he moved here. Got a gig in the restaurant industry, made some good connections, and opened this place two years ago."

"You make it sound so easy." The wheels in Blake's head started turning. When he chose to major in business, he'd been thinking about a corporate job in marketing or operations. Not entrepreneurship. He didn't know the first thing about starting and running a business. The thought of doing his own thing was tempting, though. Blake could be his own boss. No one would tell him what to do.

"It was tough at first, but he made it work. Greg's good at this sort of thing." Mina left to tend to the other customer but not before giving Blake a wink that said she'd be back.

Blake's heart beat fast. The wheels in his head turned faster.

He liked sports bars. He knew what people who frequented sports bars liked because he'd grown up with them. He knew how to build and sell a brand—he'd been selling himself as a brand for years.

It was like a dam broke. After months of not knowing what he wanted to do after graduation, the ideas flowed so fast, Blake couldn't keep up.

He asked for the check and scribbled his signature, eager to return to the dorm and put some of his ideas on paper. They might not lead anywhere, but it felt good to have a plan. He couldn't wait to tell—

Who?

His family? His father wasn't going to be happy unless Blake rejoined the football world; his mother and Joy would try their best to be supportive, but they wouldn't get it.

His friends? His Shanghai friends were in Thailand, and they didn't know him well enough to understand why he was so excited.

Meanwhile, his friends back home were far and few between since he quit the team. He and Cleo didn't part on the best terms, and Landon had his hands full with his mother.

When Blake led the TSU Mustangs to their third national championship, he had fifty thousand people cheering him on. When it came to the personal wins, he had no one.

The realization washed over him like a cold shower.

"It was nice talking to you." Mina whisked his signed receipt off the counter. "I have to keep an eye on things until my brother gets in tonight, but I'll be free after eight." She pressed another slip of paper into Blake's hand. "We could have some fun. No strings attached."

Blake raised his eyebrows. "No strings attached, huh?"

"I'm in Shanghai for a few more weeks, and you're cute." Mina shrugged. "It doesn't have to be a big thing."

Blake thought about the empty dorm waiting for him on campus and slipped her number into his pocket. "I'll see you at eight."

CHAPTER 9

THE RAYS WARMED FARRAH'S SKIN LIKE A LUXURIOUS blanket, the sound of water lapping against the shore provided a soothing natural soundtrack, and the coconut drink next to her was the best she'd ever tasted.

Life was good.

She propped herself up to take another sip of her drink.

"You're blocking my sun," Kris said.

"Sorry." Farrah lay down. Despite their idyllic setting, Kris was grumpier than usual.

"Cheer up." Courtney stretched her arms over her head. Hours of sun had darkened her freckles until they resembled a constellation of stars across her nose and cheeks. "Look at this place. How can you not be happy here?"

Koh Samui was a popular tourist destination, but the group had been lucky enough to stumble on this remote beach on their way back to the resort. Swaying coconut palms, big boulders framing the pristine stretch of powdery white sand, crystal water that glittered like a sheet of aquamarine beneath the sun. It was a tropical postcard come to life.

"It's my dad's stupid girlfriend." Kris adjusted her sunglasses. "She convinced him to spend Christmas in Aspen. Aspen! It'll be snowing and shit. I mean, who wants a white Christmas?"

The rest of the group exchanged glances.

"Uh, is that a rhetorical question?" Sammy asked.

Kris ignored him. "We've spent every Christmas in St. Barts since I was five. It's tradition. Now this girl waltzes in and tries to change everything." She sighed. "On the bright side, Daddy feels so bad, he's buying me Harry Winston for Christmas. He usually gets me Tiffany."

"Every cloud has a diamond lining," Leo deadpanned, earning himself a jab in the ribs from Courtney.

His sarcasm went over Kris's head. "True."

Farrah stifled a laugh.

Meanwhile, Olivia was trying to engage Nardo in conversation, a clear sign of how much she liked Sammy. She thought Nardo was a pompous, mansplaining jerk, but he was Sammy's best friend for reasons no one could fathom. Sammy was the most likable guy on the planet; Nardo was not.

"Whatcha reading?" Olivia flipped onto her stomach to peer at the thick tome in Nardo's hands.

"A book."

"No shit, Sherlock. What book?"

Nardo pushed his glasses up on his nose. He was the palest in the group and had slathered on half a bottle of sunscreen before they hit the beach. Even so, Farrah could see the skin on his back turning pink. "*War and Peace and War*."

"You mean *War and Peace*."

"No, that's a nineteenth-century novel by Leo Tolstoy about the French invasion of Russia. This is *War and Peace and War* by Peter Turchin. It explores the rise and fall of empires from the perspective of evolutionary biology."

Olivia's eyes glazed over. "Wow. Fun beach read."

"Do you know you talk like a human Wikipedia?" Farrah asked.

Nardo looked touched. "Thank you."

Sammy rolled over onto his side and kissed Olivia's shoulder. "He's always been this way. You should see our dorm at Harvey Mudd. It's packed with political history books."

Olivia wrinkled her nose. "Aren't you guys math majors?"

"I'm economics." Nardo returned to his book. "You can read outside your major."

"I know. I just finished *Crazy Rich Asians*."

Farrah's face split into a huge grin at the look on Nardo's face.

"*Excuse* me. I thought we were on vacation." Courtney snatched the book from Nardo's hands, ignoring his cry of protest. "Let's do something fun."

"We are doing something fun," Sammy said. "We're at the beach."

"No, something *fun*. I know!" Courtney snapped her fingers. "Let's go skinny-dipping!"

Farrah's eyes widened in horror.

"I love you, but that's the worst idea I've ever heard." Olivia's expression matched Farrah's. "It's broad daylight."

"So? We're among friends. Live and let live, Liv."

"No, thanks."

Luke raised his hand. "I'll do it."

"Me too," Nardo said.

Every head whipped in his direction.

"You will?" Sammy asked, mouth agape.

Nardo's cheeks matched his back. "Like Courtney said, we're on vacation."

"Great," Kris said. "See what you did, Court? Now we'll have to see Luke and Nardo naked."

The boys looked at each other. Without saying a word, they gathered handfuls of sand and tossed them at Kris before she could duck out of the way. Her mouth froze into a shocked O as the grains peppered her hair and cleavage.

Everyone burst into laughter.

"Blech!" Kris sputtered. "I have sand in my mouth! I'm going to *kill* you guys." She tried to wipe the sand from her face and smeared it farther across her cheeks.

They laughed harder.

"A skinny dip will get the sand off. Come on, guys, don't be boring," Courtney wheedled.

"Chill," Leo said. "The Full Moon Party is tonight. We'll have fun then."

"I am chill. Excuse me for trying to make sure everyone enjoys themselves."

"We are enjoying ourselves," Leo argued. "People know how to have fun without you. We don't have to do everything you say all the time."

The laughter stopped.

Farrah's heart pounded like a carpenter hammering a nail into the wall. Courtney and Leo didn't fight. Ever. He was too easygoing, and she was...well, she was Courtney.

"What did you say?" Courtney's face turned red.

He pinched his temple. "Let's not do this now."

"Oh, we are doing this now. You started it. Finish it." The challenge was clear.

"I'm just saying, you don't have to be such a control freak all the time."

Kris flinched.

Olivia buried her face in Farrah's shoulder.

"*Control freak?*" Courtney was Mount Etna waiting to erupt. Farrah saw steam pouring out of her ears. "Screw you! It's easy for you to be the chill, laid-back one. *I'm* the one who makes sure we have fun. I come up with the activities. I keep this group together. We wouldn't *be* here if it weren't for me!"

"Listen to yourself." Leo's sharp tone sent a ripple of shock through the group. "No one asks you to do those things. It's like you have some sort of god complex."

Courtney, Olivia, and Farrah gasped at the same time.

"Leo." Kris took off her sunglasses and flicked some sand off her shoulder. Her voice was glacial. "You should go back to the hotel."

"Gladly." Leo tossed his towel over his shoulder and walked off, leaving silence in his wake.

"That escalated quickly," Luke finally said.

"Are you ok?" Farrah wasn't sure what to say. They'd never had a big fight in the group before.

"Yeah. I can't believe him. God complex." Courtney squirted sunscreen into her palm and rubbed it onto her arms with more force than necessary. "I don't have a god complex."

Nardo coughed.

"Of course you don't. You take charge, and he can't handle it." Kris put her sunglasses back on. "Guys. If you ask me, they're not worth the trouble."

"Thanks a lot," Sammy said.

Olivia patted his hand. "Don't worry, sweetie. You're the exception."

The group settled into an uneasy silence.

Farrah tried to focus on the sound of the waves, but her mind was running a million miles a minute. She used to fantasize about Courtney and Leo breaking up. They'd part amicably, Leo would realize he'd been in love with Farrah all along, and Courtney would give them her blessing.

She didn't know when or how, but somewhere along the way, that fantasy had dissolved.

Farrah didn't want Courtney and Leo to break up. She wanted the group to stay the way it was. Their collective friendship meant more than any selfish individual desire.

Farrah squeezed her eyes shut and quieted her thoughts enough to let the warmth and waves work their magic.

It was *so nice* here. She didn't want to go back to Shanghai. She wanted to stay here forever. Who was in Shanghai, anyway?

Blake. Blake's in Shanghai.

The thought was so unexpected, it kicked Farrah right out of her dreamy state. She was in paradise. What was she doing thinking about Blake and his dimples and his muscles? Good Lord, those muscles. He could probably bench-press her without breaking a sweat.

Farrah's mouth dried. She wondered what he was doing. Going out every night? Having wild sex with a rotating cast of girls in every corner of the dorm?

Probably. She hadn't seen him hook up with anyone since the program started, but that didn't mean he didn't do it. You couldn't be a college guy who looked like that and not be getting some on a regular basis.

It was the wrong mental route to take because Farrah couldn't keep the resulting flood of images at bay.

Blake naked. Blake and faceless girl having sex in his room. Blake and faceless girl having sex in the kitchen. Blake and Farrah having sex in the student lounge.

Whoa. Where the hell did that *come from?*

Farrah's eyes flew open. She slammed her mental gate down in panic and stopped the images in their tracks. They continued to hover near the entrance, waiting for an opportunity to sneak back in.

Her heart beat double time. The last fantasy came through so vividly, she might as well have broadcast it to the world.

Farrah snuck a peek at her friends. They lolled on their beach towels, oblivious.

She squeezed her eyes shut again. *Think of Leo. Think of the Full Moon Party. Think of Grandma in her old pink pajamas.*

Nothing worked. The fantasy of her and Blake pushed against her consciousness. If she let herself, she could still see it—her soft flesh pressed against Blake's hard muscles, his hands gripping her hips, their mouths fused in a hungry embrace.

A surge of heat coursed through her body. Farrah flipped onto her stomach and buried her face in her arms. The ache remained.

"Wait! My timer didn't go off yet," Olivia protested. "We're supposed to flip every twenty minutes." She poked Farrah's back. "Hmm. You are kind of red. Maybe you should apply more sunscreen."

"I'm fine," Farrah said, her voice muffled.

"I'm reapplying for you. Stay still."

Farrah didn't resist as Olivia slathered her with SPF 50. Instead, she lay there and wondered why, exactly, she was fantasizing about sex with Blake Ryan.

Deep down, she knew the answer.

I am so screwed.

CHAPTER 10

BLAKE'S DRY SPELL? DONEZO.

Thank god. If he went any longer without sex, they'd have to wheel him into the ER for emergency blue ball surgery.

However, despite Mina's considerable skills in bed, their fling wasn't as satisfying as he'd expected. It was like junk food: good in the moment, until the high dissipated and left him emptier than ever.

Blake watched as Mina slipped into her heels and slung her bag strap over her shoulder. Luke texted a few hours ago saying he'd swing by after he dropped his luggage off at his homestay. He expected his ex-roommate to bang on his door any minute now.

Someone knocked.

Well, that was scarily accurate timing.

"That's my cue," Mina drawled. Like Blake, she had no desire for after-sex chitchat. They met up, banged, and parted ways. Easy. Simple. No strings attached.

"I'll walk you out."

Blake opened the door, expecting to see Luke's burly frame filling the doorway. To his shock, he found Farrah standing there dressed in...sheep pajamas?

Yep, those were definitely fluffy white sheep marching across her shirt and pants. They were so adorable and such a departure from Farrah's usual polished style, Blake couldn't hold back a chuckle.

"Hey, I—" Farrah stopped when she saw Mina. One look at Mina's tousled hair and swollen lips, and it didn't take a genius to figure out what she and Blake had been up to.

Surprise and another emotion Blake couldn't place flitted across her face.

Tendrils of guilt snaked up his spine.

Wait. I have nothing to be guilty about. Blake was single. He could hook up with anyone he wanted.

"I can see myself out." Mina stood on her tiptoes to plant a lingering kiss on Blake's mouth. He returned it with hesitation, hyperaware of Farrah's presence. "Call me later."

She nodded at Farrah on her way out. "Nice jammies." She sauntered down the hall and disappeared into the stairwell.

"Sorry," Farrah said, that strange expression still on her face. "I didn't know you had company."

"It's fine. She was leaving anyway." Blake leaned against the doorframe. Nope. Guilt had no business here. None at all. "To what do I owe this pleasure?"

"It's nothing."

"If it's nothing, you wouldn't be standing here."

Farrah blew out a breath. "Ok, I don't want you to read too much into this, but I got you something from Thailand and wanted to give it to you before I forgot." She handed him a small elephant figurine. He'd been so busy staring at the sheep, he hadn't noticed the elephant. "It's modeled after an elephant at the sanctuary we went to. He reminded me of you."

Blake took the elephant and rubbed his thumb over the intricate stone carving. A lump formed in his throat. He couldn't remember the last time he received a gift from someone who didn't expect something back.

The pit of loneliness that had plagued him for the past week shrank from the size of a fist to the size of a pea.

Stop being a pansy and toughen up. It's an elephant, for chrissakes.

Blake ignored the warmth flooding his veins and flashed his signature smile, the one that he knew made girls melt. To his annoyance, Farrah remained unfazed. "Was the elephant also handsome and athletic?"

"Cocky and a show-off."

"I'll take it." Blake assessed the elephant. Heck, it *was* a good-looking animal. "Thank you. This is so thoughtful."

Farrah looked embarrassed. "It's not a big deal. Just a trinket I picked up."

"Well, I appreciate it. Shows how much you missed me." He wiggled his eyebrows.

"I did not *miss* you."

"You thought about me."

"Hardly."

"You thought about me enough to buy this." Blake brandished the elephant in triumph.

Farrah's expression was priceless.

"You know what? I'm taking it back." She attempted to swipe the figurine from his hands. He held it above his head, laughing as she jumped to try to reach it. "I'm giving it to Josh."

Blake stilled. "Who's Josh?"

"My cousin."

He relaxed. "Well, Josh will have to do without because Blake Jr. is mine."

"Of course you named it after yourself. How narcissistic can you be?"

IF WE EVER MEET AGAIN | 79

"Very. Now stop trying to take him back, or you're not getting your thank-you present."

That caught her attention. "What's my present?"

"Whatever you want it to be."

"That's the laziest answer ever."

"Yet it works. Would you rather have something you want or something someone else *thinks* you want?"

Farrah frowned. "Good point. Fine. I want dinner. A *good* dinner. I'm starving."

"That's it?"

"You want me to ask for your firstborn too?"

"If you want to raise him or her for me, sure." Blake shrugged. "In the meantime, dinner it is, milady."

"I'll change."

"No. You should wear those PJs out. They're cute." He tried to keep a straight face. He failed.

"Shut up." Farrah spun on her heels and marched toward the stairs.

"I'm serious. They are cute!" Blake yelled after her.

She flipped him the finger without turning around. "Meet me in the lobby in ten."

Blake was still chuckling when he tucked the elephant into his desk drawer. He changed into street clothes and pulled out his phone to ask Luke for a rain check when a message from his friend popped up.

Can't make it tonight. Homestay fam made dinner for me.

Sometimes the universe aligns.

Cool. Next time.

On Blake's way to the lobby, he passed by Zack and Scott, who sported dark tans from their week backpacking in Vietnam. Flo was downstairs, surrounded by a pile of shopping bags stamped with Korean characters. She was showing off what looked like a pack of Jason masks to her friends.

Hmm. That reminds me, Halloween is coming up.

"I'm ready!"

Farrah bounded down the stairs in a coat, jeans, and boots. A scarf was wrapped around her throat; gloves covered her hands.

It was sixty degrees outside.

"I didn't realize we're going to Siberia for dinner."

"Har-har." Farrah flipped her hood up. "I'm from SoCal. I'm cold."

"I'm from Texas and you don't see me dressed like we're in the Arctic."

"You're a guy. Guys make terrible decisions."

"That's sexist."

"Sue me."

Blake grinned. Damn, he'd missed her.

"So where do you want to eat dinner, princess?"

She cut a glance his way but let the nickname slide. "Any chance you discovered a cool new restaurant around here?"

Hmm. He'd tried a bunch of restaurants, but none—wait. A slow grin spread across his face.

"Actually, I did. It's not new, and it's not around here, but you'll love it. Come on!"

"Where are we going?" Farrah puffed as she jogged to keep up with him. Blake had a good seven inches on her; every step he took was the equivalent of two of hers.

"You'll see."

They climbed into one of the cabs idling outside the campus gates. Blake gave the address to the driver, who stepped on the gas in a sudden move that threw Blake and Farrah against the back seat.

"The least you can do is tell me what kind of cuisine it is," Farrah said once they straightened themselves up. "Pretty please."

"And ruin the surprise? No way."

She pouted. "Fine. At least tell me whether the food is good."

"I have no idea."

"Blake!"

The driver slammed the brakes as they approached a red light. Everyone jerked forward.

Christ. This man's driving was the reason they'd invented seat belts.

"How can you not know if the food is good or not?" Farrah clutched her chest. "Are you taking me to...an *untested restaurant?*"

Blake laughed. "Olivia's spoiled you."

"Say what you will, but the girl knows her restaurants. She's never steered me wrong."

"It's not about the food. Trust me, you'll love it."

"It's dinner. Of course it's about the food."

Blake smiled in response. He refused to succumb to Farrah's pleas for more information. Instead, he distracted her with questions about Thailand, which she was more than happy to talk about. Other than what sounded like Courtney-Leo drama, the trip seemed like a blast, especially the Full Moon Party. Drinking on the beach, fire jump ropes, and bikini-clad girls (including Farrah) covered in body paint? Blake regretted staying behind.

They arrived at their destination. It was a well-known spot, just not amongst the college crowd. He doubted Farrah had heard of it.

The look on her face when the building came into sight proved him right.

"What is this place?" she breathed, her eyes wide with amazement as she took in the architectural marvel in front of her.

Tucked in the northwestern corner of the French Concession, the mansion resembled a Northern European storybook castle with its brown-tiled Gothic and Tudor steeples and spires. There were Chinese touches too, like the two stone lions guarding the front gate and Chinese-style glazed tiling along its roof. It was a radical departure from the colonial architecture that made up most of the French Concession.

Blake grinned at Farrah's reaction. "It's called Moller Villa. It belonged to some rich European guy, but it's a hotel now. Don't worry—there's a restaurant inside."

"How did you find this place? I can't believe I've never heard of it and I'm supposed to be the design student."

"It's not in a lot of Shanghai guides. I only know about it because I was hanging out in a café nearby and one of the staff recommended it."

Farrah slid a glance in his direction. "You met quite a few new people while we were gone."

She was no doubt referring to Mina. For his own sake, Blake chose not to take the bait.

They didn't have reservations, but the hostess squeezed them in after Farrah said something to her in Mandarin. He couldn't understand everything she said, but he picked up on the words *boyfriend (nan pengyou)* and *one year (yi nian)*.

"What did you tell her?" he whispered as the hostess led them to their table.

"I told her you're my boyfriend and it's our one-year anniversary. This was where we had our first date, but you forgot to make reservations."

"Throwing me under the bus. Typical girlfriend behavior."

Her silvery laugh was music to his ears.

Chill, man. Stop acting like you've never been on a date—

He caught himself in the nick of time. This wasn't a date. This was—why were they here again? Right. He was thanking her for the elephant.

It was one hundred percent not a date.

Just a guy and a girl he found wildly attractive, having dinner in a romantic hotel in Shanghai.

Shit.

They took their seats and examined their menus. Blake hadn't been lying when he said he didn't know if the food was good. Judging by the way Farrah's eyes roved the room, examining every detail, it didn't matter. They both knew what they were here for, and it wasn't the lamb.

"You really love it."

Her gaze snapped to his. "What?"

"Design. You haven't stopped staring at the architecture since we arrived."

"Sorry. I'm being a bad dinner companion." Farrah bit her lip. "This design contest is taking over my life."

"It's nothing to apologize for." In fact, her passion fascinated him. What was it like to wake up every day feeling that excited about something? Pretty nice, he'd bet. "How did you get so interested in interior design?"

"You could say it's been a lifelong dream." Farrah smiled. "Sounds cheesy but when I was seven, my parents redecorated the house, and I tagged along with them to the furniture and paint stores. Most kids my age would've found it boring. I loved it. Turns out I had a knack for matching colors and arranging furniture. My dad even took me to his office—" A shadow crossed her face. Farrah cleared her throat and sipped her water. "Anyway, the rest is history."

"A seven-year-old prodigy," Blake teased. He stabbed a piece of meat with his fork. "Do you think you like design so much because you're good at it, or you're good at it because you like it?"

"I never thought about it." Farrah traced the rim of her glass with her finger. "Both, I guess. I'm good at it *and* I like it. I love taking a space and helping it fulfill its potential. Like this restaurant is just a room, right? But with the right furniture and colors, it's a formal dinner spot. Change things up, and it could be a cozy library or a modern minimalist gallery. It could be anything. My job is to mold a space into something that's perfect for the owner—something that'll transform it from just a room into an experience, or a home. We spend most of our lives indoors. How incredible is it to shape something that's such a huge part of people's lives?"

Blake was so swept up in Farrah's enthusiasm, he could picture everything she was saying—the library, the gallery, the gasps of delight when the owners saw their redecorated homes for the first time.

"I'm rambling."

"No. I love hearing you talk about it. It's...captivating." The word slipped out without thought. Part of Blake wanted to take it back, but it was the perfect word to describe how he felt seeing the sparkle in Farrah's eyes and hearing the animation in her voice.

Farrah blushed.

Blake's stomach did a slow roll. He thought he'd gotten over the silly things his body did when he was around her. After all, he'd had enough sex the past three days to get any girl out of his system.

Guess not.

Farrah grabbed her water. "Isn't that how you feel about football?"

The warmth dissipated. Blake leaned back and fiddled with his own glass. "If that were true, I'd still be on the team."

"You were so good. Or so I heard." Farrah shrugged. "I don't follow football."

A smile touched his lips. "Thank god. I'm the opposite of you—good at what I did, didn't particularly like it. Not enough to do it for the next ten, twenty years of my life."

"That's why you quit?"

Blake swallowed. "It's part of it."

Fortunately, Farrah didn't press him on the issue. Unfortunately, she asked him a harder question. "If not football, then what do you want to do?"

Blake remembered his excitement at The End Zone. He'd thought he could do it—start his own business. After sleeping on it, it seemed ridiculous. Sure, he'd already designed the menu in his mind, and he had a million ideas for marketing and how he wanted the place to look, but dreams don't require capital. Businesses do.

The only capital he had was a couple thousand bucks in savings. A liquor license alone cost more than that.

Blake forced himself to smile bigger. "I'll figure it out."

CHAPTER 11

"HE CAN'T DO THIS TO ME." KRIS SNATCHED A DRESS off the rack and tossed it on the growing pile of clothes draped over her arm without glancing at the price tag. "I won't let him."

"Be careful!" Olivia winced. "That dress is like a thousand bucks."

"Good. I'll get one in every color." Kris added the red, gold, and blue versions before moving on to the skirt section.

Farrah trailed after her, trying to ignore the fact that the total value of the items in Kris's arms equaled that of a small country's GDP.

"She always does this when she's upset," Courtney whispered. "She'll be fine after some retail therapy."

"Honey, that's not 'some.' That's a *lot* of retail therapy," Olivia said as Kris dumped her haul into a nearby saleswoman's arms so she could flick through a rack of Maison Margiela skirts. "Besides, I don't think shopping will cut it this time. Her dad is getting married to someone five years older than her. That's gotta sting."

"I can hear you." Kris yanked a skirt so hard off the hanger the delicate material ripped. Everyone gasped. The saleswoman looked like she was going to have a heart attack. "Calm down. I'll pay for it."

"Sweetie, slow down," Farrah said gently. "We can't carry all of this back to the dorm."

"I'll hire someone to carry it back. Don't you know? Money can buy anything, including a twenty-six-year-old redheaded bimbo who thinks she can take my mom's place." Kris's lips trembled before she caught herself. She tossed her hair over her shoulder, her jaw set in defiance.

"Oh, honey." Courtney's eyes swam with sympathy. "It'll be all right."

"Maybe she isn't so bad," Olivia said. "Maybe she really loves your dad."

"*Please.*" Kris sniffled. "He's twice her age, and I love my dad, but he's not George Clooney. The only thing she loves about him is his bank account."

"Soo...the strategy is to drain it before they get married?" Farrah joked, trying to lighten the mood.

It didn't work.

"Hilarious," Kris said. "I can't stop the wedding while I'm in Shanghai, but I can strategize. They're not getting married until next November. In the meantime, I'm going to let Daddy know exactly how upset I am."

"Oh, I think he knows," Courtney said. "The entire girls' hall heard you screaming yesterday."

Farrah and Olivia nodded in affirmation.

"The only language my dad understands is money, and he has tons of it. What I spend today won't even make a—" Kris stopped and held up a finger. "Wait."

They waited.

"Court, your birthday is coming up."

"Two weeks." Courtney rubbed her hands in anticipation. "We're going to *rage*. Gino's and 808 will never be the same."

"Forget Gino's and 808." Kris fished her black Amex out of her purse and handed it to the saleswoman, who snatched it up and hurried to the cashier without dropping any of the clothes items on the floor. "I've got something better in mind."

What that something was, no one knew. Kris refused to tell them because she wanted it to be a "surprise." All she said was not to schedule anything for the entirety of Courtney's birthday weekend and to let the rest of the group know.

When they returned to the dorm, Kris hightailed it to her room with her purchases. Olivia, who'd made it to the interview round for the CB Lippmann internship, went to prep for her video call tomorrow, while Courtney had a Skype date with her family.

That left Farrah with the rest of the afternoon to herself. She'd finished her homework and didn't feel like wrestling with YouTube or Netflix. Between her VPN and the dorm's slow-as-a-snail Wi-Fi, streaming video was a constant struggle.

She wandered down to the boys' floor to find Sammy. He wasn't there. Neither was Blake. Farrah wondered whether he was with the brunette she'd seen coming out of his room the other day. Her stomach twisted at the thought.

Were they dating? Where did they meet? If they were dating, Blake and Farrah's dinner seemed quite intimate for a guy who had a girlfriend, no? Farrah could've sworn—

No. Stop it.

Farrah forced herself to stop thinking about Blake and ran through her other options for company. Luke and Leo lived in homestays, and she wasn't desperate enough to seek out Nardo.

As a last resort, she checked the student lounge, which FEAers never used. Why would they when they had a whole city to play in?

The quiet lounge carried the musty smell of a place that hadn't been disturbed for a while. Farrah was about to leave when she noticed the person reading in the armchair in the corner. A faint sliver of sunlight illuminated Leo's sculpted features.

"Dostoyevsky," she said, making out the book cover from a distance. "Impressive."

Leo's head jerked up. His shoulders eased when he saw who it was. "You should work for the CIA. I didn't hear you come in."

"I'm guessing it's less my spy skills and more the *Crime and Punishment*." Farrah pulled up the chair opposite Leo. "Not a lot of college students spend their Saturday afternoons reading Russian literature."

"They're missing out. What's more exciting than crime *and* punishment?"

Farrah's mouth quirked up. "You have a point."

This was the first time she'd seen Leo since Thailand. He and Courtney said they made up after their fight, but the air between them remained tense. Leo had begged off every group dinner since they returned, citing schoolwork or homestay obligations.

"You look like you just ran a marathon."

"Sort of. I went shopping with Kris."

"Ah, that explains it."

"I don't know if Courtney told you, but Kris found out her dad's getting remarried to some twenty-six-year-old he met at a cocktail bar a few months ago. She's pissed." Farrah watched for a reaction to Courtney's name.

"I wasn't aware." Leo's face was as smooth and blank as marble. "That sucks."

Time to stop beating around the bush. "What's going on with you and Courtney?" Whatever it was, they needed to suck it up and make up—for real.

"I don't know what you mean."

"You had that big fight in Thailand, and things haven't been the same since."

Leo thumbed through his book. "They've been fine."

"You've avoided us—correction, you've avoided Courtney—since we got back."

"I've been busy."

"Bullshit." Farrah slammed her hands on the armrests, causing Leo to jump. "Tell the truth. What's going on? Are you guys breaking up?"

"We're not dating."

"I'm not an idiot. Neither of you has been with anyone else since the year started. In college world, that's dating."

"Really?" Leo arched an eyebrow. "Shall I pull out a dictionary?"

"Don't change the subject."

He flipped his book open and closed. "Look, Courtney's a cool girl. She's fun, and I enjoy hanging out with her. But..." He trailed off. His brows drew together in a deep *V*. "She can be a little..."

"Bossy?"

Leo shrugged.

"We all know she's bossy. *She* knows she's bossy. That's part of her charm."

"I guess." Leo sighed. "Sometimes I wonder what it'd be like to be with someone more chill. Someone like you, for example."

Farrah choked on her spit. He didn't say that. *Did he just say that?*

This was the moment she'd fantasized about since she first laid eyes on Leo.

She expected fireworks.

She expected sweaty palms and jitters in her stomach.

Instead, there was...nothing. The butterflies that used to take flight whenever she saw Leo didn't so much as stir.

"Um, I—"

"Hypothetically." Leo's face crinkled into a smile. "I know I'm not your type."

"You're not?" That was news to her. Leo was *exactly* her type: tall, dark, handsome, sensitive, intelligent. He checked every box on her Ideal Guy checklist.

And yet, nothing.

Maybe she was so used to pining after him, she didn't notice the flutters anymore.

"Nah, you need someone who can challenge you. You'd get bored with me. The two of us would just sit around all day in our thoughts."

She laughed. "There are worse things in life."

"True, but it wouldn't be very exciting."

"Which is why you and Courtney are perfect. She talks enough for both of you."

Leo's laugh joined hers. "That she does."

In the approaching dusk, Leo looked like a sculpture come to life. But as Farrah sat there across from the boy she'd fantasized about since the beginning of the semester, she felt nothing. No butterflies, no skipped heartbeats, no giddiness from his mere presence.

There was only one person who made her feel that way.

He was blond and cocky and infuriating—everything Farrah thought she didn't want. But he was also sweet, thoughtful, and made her laugh in a way no one else could.

Oh god.

Farrah slid down in her chair. She ignored Leo's questioning look and instead wondered how the hell she'd ended up falling for Blake Ryan.

CHAPTER 12

BLAKE WAS GOING TO JUMP.

Seventy stories, 764 feet, and nothing but a rope to keep him from sailing into the afterlife at the tender young age of twenty-one.

It was a helluva bet.

Courtney's birthday weekend could very well turn into Blake's death weekend, but fuck it. What was life without some risks?

Beside him, Farrah clutched the railing with one hand and her necklace with the other, eyes wide and face deathly white. Terror emanated from her in waves.

"I can't do this." She tugged at her harness like it was too tight. "Take this off me. I can't do it. I'm going to die."

"It'll be ok," the bungee jump operator said soothingly. "We've done thousands of these jumps; we know what we're doing. Our safety equipment is top of the line."

"Pass." Farrah backed away and tugged at her harness again. Her breath came out in short, panicked puffs.

The operator looked at Blake, the only person in their group who had yet to jump besides Farrah.

"I'll talk to her," Blake said. "Give us a minute."

He walked over to Farrah and placed his hands on her shoulders. She trembled beneath his hold. "Take a deep breath. In one, two; out one, two. That's it. How are you feeling?"

"Not good. I hate heights." Farrah gulped in another breath. "I don't know why I agreed to this. Tell Court I'm sorry, and that I'll refund Kris her money. Wait, no. I'll tell them myself when I go down." She raised her hand to beckon the operator once.

Blake grabbed her wrist and eased it down. "Whoa. Before you leave, hear me out."

"Don't waste your time. I'm not changing my mind. Do your jump, and I'll meet—"

"Seven thousand miles."

Farrah's brow knit in confusion. "Excuse me?"

"That's how many miles you flew to get from the U.S. to China. Seven thousand miles."

"Um, ok?"

"Did you spend all that time and money to get here so you could stand on the sidelines and watch other people live their lives?"

Farrah's jaw dropped. The words sounded harsh to Blake's own ears, but they needed to be said.

"That's not living." Farrah jabbed her finger at the jumping platform. "That's dying. If I jump off that platform, I'll die."

"Bullshit."

"It's not bullshit!"

"Farrah, think of everyone that's jumped tonight and survived. Fuck, even Luke did it, and he weighs three times more than you do. If he can't break that rope, no one can." Blake's eyes twinkled. "I hate to break it to you, but you're not that special."

"Ha-ha." Farrah's expression lightened before it tensed again.

"I'm still not doing it. Even if the rope doesn't break, I'll have a heart attack in midair."

"Ok." Blake released her. "We're not going to force you to do something you don't want to do. If you're really uncomfortable with the idea, you can leave, and no one will judge you for it. But before you do, look around and tell me what you see."

She did. Blake followed her gaze and took in their surroundings. They stood atop the Macau Tower, home to the world's highest bungee jump. Beneath them, the city's lights and sprawling casino hotels glittered like a carpet of fallen stars.

"I see Macau?"

"You see Macau; I see a choice." Six months ago, Blake would've punched himself in the face if he heard these words coming out of his mouth. He sounded like a damn self-help book. But this wasn't about him; this was about Farrah. "You can either stay in your comfort zone or do something that makes your heart goddamn race. One's safe. The other is scary as hell. You know where the safe path takes you—but it *only* takes you that far. The scary path? No one knows. It could be awful. Or it could be the best decision you'll ever make."

Blake got so caught up in his speech, he forgot whether they were talking about the bungee jump or something else.

Damn, I should be a motivational speaker.

Farrah's eyes swam with uncertainty. "I—" She looked around once more. "I'm *really* scared."

"You should be. So am I. But think of how good it will feel after you do it. Bungee jump: five hundred dollars. Facing your fears: priceless."

Farrah's laughter was music to Blake's ears. She loosened her grip on her necklace. "You are such a cheeseball."

"There's nothing wrong with cheese. It's delicious." Blake's face softened. "How about this? If you don't jump, I won't either."

Her eyes grew round. "You don't have to do that."

"I want to. What are friends for?" Blake smiled a crooked smile. "Second option: if you jump, I'll jump first. I'll catch you if you fall. Not that you will," he added quickly.

A slideshow of emotions played out across Farrah's face. Fear, nervousness, and ultimately, determination. "No," she said. "I'll go first. I need you here for moral support."

Blake grinned. "You got it."

He flagged down the operator. Good thing Kris reserved the entire hour for them. Otherwise, the staff would've kicked them out a long time ago.

"If I die, it's your fault," Farrah said while the operator checked her harness to make sure it was tight enough and buckled correctly.

"Noted." Without thinking, Blake reached out and squeezed her hand. The touch of her skin against his sent his heart racing in a way that had nothing to do with their impending jump off a seventy-story tower. "You'll be ok. I'll buy you a drink after we're done."

"Ready?" the operator asked.

Farrah took a deep breath. Her skin had a faint green tint. "No." She took her position on the jumping platform and looked over her shoulder at Blake. "Make that drink a double."

"Done."

Farrah faced forward. Blake held his breath, his heart pounding in triple time. She hesitated, and for a second he thought she was going to back out again. But she took the leap, and her scream echoed in the cold night air. He could pinpoint the moment the rebound happened because he heard another scream—fainter this time—and then…silence.

A grin spread across Blake's face. Damn, she did it. She really did it.

A wave of pride flooded him.

"You're up." The operator beckoned to Blake.

After he passed the safety check, Blake took Farrah's spot on the jumping platform and looked down. 764 feet was a long way to fall.

"Ready?" The operator and an assistant grasped the back of Blake's harness.

He nodded.

They let go.

Blake pictured Farrah's face. If she could do this, so could he. *Fuck it.*

He was in Macau. He was on top of the world. It was now or never.

Blake closed his eyes and took the fall.

CHAPTER 13

FARRAH DIDN'T DIE. ON THE CONTRARY, SHE'D NEVER felt more alive.

She grabbed Kris's hand and spun her around, her skin buzzing with energy. She couldn't stop smiling. She was on top of the freakin' world.

"Thank you for this!" she shouted over the music.

The idea Kris had during her retail therapy session turned out to be a *humongous* idea—an all-expenses-paid trip to Macau for Courtney's birthday weekend. The bungee jump packages alone cost $4,500 for the group. That wasn't counting the flights, meals, drinks, suites at a five-star hotel, and various other activities. The total bill must have run in the five figures.

Farrah couldn't fathom any parent being okay with their kid dropping that much money in one weekend, but she couldn't bring herself to care. She was too happy, too buzzed, too...*everything*.

"Anytime. I love Macau!" Kris shouted back. Her eyes glowed with a mixture of triumph, defiance, and satisfaction. "And Daddy's going to *freak* when he sees next month's credit card bill. I can't wait! He'll finally understand how upset I am about Gloria."

So the redhead had a name.

The music transitioned from the down-tempo, hypnotic beats of EDM to a sultrier club remix of the latest R&B hit. Farrah smiled when she saw Courtney and Leo making out in the corner. Guess her talk with him worked.

Courtney's birthday fell a day before Halloween, and she had insisted on wearing a costume-esque outfit. Her gold flapper dress glittered like a ray of sunlight in the dark nightclub.

Farrah's gaze flitted around the club and landed on Blake, who was drinking with Luke at the bar. In the club's dim reddish lighting, he looked like sin and temptation rolled into one. Blake turned his head to say something to Luke, and the move threw his profile into sharp relief—the sculpted cheekbones, the high straight nose, the strong jaw. How was it possible for someone's face to be *that* perfect? It wasn't fair.

Yet when Farrah looked at him, she didn't think about how Blake resembled a Greek god. Ok, she thought about it a little, but all she could focus on was the way he'd held her at the top of the Macau Tower. The warmth that rolled through her when he offered to skip the jump with her. How he made her feel like she could conquer her biggest physical fear—and she had.

"You've got it bad."

"What?" Farrah asked, distracted. Blake laughed at something Luke said. The butterflies in her stomach performed a somersault that would have made Simone Biles proud.

"You have a crush on Blake," Kris sang.

Farrah whipped around to face her friend. She flushed crimson. "I do not."

"Please. I recognize that look. You *totally* want to jump Blake's bones."

"Shh!" Farrah glanced back at the bar. Blake remained deep in conversation with Luke. "Do you want everyone to hear you?"

"No one can hear shit. It's loud in here."

"He can hear you!" Farrah gestured at Nardo.

"Thanks for realizing I'm here," he said sardonically. "Don't worry, I won't tell anyone. A girl liking Blake Ryan is hardly news. Guys like that always have a line of girls waiting to get with them." Nardo sniffed. "It's an uninspired choice, really."

"Thank you for your unsolicited opinion." Kris pushed Farrah toward the bar. "Ask him to dance."

"I don't think so." So much for her earlier I-can-conquer-the-world high.

Farrah didn't make the first move. Ever. The thought of rejection and the accompanying humiliation was too much to bear.

"Why not? You like him, don't you?"

"That's not the point. I can't just go up there and ask him."

"Honey, it's the twenty-first century. Girls can make the first move."

"What if he says no?"

"Then he's an idiot. You're hot!"

"Ok, but that doesn't mean—"

"Farrah Lin, if you make one more excuse, I'm going to shove my foot up your ass. Go!"

Ok. She could do this. She was asking Blake to dance, not to marry her.

Farrah forced herself to walk to the bar. Her stomach cramped harder with every step.

Luke noticed her first. "'Sup?"

"'Sup. I mean, hi." *Nice.*

Blake's eyes crinkled into a smile. "I see you're here to claim your drink."

"What? Oh, my drink!" Right. The postjump drink he'd promised her. "That's why I'm here," Farrah said, relieved to have an excuse.

"How does a double tequila shot sound?"

It sounded terrible, but she needed liquid courage. "Perfect."

As Blake placed the order, Farrah worked on taming her nerves. She'd jumped off a fucking tower tonight, for Pete's sake. She shouldn't be this nervous over a simple dance.

"I need to pee before I drink more tequila," Luke announced.

Farrah eyed the yellowish-brown liquid in her shot glass and wrinkled her nose.

"Uh, thanks for letting us know." Blake clapped Luke on the shoulder. "Go do your thing, man."

"Peace." Luke threw up the peace sign and ambled off. He was so tall, he towered over everyone else in the club.

"He's so gone," Farrah said.

"Oh yeah, he's done. I'll be lucky if he doesn't puke all over our bathroom tonight." Blake sprinkled salt on the skin between his thumb and forefinger and handed the shaker to her.

She did the same.

"To conquering fears."

"To conquering fears." Farrah clinked her glass against Blake's and downed the tequila. She grimaced and bit into her lime wedge, letting the sour fruit balance the flavor of the alcohol burning its way down her throat.

God, tequila shots were gross. On the bright side, it didn't take long for her buzz to return and smooth her frayed nerves.

This was it. Time to ask him. "Who's the girl?"

Wait. That wasn't the right question.

Blake tilted his head. "What girl?"

"The girl I saw coming out of your room the night we went to Moller Villa." Farrah had avoided asking or thinking about Mystery Girl since that night, but now she couldn't *stop* thinking about her. It didn't take a genius to realize what Blake and Mystery Girl had been up to.

Was it a onetime thing, or was he still seeing her?

Farrah fought the urge to dry heave. Yep, the postjump high was one hundred percent gone.

Discomfort filled Blake's face. "She's a girl I was seeing."

Seeing meaning more than once.

Was as in past tense.

"Oh." Farrah fiddled with her empty glass. "What's her name?"

"Mina."

"She's really pretty."

The discomfort deepened. "I guess."

"Are you still seeing her?"

"She's leaving Shanghai next week. I might say goodbye."

"Wow, that's romantic." It came out more sarcastic than she intended. What was wrong with her?

Farrah's head swam. The tequila shot was not a good idea.

Blake scowled. "Ours isn't a romantic relationship. We knew going in that it was going to be purely physical. I know that's hard for you to understand—"

"Wow." Farrah sucked in a breath. "Why is it hard for me to understand? Because I'm a virgin? That doesn't mean I grew up in a nunnery, Blake. I know what hookup buddies are."

"No! You're taking this the wrong way." Blake raked a hand through his hair, his face taut with frustration. "I meant you're a romantic. You said it yourself. You believe in The One and epic love and all that. I don't. That's not what I came here for."

He was right. He'd said it all along. Blake didn't believe in love. Farrah was a fool to forget that. She'd been so caught up in her daydreams, she ignored what was right in front of her and read too much into every glance, every word, every action. When Blake took her to dinner and gave her that pep talk on the tower, it wasn't because he liked her. He was just being a good friend.

Good friends had their place, but Farrah was sick of falling for guys she couldn't have. They were always either emotionally unavailable, like Blake, or literally unavailable, like Leo.

She needed to stop living in the clouds and return to reality.

"Maybe it's not what I came here for either." Farrah grabbed the drink nearest to her and chugged it. Vodka. *Blech.*

"Hey!" the owner of the drink protested.

The buzz intensified. Her heart beat fast with adrenaline.

"I can have casual hookups," Farrah said. "I'll prove it."

Blake's brow knit into a frown. "Farrah..." His voice carried a warning.

Farrah ignored it. She grabbed the drink owner's shirt. He was young. Decent-looking. He'd do. "You. Are you single?"

"Uh, yeah."

"Good. Let's dance."

Farrah dragged him onto the dance floor without sparing Blake another glance. She bypassed her surprised friends and wrapped her arms around the guy's neck.

The music segued into another, even sexier R&B song. Farrah ground her hips against Drink Guy's, gyrating to the beat of the music. He was wearing too much cologne, and his breath smelled like cheap vodka.

Luckily, she was drunk enough to overlook both of those things.

Fuck Blake. Farrah wasn't waiting for Prince Charming, and she wasn't naive enough to think she'd find him during study abroad. Her mistake was tunnel vision—focusing on one guy she liked and ignoring the rest of her options.

It was time to give other guys a chance. She didn't need butterflies and skipped heartbeats to have a good time.

"Wow." Drink Guy's eyes glazed over. "I'm so glad you took my drink. I'm Greg."

"Greg, I'm Farrah. Now shut up."

"Ok." A minute passed. "So where are you from?"

Farrah groaned. Instead of answering, she grabbed the back of his head and kissed him. *That'll shut him up.*

Greg wasn't a great kisser, but what he lacked in skill he made up for in enthusiasm. His lips moved eagerly over hers, and his hands cupped her bottom—

Greg was gone.

Farrah frowned. Her eyes fluttered open to see Blake towering over them with a face like thunder. He gripped Greg's shoulder so hard his knuckles turned white.

"You've made your point." His voice was calm but edged in steel. A muscle ticked in his jaw.

"I'm not making a point. I'm making out." Farrah giggled at her play on words. "Now let him go so we can continue making out."

"Yeah, man, you're hurting me," Greg complained. He tried to twist out of Blake's grasp.

Blake clamped down harder. "I'll give you to the count of three before I rearrange your face," he said, still in that deadly calm voice.

Greg looked at Blake, then at Farrah, then at Blake again. He held up his hands. "Don't need to shoot me twice."

He scampered off.

Coward.

"Look what you did. Happy now?" The room tilted to the right. Farrah shook her head until it corrected itself.

"Not even a little bit. You're drunk."

"No shit. We're in a bar."

"That guy had his hands all over you!"

"So? If I *didn't* want his hands all over me, I would've taken care of it myself." Farrah shoved Blake's chest, her buzz giving way to anger. Blake didn't budge. It was like trying to shove a tree. One with stupid dimples and stupid blue eyes the color of crystals. Only now, the dimples were nowhere to be seen, and his eyes had darkened to a furious shade of sapphire. "You had no right to scare him away like that."

"I was trying to help you!"

"I don't need your help!"

"Guys." Sammy stepped in between them. Olivia must've put him up to it because he looked like he would rather be anywhere but here. "Let's take it down a notch. Why don't we—"

"Shut up, Sammy," Farrah and Blake said in unison.

"Yeah, ok." Sammy returned to where Olivia stood with the rest of their friends. She glared at him. "What? I tried."

"We'll discuss this outside," Blake said through gritted teeth. "Everyone's staring."

He was right. A crowd had formed, and people were watching the drama play out with wide eyes. She half expected one of them to bust out a bucket of popcorn.

"There's nothing to discuss."

"Farrah, please."

"Fine," she snapped. She followed Blake out of the VIP room to the exit. Sweat trickled down her forehead. Maybe the fresh air would do her some good.

"No reentry after you leave," the bouncer warned.

"VIP." Farrah flashed her purple wristband as proof.

The bouncer squinted at it and nodded.

There was no one near the exit except for a handful of cabbies smoking and chatting by their cars. Farrah gulped in a breath of fresh air.

Blake faced her. "You're not acting like yourself."

"Neither are you. You're acting like a dick."

"*I'm* acting like a dick? You chewed me out for trying to help you!"

"I told you I *don't need your help.*"

Blake's nostrils flared. "Fine. My bad. Go make out with that guy. In fact, go have wild monkey sex and swing from the chandeliers. See if I care."

"You do." The words slipped out before Farrah could stop them.

"Excuse me?"

She crossed her arms over her chest. "You do care, or you wouldn't have pulled him away from me." Maybe she was reading too much into things again. Maybe not. The crisp fall air cleared the fog in her head enough for her to realize Blake was not acting the way a normal friend would act when he saw her kissing someone else. "Why?"

Blake stiffened. "I don't know what you're talking about."

"I'm talking about why you're so worked up about who I hook up with."

"I'm not!"

"You're yelling!"

"I'm not yelling!" he yelled louder. "I—" Blake rubbed his face. His shoulders slumped. "Fuck."

"Tell me." Farrah's heart raced like she was on the edge of the jumping platform again, ready to fall. She was going down a dangerous path, but maybe, just maybe... "Why do you care?"

"Maybe it's the same reason you care," Blake said quietly. "Why all the questions about Mina tonight?"

Farrah's head pounded in time with her pulse.

They stared at each other, the air between them heavy with words neither wanted to say. "Because." She licked her lips. Her mouth was so dry it didn't help. "Blake, I..."

"I love you."

Farrah's breath caught in her throat. Giddiness bubbled up inside her. *Did he say—*

"I love you like a sister, and I don't want to see you get hurt."

The giddiness collapsed. "You love me like a sister," she repeated numbly.

Sister. Worse than *friend.* Worse than *enemy.* Those things, under the right conditions, could morph into something more. *Sister* was untouchable.

Blake didn't see her as a romantic or sexual prospect at all. Why should he when he had girls like Mina waiting in the wings? Girls who were beautiful and experienced and looked like a cross between Megan Fox and a young Angelina Jolie. How could Farrah compete with that?

She couldn't, and she didn't want to.

Farrah lifted her chin. She'd be damned if she let herself pine over someone who didn't want her back.

She got over Leo. She'd get over Blake.

"Good to know," she said. To her relief, her voice came out even. "I'm glad we got that sorted out." She turned to reenter the club when Blake grabbed her arm.

"Farrah, you are—" Blake stopped and swallowed. He looked tortured, as if there was a war raging inside him. "I don't—"

"You don't have to say anything else. I understand." Farrah extricated herself from his grasp and resumed her walk into the bar. She blinked back the burning sensation behind her eyelids. "Now, if you'll excuse me, I have a friend's birthday to celebrate."

Farrah didn't know if Blake followed her. She didn't look back to check.

CHAPTER 14

BLAKE KEPT AN EYE ON THE GROUND AS HE PICKED HIS way up a steep slope of crumbling stairs. There were no handrails, and while he may not have a life plan yet, he knew it didn't include tumbling off the Great Wall of China.

FEA had arrived in Beijing yesterday for their big fall semester trip. After a short night's rest, the *laoshis* had hustled them to the Great Wall this morning. Instead of going to Badaling or Mutianyu—the most touristy and therefore easiest-to-navigate sections of the Wall—they were hiking from Jinshanling to Simatai by foot. No cable cars, just steep stairs and more vertical climbs than Blake cared for.

On a normal day, Blake could've completed the hike in three hours instead of the usual four, but he was so distracted, he lagged behind his friends, even Kris.

Well, not *all* of his friends.

Blake reached the next watchtower and drank from his water bottle. He watched Farrah out of the corner of his eye as she inched her way up the stairs toward him, her face pink with exertion.

She stumbled on a loose stone and pitched forward. Blake's heart stopped. He reached out to help her, but Farrah regained her balance and scrambled up the rest of the stairs.

Blake's heartbeat returned to normal.

"Are you ok?" he asked.

"Yeah." Farrah brushed a stray strand of hair out of her eyes.

It was the first word she'd said to him in six days (not that he was counting). She'd avoided him since Macau, and he didn't blame her. He'd acted like a dick that night.

Farrah brushed past him and hauled herself through the watchtower window, onto the next stretch of the wall. Blake followed suit. He waited until they edged across the narrow path beneath the watchtower and reached the broader main section before he spoke.

"So how are you liking the hike?" He winced the instant the words left his mouth. *Lame.*

"Fine."

Blake tried a different tack. "Have you been to Beijing before?"

"No."

"It's an interesting city."

"Mm-hmm."

"Heard the *laoshis* are serving us poisonous mushrooms for dinner tonight."

"Great."

Blake groaned. "Farrah."

"What?"

"Talk to me."

"I am talking to you."

Multiple words. That was an improvement. "Look, I know I acted like an asshole last week. I'm sorry." Blake stumbled over the last word because he'd still tear that guy's arm off if he had the chance.

The image of Farrah and Douchebag making out flashed through his mind. Blake's jaw clenched.

He wasn't sorry about tearing Douchebag away from her. He was sorry about the way he treated Farrah. He'd been hopped up on his own issues and jealousy and taken them out on her.

Plus, that bit about loving her like a sister? Complete bullshit.

If Blake thought about Joy the way he thought about Farrah, he was in for some serious hell in the afterlife.

"Apology accepted."

Silence fell.

Blake struggled to come up with the right words to say. Farrah walked beside him, yet she was so distant, he expected her to slip through his fingers and fade into the air at any moment.

They passed through the next few watchtowers without a word. Slope after slope, one step after another.

After an hour, they stopped to rest. Farrah sank onto the ground. "You can go ahead," she said. "You don't have to stay with me."

"I want to."

Farrah slid a puzzled glance in his direction before turning to survey the landscape. Blake followed her gaze. It was a scene he'd seen multiple times in pictures, but nothing compared to the real thing. Not even close.

Rugged mountains encircled them like sentinels, draped in cloaks of silence. The ancient wall sighed as they stood on its back, following in the footsteps of the thousands who came before them. Nevertheless, it snaked through the rough terrain, endlessly and persistently, as it had for millennia.

The wall cut a striking figure amongst the explosion of red, orange, and green foliage before it disappeared into the low-hanging mist in the distance. Every so often a breeze swept by, carrying with it the whispers of history—the dynasties that rose and fell, the ghosts of emperors past and lives sacrificed, the faded screams of ancient warriors who'd fought on this very land.

Goose bumps erupted on Blake's skin. He found it hard to wrap his mind around the fact that he was standing on thousands of years of history. He remembered visiting the Alamo as a kid and marveling at how old it was.

Compared to the Great Wall, the Alamo was a freakin' fetus.

"He always wanted to come here."

Blake sat next to Farrah. His feet sighed in relief. "Who?"

"My dad."

"There's still time. I have a feeling the wall will be here for a while," Blake joked.

Farrah looked down. "He died four years ago."

Ah, fuck. "I'm so sorry." Blake felt like an ass. He couldn't do anything right these days.

"It's ok. You didn't know." Her smile wobbled and lasted five seconds before it fell.

It broke Blake's heart. He was shit at comforting people. He never knew what to say, and tears made him more uncomfortable than a nun who stumbled into an orgy. If this were anyone else, Blake would've gotten the fuck outta there.

But this wasn't anyone else. This was Farrah.

He placed a tentative arm around her shoulders. To his relief, she didn't pull away.

"My dad spent most of his life in China and never saw its most famous landmark." Farrah played with the pendant around her neck. "He used to tell me we'd visit together. One day, he said, we'd fly to Beijing and walk the entire wall, from one end to the other. It'd be the greatest father-daughter hike ever taken. I was only seven at the time, but even I knew it was impossible to walk the *entire* wall. Still, I liked imagining it. It seemed like a great adventure."

Her voice thickened with unshed tears.

Blake squeezed her tight, wishing he could do more to help.

Farrah sniffled and wiped her nose with the back of her hand. "Anyway, tell me about your dad. Are you guys close?"

Blake swallowed. He had to battle his instinct to avoid the question before he got his answer out. "We were. Once. A long time ago."

When he was a kid, his dad would take him to the zoo and make funny faces imitating the animals until Blake howled with laughter. He took Blake fishing every two months and almost came to blows with Ted Crenshaw's dad after Ted pushed Blake at recess and Blake skinned his knee.

Then Blake grew up and displayed a talent for football. His dad stopped being his dad and started being his coach. He never switched back.

"What happened?"

"We grew apart." Blake played with the ends of Farrah's hair. They slipped across his fingers like silk. "We have different ideas of how I should live my life."

"I'm guessing he didn't want you to quit football."

He barked out a laugh devoid of humor. "That's putting it mildly. His biggest dream is for me to sign with the NFL. He played college ball too, you know, but he tore his ACL and that ended his pro dreams. So he lived those dreams through me until I quote-unquote 'threw my future away' because I'm an idiot who can't do anything right except throw a ball."

Farrah lifted her head to look at him. "That's not true. I've seen how hard you work. You're definitely more than a meathead."

"Maybe." Blake wasn't sure. He spent most of his life so focused on football he didn't have time to do much else. He was a business major, and he did well in his classes, but he didn't have any business experience except for a summer internship after his sophomore year. He'd had to fight his father tooth and nail on that one. Joe Ryan didn't understand why Blake would throw away a summer's worth of preseason prep to toil in an office.

He thought about his idea to start his own sports bar, but that was all he did—think about it. Blake was too afraid of what might happen if he tried to do it. The last thing he wanted was to fail and prove his father right.

"Not maybe. For sure." Farrah's tone brooked no opposition. "Trust me, meatheads do not pick up Mandarin as quickly as you have."

Blake's mouth quirked up. "Know a lot of Mandarin-learning meatheads, do you?"

"I'm from LA You'd be surprised." She rubbed her arms. Blake pulled her closer. The nip in the air felt good when they were walking, but it started to bite after they stopped moving. "So why did you quit football? Most guys would kill for a chance to join the NFL."

She wasn't the first person to ask him that question, but she was the first person he wanted to tell the truth to.

Blake weighed his words before he answered.

"A week after we won the national championship, I ran into Dan Griffin's wife at an alumni event. He was a Mustangs quarterback back in the day. One of the best. Played for sixteen seasons in the NFL before he retired and became a sports broadcaster." A lump formed in Blake's throat when he remembered the look in her eyes. She'd been so sad and angry, it wrenched his heart. "He died of CTE a few days before the event."

Chronic traumatic encephalopathy, a degenerative brain disease found in those with a history of repetitive brain trauma— such as the concussions football players often endured on the field.

Blake had heard of CTE before. He never expected it to affect someone he knew, especially not someone as larger-than-life as Dan. He was invincible—or so it seemed.

Farrah's eyes widened. "Oh my god."

"I was close to Dan. He came to all the games and was my mentor, in a way, but I only met his wife a few times. She wasn't much into the football world, and I didn't know why she wanted to talk to me specifically except..." Blake looked down. "To warn me, I guess. To get out while I can. She didn't want what happened to Dan to happen to me."

Their paths were similar. Both Blake and Dan were Texas born and bred, high school football stars who chose to attend TSU after a recruitment war between the country's top Division I schools. Both Heisman winners groomed for the NFL. Both buoyed and weighed down by the expectations of those around them.

There was only one difference.

"Dan loved football," Blake said. "He lived for it and, in the end, died for it. I like football, but it was always more for my father than myself. I would've been happy being a normal student instead of a so-called sports star." Sometimes he fantasized about what his life would've been like had that been the case. Would his relationship with his father be any different, or would they have been at odds over something else? Would his father have resented Blake for not following the football path he himself wanted but couldn't take? "I don't want to die for something I don't love."

When Blake found out what happened to Dan, he remembered all the hits he'd taken on the field. Every tackle replayed itself in his mind, including a brutal takedown by Oklahoma's defense his sophomore year. It had led to pain so sharp, he was sure he had a concussion, but he played through it because the team was counting on him and that's what you did.

The Mustangs won. The pain went away. But what if one day

it didn't? Blake was healthy now. If he continued along his path, he might not be.

Dan's death wiped away the dust, and he saw the writing on the wall. Could he say the same for his friends, family, and fans? Probably not. Football was a religion in Texas. Blake would get pilloried for being selfish and overdramatic if he revealed he quit because he was worried about CTE. So he kept his mouth shut and let the speculation run wild. It was better than the alternative.

Farrah squeezed his hand. "That's understandable. I can't imagine anyone would be mad about that."

"You haven't met my father."

Farrah's gaze swept down.

Blake winced when he realized how callous his complaint must sound. "I'm sorry. He and I have our differences, but I know I'm lucky he's still here."

"It's ok." Farrah fiddled with her necklace again. "My dad wasn't the greatest dad either when he was alive. I feel terrible saying that because he *was* a good dad for a while." Her voice wobbled. "He had an...interesting life before he married my mom. They settled down and had me, and everything was great until it wasn't. My parents started fighting every night over stupid stuff—what channel to watch, whose turn it was to take out the trash—until my dad moved out. I was thirteen."

Blake's chest tightened as Farrah spoke. Thirteen was hard enough without having to deal with your parents' separation.

"They separated for a year before divorcing. In that year, without my mom keeping an eye on him, my dad fell back into old bad habits—smoking, drinking, gambling. He racked up a ton of debt, and he and my mom still had some joint accounts, so you can imagine how that went down. I remember walking into my mom's bedroom one day after they divorced and seeing her cry. My mom *never* cries. I was so pissed at my dad for putting us through all of that pain that when I saw him during our next visit, I called him all these horrible names, and I—" Farrah swallowed hard. "I said I wished he were dead."

The tightness increased until Blake couldn't breathe.

"A few days later, we got a call from my uncle. My dad had been dealing with liver cirrhosis for years, but it got worse without my mom looking after him. My uncle called to tell us my dad was in a coma."

A sense of foreboding fell over Blake.

"A few days later, he died."

His heart exploded. Farrah radiated so much pain, Blake felt it deep within his bones.

He hugged her tight, unable to do anything but hold her and keep the pieces together as she fell apart.

"Can you imagine if the last thing your daughter ever said to you was that she wished you were dead?" The only way Blake knew how much Farrah hurt was by the way her shoulders heaved as she collapsed into silent sobs.

"Shh. It's ok." He rubbed her back and pressed his lips to the top of her head, feeling helpless. "It's ok."

"I'm a terrible person. No matter what he did, he was my dad and I loved him. And now I'll—" She hiccupped. "I'll never get the chance to tell him."

"He knows."

Farrah shook her head.

"He does," Blake insisted. "We've all said things we regret out of anger. I'm sure your dad did too. He knew you didn't mean it. And those were only a few words out of how many you'd spoken to him throughout your life?" He tilted her chin up. Despite her red nose and swollen eyes, she took his breath away. Her true beauty wasn't physical; it was in her soul. He saw it shining through in everything she did, and it was as bright and warm as the sun on a summer day. "You're an incredible person. You would never hurt someone on purpose. This is coming from me, someone who's known you for three months. Your dad knew you your entire life."

Farrah's lips trembled. She nodded once before burying her face in his chest again. Blake sat there, holding her until her sobs slowed.

Once they did, she pulled away and wiped her cheeks dry. "I'm sorry. I ruined your shirt."

"It's a stupid shirt. I can buy another one." Blake brushed away her remaining tears. "How are you feeling?"

"Better." Farrah sniffled. "I've never told anyone what happened with my dad before. Not even my mom."

Damn. Blake was about to cry himself. *Toughen up, man.* "Thank you for trusting me."

She gave him a wobbly smile. "Thank you for trusting *me.*"

They sat there on their little corner of the wall, each the keeper of the other's secrets. Their fight in Macau was a faded memory, but one thing from that night remained crystal clear in Blake's mind: the look in Farrah's eyes when he asked why she cared about him and Mina.

Deep down, he knew what she was going to say. He'd interrupted her with a lie because he was too scared to admit what he'd known all along, but after today there was no use denying it: Blake was in love with Farrah. He was in so deep, he didn't have a devil's chance of getting out, and what's more, he didn't want to.

Blake closed his eyes and leaned his head against the wall.

I am so fucked.

CHAPTER 15

THE PEBBLES CRUNCHED BENEATH FARRAH'S FEET AS she and Blake followed Wang *laoshi* to their hostel in Gubei, a water town at the foot of the Simatai section of the wall. As Farrah expected, they were the last FEAers to arrive.

Farrah was exhausted, but she had enough wits about her to admire the view. Despite being an artificial "ancient" town (modeled after the actual historic town of Wuzhen in southern China), Gubei was beautiful. Its traditional architecture harkened back to the days of imperial China. Stone streets wound past wooden houses with tile roofs and sweeping eaves; small arch bridges curved over narrow canals. As the sun sank beneath the horizon, the lights flicked on, one by one, until the entire town glowed with their warmth. The orange spots danced and shimmered on the water, competing with the pale fire skies for attention.

"Toto, we're not in Texas anymore," Blake murmured.

Laughter bubbled up inside her. It was a relief after the heavy emotions of earlier that day. "No, Dorothy, we're not."

Farrah was coming to terms with her unrequited feelings for Blake. She wasn't even mad about what happened in Macau anymore. She'd missed Blake too much during the past week to stay angry with him. Her romantic feelings were one thing; their friendship was another. What happened on the wall was proof of that.

She'd kept her guilt over what happened with her dad a secret for so long that talking about it felt like a thousand-ton weight had lifted off her shoulders.

Farrah had had opportunities to talk about it before, but she'd been too afraid. Afraid people would judge her for being a terrible person and a terrible daughter, afraid they would never look at her the same afterward.

She didn't have that fear with Blake. Somehow, she knew he would understand.

Blake slanted a glance in her direction. His mouth curled up to reveal those devastating dimples.

"I'm glad we're talking again," he whispered. "I missed you."

There went the damned butterflies. Farrah loved all living creatures, but those butterflies needed to die.

"I missed you too...brother." She punched him in the shoulder.

Oh god, I did not just say that.

Blake frowned.

By the time they reached their hostel, dusk had settled over the town. Voices filtered through the open doorway of the complex. FEA had booked the entire building, which was large enough to house all seventy students if they crammed four to a room.

Farrah stepped into the courtyard and found the rest of FEA eating dinner at the tables scattered throughout the space. The smell of pork and noodles wafted through the air, eliciting a growl from her stomach. She'd planned on showering before she ate, but she was ravenous.

"Guys, over here!" Courtney waved them over to the group's table in the back corner.

"Took you guys long enough. We thought you died." Luke

reached for the near-empty plate of dumplings. "I understand why Farrah took so long, but what happened to you?" he asked Blake. "You're supposed to be in good shape."

Farrah stuck her tongue out at him. "Thanks a lot."

"Dude. Blake and Farrah haven't eaten yet." Sammy knocked Luke's hand away.

"I took it easy." Blake glanced at Farrah as the hostel staff brought out another round of steaming home-cooked food: stir-fried tomato with scrambled eggs, kung pao chicken with white rice, spicy dry-fried green beans, and shredded pork in sweet bean sauce.

Farrah wolfed down her first portion and went for seconds. She'd endured more physical activity today than she had in months. She could eat a cow right now.

The staff watched in stunned silence as the students devoured every morsel of food in fifteen minutes flat.

"Damn. That hit the spot." Luke leaned back in his chair, patted his stomach, and burped.

Beside him, Kris wrinkled her nose and scooted closer to Blake.

"I'm showered. I'm fed. I'm ready for bed." Olivia yawned. Her eyes drooped with exhaustion.

"You can't go to bed!" Courtney checked her watch. "It's only seven."

"How? It feels like midnight," Olivia moaned.

"We woke up at seven this morning," Farrah pointed out.

"Great. A twelve-hour day is enough for me. I'm beat."

"I agree." Leo, too, failed to stifle a yawn.

"Stop. We're young and so is the night. We are not going to bed." Courtney planted her hands on the table. "We're playing a game. Does anyone have cards?"

Silence.

She sighed. "Fine. Never Have I Ever it is."

The last thing Farrah wanted was to play Never Have I Ever, but she sat through one game to indulge Courtney. Otherwise, she'd never hear the end of it.

"Never have I ever received a grade below an A," Nardo said, causing a wave of eye rolls around the table. "What? I haven't."

"Big. Effing. Deal," Olivia said. "Neither have I."

"Then keep your finger up. That's how it works."

"Fine. Never have *I* ever been rejected from a college."

Nardo glared at Sammy. "You told her?"

"No. Yes." Sammy cleared his throat. "Getting wait-listed at MIT is still an honor."

Nardo pressed his lips together and folded one finger down. "Never have I ever not made it to the interview round for an internship."

"Never have I ever—"

"Stop!" Courtney slashed the air with her hands. "This is not the Olivia and Nardo Show. You're both smart, we get it. Let's move on. Farrah, it's your turn. Please, make it good."

"No pressure." Farrah tried to think of something no one had said yet. "Never have I ever…had a threesome."

"Duh," Luke said. "You're a virgin. You've never had a twosome—ow!"

"Sorry," Farrah said sweetly. "My foot slipped."

"Yeah right," he grumbled.

Two people at the table put their fingers down: Blake and Sammy.

"High school prom." Blake shrugged.

It didn't come as a surprise—she knew he was experienced— but jealousy still fluttered in her chest at the thought of Blake with two nameless, faceless girls.

Sammy, on the other hand, *was* a surprise.

"You've had a threesome?" Olivia's mouth formed a sur-prised O.

"Years ago." Sammy shifted in his seat. "It's not a big deal."

"Sammy Sam." Kris eyed him with newfound respect. "Aren't you full of surprises?"

"Dude, you can't leave us hanging. Tell us the deets!" Luke urged.

"No way."

"Come on!"

Farrah tilted her head up to the sky. The moon shone bright and clear. Even the stars made an appearance.

"I'm going for a walk," she said.

"We're at the edge of town. There's nothing nearby," Sammy pointed out, clearly eager to shift the attention away from himself.

"I just need to walk off the food." Farrah stood up. "I'll be back soon."

"I'll go with you." Blake pushed back his chair. "I could use a walk too."

"A walk sounds like a good idea." Kris nudged Courtney, who looked like she was about to argue. "Right, Court?"

Realization dawned on Courtney's face. "Right. Wish I could bring myself to get up, but I can't." She stretched her arms over her head. "Have fun, guys. Remember, we don't have curfew."

Luke's face scrunched in confusion. "We do have curfew. The *laoshis* said—ow! Would you guys *stop kicking me?*"

"Stop saying kick-worthy stuff," Kris said.

While her friends bickered, Farrah slipped out the hostel entrance with Blake in tow.

"You didn't have to come with me." She pulled her jacket tighter around her body. The wind skimmed over the exposed skin on her face and hands, causing her to shiver.

"I was planning to take a walk, anyway. Might as well have company." Blake's arm brushed hers as they walked.

Her heart skipped. The layers of clothing between them did nothing to dull the effect he had on her.

They wandered through the maze of buildings until they reached one of the little arched bridges closer to the main part of town.

"I can't believe this place is real," Blake said. "There's nothing like this in Texas."

"Depends on how you define *real*." Farrah rested her arms on the railing. "The government built it as a tourist site. It didn't exist until a few years ago."

Blake ran his hands over the smooth stone. "It feels real to me."

"Yeah." Farrah inhaled the crisp, cold air. It burned her lungs in a good way. "How'd you end up here, Blake?"

"Same way you did. I walked from the hostel."

"I meant in China."

"I took a plane." His mouth quirked at her expression. "I'm guessing that's not the answer you were looking for."

"You don't have personal ties to China, and you didn't study Chinese. Why'd you choose Shanghai? Not saying you have to have those things to be here," she added. "I'm just curious. Most people prefer to go to Europe or Australia. China is too…foreign for them."

"It's going to sound stupid."

"Try me."

Blake's cheeks tinged pink. "I watched *Skyfall*," he admitted.

Farrah's laughter pealed through the air. "That is a great scene," she agreed, remembering Bond's fight with an assassin at the top of a Shanghai skyscraper.

"One of the best-choreographed scenes in Bond history, if

you ask me." Blake joined in Farrah's mirth. "I know someone who chose their study abroad destination by closing their eyes and pointing to a map, so it could've been worse."

"Where'd they end up?"

Blake's grin widened. "Moscow. In December."

She cracked up again. "And they went through with it?"

"Yep. Fortunately for them, it was only a three-week program." Blake moved closer. "What about you? Why Shanghai?"

"I wanted to see this place for myself. My mom's always talking about China, but I'd never been." Farrah traced her initials with her finger on the railing. "I almost didn't choose Shanghai. I studied Mandarin to make my mom happy. I went against her wishes and majored in interior design instead of engineering or whatever, so I thought it would be a good compromise. It worked, kind of. She still gives me shit for not learning Mandarin sooner. Apparently, I wasted my high school years on French."

"Still better than me. I only speak English."

"And some Mandarin," Farrah corrected him. "I've forgotten most of my French, so she may have a point. I was going to brush up on it in Paris. But when it came time to choose my study abroad location...I don't know. I meant to click Paris but somehow clicked Shanghai. And here I am." She flashed a lopsided smile. "In some ways, I chose it with even less thought than you."

"Hey!" Blake pretended to take offense. "What do you mean *less* thought? I put a lot of effort into the decision-making process."

She patted his hand. "Sure you did."

To her surprise, Blake wrapped his fingers around hers. The warmth from his skin heated her from head to toe. "Either way, I'm glad you're here."

Farrah's breath caught in her throat. Blake was so close she could see every detail of his face—the dark lashes, the cheekbones that cut through the night like knives, the ice-blue eyes darkening to the color of sapphires. She saw him clearer than she'd seen anyone in her life.

"Blake." His name was a whisper in the night.

His Adam's apple bobbed. "Yes?"

"Do you really think of me as a sister?"

It was a dangerous question. There was every chance she wouldn't like the answer. But dammit, something about this place made her believe in magic, and she deserved to give it one last shot. She owed it to herself.

No regrets.

A thousand emotions passed over Blake's face. His hand trembled against hers. All the while, Farrah's heart banged against her chest, desperate to reach something on the other side.

"No." His hand remained entwined with hers.

The banging intensified. "What do you think of me?"

Blake was silent for so long, she thought he didn't hear her. She was debating whether to repeat the question or flee in mortification when he stepped closer.

"I think—" Blake's voice turned rough. "You're a smart-ass who's too stubborn for your own good. I think you drive me crazier than any person ought to. And I think I might die if I can't be with you."

The air whooshed out of Farrah's lungs. She had the moment-by-moment clarity of someone speeding down the road in a car without brakes. The road would lead to either the most terrifying or most amazing place she'd ever see.

There was only one way to find out.

Farrah grabbed Blake Ryan's face and kissed him.

Their mouths explored each other, hungrily and desperately, as if they'd longed for each other their whole lives and were only now getting the chance to meet. Farrah moaned and tangled her hands in his hair, her entire body aching. Blake tasted like ice and fire, like love and danger, like an angel and the devil, and she couldn't get enough. She wanted to drink up every last drop of him.

He pushed her against the railing and molded his body to hers until she didn't know where she ended and he began. They poured everything they had into each other—every feeling, every thought, every memory, both good and bad. They left themselves open so the other could rush in and fill the space that had been empty for too long.

Time fell away, taking with it everything that happened before or would happen and leaving them with only this moment. The surrounding buildings crumbled. The wall collapsed, the trees disappeared, and the hills flattened out, retreating into nonexistence while they waited for the world to be born. Then, just like that, the world was there, bursting forth with such excitement, it sped past everything. Past civilization, past nature, past the sun and moon and stars until it all fell quiet again.

Through it all, Blake and Farrah stood, unmoved by the creation and destruction around them. Here, at last, they found a place time couldn't touch.

But in the end, the universe gets its way, and though they fought it until their lungs ran out of breath, they eventually had to ease apart.

They stared at each other.

Elation coursed through Farrah's veins. It filled her up until she thought she might burst, so she did the only thing she could do: she laughed. The sound danced in the air and echoed back at her, causing her to laugh harder. Blake's face broke into a grin. His laughter joined hers, their harmony saying everything they couldn't say in words.

"Let's not go back," Blake said. "Let's stay awhile longer."

"Yes." Farrah sank into his arms. "Let's."

They stared up at the sky. The stars beamed back, twinkling with joy.

Farrah had always equated the stars with love, which seemed as nebulous and out of reach as the diamonds in the sky. But as she stood there next to Blake, beneath the infinite skies of a foreign land, the stars felt a little closer.

CHAPTER 16

ONE MOMENT CAN CHANGE YOUR LIFE.

It can happen anywhere, anytime, and it usually happens when you least expect it.

For Blake, it happened on a little bridge in a little town halfway across the world from home.

The moment his lips touched Farrah's, he was a goner. His excuses for why he shouldn't get involved with anyone from FEA crumbled into dust, as did his aversion to virgins. In fact, jealousy streaked through him at the thought of Farrah sleeping with anyone else.

Farrah wasn't like Lorna. She wasn't like anyone he'd ever met before.

For the first time in his life Blake believed in the Hollywood romance and the butterflies and the fireworks because he saw them. They were as bright and unexpected as the girl who entered his life like a meteor streaking through the night, illuminating the darkness and showing him what was possible if only he would believe in the stars.

"I'm going to tell you a secret, but you can't tell anyone."

Blake held Farrah's hand as they walked along the Bund. The lights from the buildings shimmered on the Huangpu River, turning its waters into a rainbow of hues.

The past few weeks had passed by in a blur of nights on the town, stolen kisses between classes, and heated make-out sessions in Blake's room. He found himself doing things that used to make him cringe, like leaving Farrah cheesy Post-it Notes in random places and buying her flowers for no reason. What's worse, he *enjoyed* doing those things.

Yep, he was a goner, and he didn't care.

"Color me intrigued." Farrah tapped a finger to her chin. "Let me guess. You're a spy, sent on a mission to infiltrate a group of hapless American study abroad students who may or may not be harboring state secrets."

"Right on the first try. Mission: get close to the target." Blake stopped and faced Farrah, closing the gap between them until their mouths were inches apart. "How am I doing?"

"You're doing a bang-up job, Agent Ryan." Farrah's breath whispered across his lips. "Keep this up and you might get a promotion."

"Might? Guess I have to work harder." Blake traced her lips with his tongue, teasing her until she caught his head in her hands and brought their mouths together in a searing kiss. She tasted like sunshine and honey and warmth, and he wanted to drown in her. To get so swept up in her depths, no one could find him. It'd be just the two of them, lost in infinity.

"Mom, look!" The high-pitched voice sliced through his bliss.

Blake cracked one eye open to see a little boy staring at them with curiosity and disgust.

"What are they doing?"

The boy's mother frowned. "Nothing. They're...doing adult things. You're too young to know."

"But—"

"Let's go." She grabbed her son's hand and hurried him along, but not before glaring at Blake. If looks could kill, his corpse would be eating dirt.

"Oops." Farrah giggled against his mouth. "I think we offended her sensibilities."

"Did you see the way she looked at me? You'd think I was having an orgy on the riverfront instead of kissing my girlfriend."

The word slipped out without thinking.

Farrah's eyebrows rose. "Girlfriend?"

Fuck.

It had been two weeks since their first kiss, and they'd yet to discuss their relationship status. Exclusivity wasn't official but implied.

Blake licked his lips. "Sorry, I didn't mean *girlfriend.* I meant girl. Friend."

"I see."

"No pressure."

"Ok."

He had a horrible feeling he was digging himself into a deeper hole with each word coming out of his mouth.

"So, how about that kiss?" Blake flashed his dimples in an attempt to warm Farrah's expression. It didn't work. "Pretty great, huh?"

"Mm-hmm."

Ah, dammit. It was time to stop beating around the bush. "Look. It's not that I don't *want* you to be my girlfriend. It's just—" He searched for the right words to say. "We haven't talked about it, and I don't want to assume. We're here for a year. We don't know what'll happen once we leave. I don't want to put too much pressure on us and the time we have together."

"So you want us to be friends with benefits like you and Mina?"

"Fuck no!" Friends with benefits were, by definition, *not* exclusive. The thought of Farrah touching another guy—or another guy touching Farrah—caused Blake to see red. Then he saw the hurt expression on her face and realized how his interjection must've come across. "Don't get me wrong. I'd love to have sex with you. But it's not—I mean, we don't *have* to have sex. No pressure on that either. Or with the relationship. Not that we have a relationship."

He didn't make sense, even to himself.

Blake finally understood how guys with no game must feel. He wanted to sink into the ground.

Farrah's frown deepened.

He considered throwing himself over the railing into the Huangpu when the frown disappeared, replaced by a wide grin.

"You're adorable when you're flustered."

"I am not *flustered*." Blake narrowed his eyes. "Wait. Were you putting me on this entire time?"

Farrah giggled. "You should see your face. You're so red."

She squealed in surprise when he picked her up and spun her around. "I can't believe you did that to me. I have half a mind to throw you into the river," he threatened.

"You would never!" She wrapped her arms and legs around him and held on tight. "Besides, can you blame me? The chance to see Blake Ryan tripping over himself was too good to resist."

"It's inhumane."

"Oh, come on." Farrah rested her forehead on his. "I think it's cute."

Blake was horrified. "Teddy bears are cute. Puppies are cute. Guys don't want to be cute. It's the sexual equivalent of Siberia."

"Cute is sexy." Farrah lowered herself to the ground, sliding her body against his as she did so. Need sliced through him, deep and heady.

"Don't think that'll get you off the hook."

"What?" She blinked, innocent as a doe.

"This thing you're doing." Blake groaned when she hooked her fingers through his belt loops and pulled him close. Her soft curves melted into the hard lines of his body, and the need ratcheted up five levels.

"I'm not the one on the hook. You're the one who said I'm not your girlfriend."

"Do you want to be?"

Her smile faded at his serious tone. "Are you serious?"

Blake's heart slammed against his rib cage. He nodded.

Farrah's eyes grew round. Was that a good thing? He couldn't tell.

One beat, one eternity. Two beats, two eternities.

The longer Blake waited for an answer, the more he wanted to die. He wasn't used to feeling this way—out of control, helpless, and ready to tumble off the precipice at another's command.

He was so caught up waiting for a verbal answer, it took him a second to register the warmth of Farrah's lips on his. Her tongue dueled with his; his hands tangled in her hair. Every inch of him ached for her—body, heart, and soul.

Blake was lost, and he never wanted to be found.

"So." His breath came hard and heavy when they broke for air. "Is that a yes?"

Farrah's eyes twinkled. "That's a yes."

Blake grinned so wide, his face might split in two. "You don't know what you got yourself into."

"Trying to make me regret my decision already?"

"Never." He brushed a stray strand of hair from her eyes. "It's you and me, babe. There's no backing out now."

"I suppose there are worse things in life." Farrah snuggled closer to him. "Was that the secret you wanted to tell me?"

Right. The secret.

"No." Blake hesitated, debating whether to say it out loud.

What the hell. He'd taken one plunge today. Might as well knock them all out.

"I've been working on a project. For after graduation." *Here goes nothing.* "I want to open a sports bar. I've been working on a business plan, and it's only a rough outline at this point, but I'm hoping to have something ready by Christmas."

Blake tried to gauge Farrah's reaction. Nerves churned his stomach into knots. Saying it out loud made his plan real. It was crazy and far-fetched, but it was real, and though the thought of starting his own business made him nauseous, he also felt... excited?

Yep, that was definitely a glimmer of excitement beneath the nerves.

"Blake."

He held his breath.

"That's amazing!" Farrah threw her arms around his neck. "Can I see your business plan? What are you going to call the bar? You should have a signature drink!"

"Whoa, slow down." Blake laughed. Relief bubbled inside him. She didn't think his idea was stupid. "Yes, you can see it after I'm done, I haven't decided on a name yet, and let's cross the signature-drink bridge when we get there."

"It'll all work out. I am so excited for you." Farrah's eyes shone bright in the moonlight.

"You don't think it's a dumb idea?"

"Of course not! Why would I think it's a dumb idea?"

"I have no experience running a business, and there are a million sports bars out there." Blake frowned. "What if it's a failure?"

"No one has experience running a business until they run a

business, and there may be a million sports bars out there, but they're not *your* sports bar." Farrah cupped his face in her hands. "You are one of the smartest, hardest-working people I know. If this is what you want to do and you give it your all, you'll succeed. I have faith in you."

Rich warmth suffused him, washing away the doubt and uncertainty. Blake couldn't remember the last time someone had such unconditional faith in him.

"I don't know what I did to deserve you, but it must've been a helluva thing." He tried not to let too much emotion show in his voice.

"You can repay me with unlimited drinks at your bar." She gave him a soft kiss. "And unlimited kisses."

"Yes, ma'am. Your wish is my command."

Blake intertwined her fingers with his as they resumed their walk along the Bund. It was late, and they had class tomorrow, but he couldn't bring himself to leave. The electricity of Shanghai's skyline beckoned, drawing him in like a magnet for lost souls.

"I can't get over this view." Farrah sounded nostalgic, as if she were speaking of a place lost in the sands of time.

Blake gazed across the river at the city's iconic skyline. The jungle of high-rises pulsed with energy, lighting up the night with a rainbow of electric blues, neon purples, glowing yellows, and fiery reds. In its midst stood the Pearl Tower, stretching toward the sky with the ambition of one determined to be on top of the world. And in certain fleeting moments, when the glittering sprawl of man-made wonders blended with the diamonds in the sky, that ambition became a reality.

Shanghai, the Paris of the East. It was as different from Texas as you could get, but it reminded Blake of New York. Like New York, it was a city that defined a nation, and it held the dreams of millions of people in its concrete palms. Unlike New York,

Shanghai was a city that still woke up and wondered at its success every day, both intoxicated by and unaccustomed to the power it wielded.

Blake inhaled sharply. The cold, crisp air burned his lungs.

In that moment, he saw it—his future, reflected in the lights and shadows before him.

In that moment, looking at that view, with Farrah in his arms, he believed it.

He could do anything.

He could be his own boss.

He could be free.

CHAPTER 17

"YOU'VE KNOWN ME FOR FOUR MONTHS, AND YOU want fast food." Olivia crossed her arms over her chest. "I've failed you as a friend."

Farrah laughed. "It's not that serious. I'm craving a McFlurry, that's all."

Olivia grimaced. "I'm in a good mood, so I'm not going to say anything."

"Thank you, CB Lippmann," Farrah quipped.

Olivia received the email that morning: she was officially a summer intern for the prestigious investment firm. Farrah heard her excited scream all the way down the hall. Olivia had been floating on air since, at least until Farrah dragged her, Sammy, and Blake into McDonald's.

The place was packed, so the guys were saving them seats while they waited in line.

Farrah examined the menu. There were staples like the Big Mac and McChicken, but there were also items tailored for a Chinese audience, including taro pies, bubble milk tea, and a Sichuan spicy chicken burger.

The taro pies looked tempting, but she ordered a McFlurry like she'd intended instead, plus two burgers and fries for Blake and Sammy (each).

"You sure you don't want anything, Liv?" Farrah teased.

"Ugh. No, thanks. Don't ask me again." A sly gleam entered Olivia's eyes. "Let's talk about a more savory topic. Have you and Blake done the deed yet?"

Farrah blushed. "Define *deed*."

"Don't be coy. Have you had sex yet?"

"Define *sex*."

"Farrah Lin!"

Farrah looked around. Sammy and Blake sat at a table in the back corner. There was no way they could hear her.

Blake caught her eye and winked.

She smiled as her heart did a happy skip.

"We've made it to second," she said. "No third or home base yet."

"Why not? He looks like he's good at bat." Olivia grinned. "Sammy would be proud of my baseball analogy."

"Maybe not when you're using it to discuss another guy's sex skills. Anyway, to answer your question, Blake wants to take things slow."

Olivia's eyebrows shot up in surprise.

A pinprick of insecurity dampened Farrah's mood. On the one hand, it was sweet that Blake didn't want to rush things. On the other, didn't college guys want to have sex, like, all the time? Was it normal that he didn't seem to have a problem saying no every time sex came up?

She was the virgin. *She* should be the one saying no.

The server called their order number. They picked up their food and walked toward their table.

"Don't overthink it," Olivia said when she saw the expression on Farrah's face. "He knows you've never done it before, so he probably doesn't want to rush you before you're ready."

"I *am* ready." Farrah knew she was whining, but she didn't care. Seriously, how hard was it to give away your virginity these days?

Olivia giggled. "Hashtag Farrah problems."

"Shh! Keep your voice down; they can hear."

"What's so funny?" Sammy asked. The tray hadn't hit the table before he reached for a fry.

"Nothing," Olivia and Farrah chorused.

"Sammy, there are some things guys are better off not knowing," Blake said.

"You're right, you're right. By the way," Sammy said through the mouthful of burger. "There's something I have to tell you guys."

"Including me?" Olivia pointed to herself.

"Yeah." He chewed and swallowed. "I'm, uh, going to be an intern at NASA this summer."

There was a beat of silence before a loud squeal caused every head in the restaurant to swivel in their direction.

"We're going to be in New York together?!" Olivia threw her arms around Sammy's neck. She seemed thrilled for someone who always said study abroad relationships don't last after the program ends.

Sammy grinned. "Yep."

"Congrats!" Farrah reached across the table to hug her friend. "You rocket scientist, you."

"Hardly. I'll be working on mathematical models for a climate change project. Not exactly Neil Armstrong stuff."

"Whatever. Anyone who works at NASA is a rocket scientist in my eyes." Farrah wiped her mouth with a napkin. "You're my mom's dream. If I majored in math and got a NASA internship, she'd faint from happiness."

"Maybe it's a good thing you didn't," Sammy joked.

"Congrats, man." Blake clapped Sammy on the shoulder. His smile didn't quite reach his eyes.

"I can't wait to start my New York spreadsheet." Olivia whipped out her phone. "There are *so many* amazing restaurants we have to try. Let's start in the West Village and work our way to the other neighborhoods."

Farrah hid a grin. Some things never changed.

When they returned to the dorm, Olivia and Sammy split to plan their summer in New York while Farrah lingered in the hall outside Blake's room. His uncharacteristic moodiness stopped her from breezing inside like normal.

"What's wrong?" She leaned against the doorway and watched Blake hang his jacket in the closet with more care than usual.

"Nothing."

"You're quiet."

"I have nothing to say."

"You always have something to say, even when no one wants you to say anything."

Not a hint of a smile. It wasn't Farrah's best joke, but Blake usually indulged her with at least a chuckle.

She walked inside and placed her hands on Blake's shoulders, forcing him to look at her. "You can tell me anything. You know that."

"I know." Blake blew out a breath. "It's going to sound stupid."

"Try me."

"Everyone has amazing summer plans. Sammy with NASA, Olivia with CB, you with your design internship—"

"I haven't submitted my application yet," Farrah reminded him. She needed to put the finishing touches on her final design. She didn't love it, but it was good enough. At this point, Farrah was just glad she had *something* on paper, especially since the deadline was coming up fast.

"You will, and you'll get it." Blake's matter-of-fact confidence eased her nerves somewhat.

"Thanks. You'll have an amazing summer too." She rubbed his arm. "Don't worry."

"Doing what? At least you guys have something concrete lined up." Blake broke away and sat on his bed. "All I have is a crazy dream to start a bar."

"It's not crazy." Farrah's fierce tone surprised herself. "You know what else started as a crazy dream? Apple. Microsoft. Every small business and company in the world. You won't know whether something is achievable unless you try."

"There's so much to think about," Blake argued. "The leasing, the marketing, the liquor licenses, the food. I don't have the capital to rent a commercial space, much less hire staff. The expenses are too big for my parents to help with, even if they want to help, which isn't a guarantee." He noticed her smile. "What's so funny?"

"You're thinking like a business owner already."

"Thanks, but that doesn't solve my problem."

She sat next to him. "Let me ask you this. Is a sports bar what you really want?"

Blake's face softened. "It is. I don't want to play sports for a living, but I love the community aspect of it. It brings people together. Well, unless you're rooting for rival teams. You can watch games at home, but there's nothing like being surrounded by people as excited as you are about every goal, every point scored. It's hype."

Farrah laughed. "I'll take your word for it." The only sport she watched was the gymnastics portion of the Olympics every four years. "If this is what you really want, go for it. It may not be as 'concrete' as an internship at an established firm, but this is *your* dream. So many people have started their own businesses, and I guarantee you're just as capable."

"You're right. But I still need to find the money." Blake shook his head. "Unless I win the lottery, I won't have enough for rent, much less everything else."

"There are loans and investors. You'll figure it out. You're Blake Ryan."

"I'm Blake Ryan, football star. Not Blake Ryan, business-man." His eyes flickered with vulnerability.

Farrah's heart ached. The world saw Blake the football player. Cocky, athletic, good-looking. The one every girl wanted and every guy wanted to be.

That was how she'd once seen him too.

While those things may be a part of him, he'd opened up enough for her to see past the winks and irreverent quips to the person deep inside—the boy whose life was defined by something someone else chose for him, who'd been told over and over again his worth was based on his skills with a ball, and who wanted to be loved as a person instead of a commodity.

Tears stung her eyes. "You will be," Farrah said fiercely. "You're Blake Ryan, anything you want to be. Businessman. President. CEO of fucking space. If Elon Musk can do it, so can you."

He laughed softly. "I'm not Elon Musk, either."

"No." Farrah pressed her forehead against his. "You're better. You're you."

CHAPTER 18

BLAKE DIDN'T KNOW WHAT GOOD DEED HE PERFORMED in his past life, but it must've been a helluva big one because it brought the girl of his dreams into his life.

His chest squeezed every time he remembered the look in Farrah's eyes when she gave him a much-needed pep talk the other day. The look that told him she meant every word she said, that she believed he could do this. That she believed in him.

No one had ever looked at him like that before.

Blake was so caught up in his thoughts, he didn't notice his mom pick up the Skype call until her voice broke through his consciousness.

"Blake!" Helen's face filled the screen. She was wearing her old sorority sweatshirt, the one she always wore when she cleaned the house. Blake did a quick mental calculation. It was nine at night in Shanghai, which meant it was seven in the morning in Austin. Trust his mom to be cleaning this early on a Saturday. "How are you, sweetie? I haven't heard from you in weeks." Her voice carried a gentle rebuke.

Blake's stomach twisted with guilt. "I know. I'm sorry. Things have been kinda chaotic."

"It's all right, dear, as long as you promise to call more often. Now tell me about these 'chaotic' things you've been up to."

Blake filled his mom in on his classes, friends, and favorite places in the city. He hesitated before adding, "I've been seeing someone in the program. Her name's Farrah."

He tensed in anticipation of his mom's response. She'd been planning his and Cleo's wedding since they were toddlers, and she had taken their breakup hard. He had no idea how she'd react to this news.

Helen's eyebrows shot up. "How long have you been seeing her?"

"A few weeks."

"And this is the first I'm hearing of her?" There was that rebuke again. "Well, don't keep me in suspense. What's she like?"

"She's amazing. Beautiful, smart, funny. When I'm around her, I..." Blake's voice trailed off. Just thinking about Farrah made him giddy as a schoolboy. He'd turned into one of those sappy boyfriends he used to make fun of. "I dunno. I feel great."

"She sounds lovely." Helen paused. "Where is she from?"

"LA"

"I see."

Warning bells rang in his head. "Why do you sound relieved?"

"I'm not relieved." Helen's guilty expression said otherwise. "I'm glad you're having fun in Shanghai. It's a good break from... everything that happened this past year. Hopefully, once you're home, you'll be ready to set everything straight."

The warning bells rang louder. "What is 'everything'?"

"Oh, you know. This whole football business with your father and your relationship with Cleo. It's a shame you won't be coming home for Thanksgiving. She's bringing her famous mac 'n' cheese. I know how much you love that dish."

Blake took a deep, controlled breath. "There's nothing to sort out. I'm done with football, and Dad will have to get it over it. As for Cleo, we're not getting back together."

"Of course you are. You love her," Helen said. "I understand you needed a break to clear your head, but the two of you are meant to be. You've been friends since you were children."

"That's all we are, Mom. Friends."

"You dated for a year!"

It was a mistake, Blake wanted to say. He should've known better than to cave to his family's expectations. They were the ones who'd wanted him to date Cleo. He did love her—just not in the way they wanted him to. If he had any doubt before, his relationship with Farrah cleared it up. The feelings he had for Cleo at the height of their relationship didn't come close to his feelings for Farrah now. "Yes, and I realized we're better off as friends."

Helen pinched her temple. "This Farrah girl..."

"I love her."

The words spilled out without thought. Helen's jaw dropped.

Meanwhile, Blake's heart raced with adrenaline at the admission. Neither he nor Farrah had broached the *L* word yet. He should've been terrified—love was the ultimate commitment. But he wasn't. Because if he was being honest, he'd known deep down he was in love with Farrah long before he said the words out loud.

He'd been falling in love with her, bit by bit, since the moment they met.

It wasn't scary.

It was inevitable.

"Oh, honey." Helen sighed. "You've known her for what? Three months? I know it must be exciting, being in a foreign country and all, but you have to be practical. She lives in LA; you live in Texas. Long-distance relationships are difficult. Meanwhile, Cleo is right here. She stood by you through everything, including after you quit the team."

"Maybe I don't want to stay in Texas."

Once again, the words slipped out.

Blake had never considered moving out of Texas. That's where his family and friends were. No one he knew left the state for good. However, now that he'd floated the possibility, the idea seemed more and more appealing.

He could go anywhere—New York, LA Hell, he could move to Shanghai if he wanted to.

The adrenaline kicked up another notch.

Helen paled. "Don't be ridiculous."

"It's not ridiculous. I graduate soon. I don't *have* to stay in Texas like everyone else."

"Where are you going to go? How will you afford it?"

Blake repeated Farrah's mantra. "I'll figure it out."

His mom was at her wit's end. "Why don't you speak to your father? I'm sure he'll have some thoughts about this."

Blake bet he would.

Helen turned her head toward the living room. "Joe! Blake wants to talk to you."

"No! Mom—"

Too late.

Helen stood up to make way for Blake's father.

Fuck.

"So." Joe Ryan sat and pinned his piercing gaze on Blake. Older and world-wearier, with wrinkles, otherwise Joe looked the same as when he was Blake's age. The same thick blond hair—thank god Blake didn't have to worry about balding when he was older—the same blue eyes and square jaw, the same gruff, determined expression.

"So."

Silence.

"How's China?" Joe looked like he would rather be anywhere but there.

That made two of them.

"Fine."

Blake's response earned him a stern glare. "Try again with a real answer."

Blake bit back a caustic reply. Instead, he gave his father a quick rundown of the semester. He omitted the details he gave his mom and focused on his classes. He didn't need his father giving him shit about going out when he should be "getting his life together."

"What about outside of class? What are you doing?"

"Hanging out."

Another withering stare. "You're telling me we paid thousands of dollars for you to fly across the world and *hang out*?" Joe's face twisted like the words left a bad taste in his mouth.

Blake gripped his laptop so hard he was surprised it didn't crack. "There's the matter of my classes, which I just mentioned," he said, struggling to remain calm. "Cultural exchange, foreign-language learning. You know, small stuff."

"How useful is that going to be? I didn't swan off to another country when I was in college and I turned out fine."

Yeah, if you consider being a bitter old man who lives vicariously through his son "fine."

"What I want to know is what you're going to do when you come back." Joe drummed his fingers on the table. "You're graduating this year. Did you think about that? Or are you so busy running around Shanghai that you haven't given a single thought to your future since you threw it away?"

"I did not throw my future away." Blake's jaw clenched with a mixture of fear and irritation. "I have—I *will* have—a business degree."

"That degree is a formality. When was the last time you did anything business related?"

"I interned at Z Hotels."

"Yes, you interned at the company your best friend's family runs." Joe snorted. "Laura Zinterhofer won't give you a management role just because you run around with her son."

Blake's jaw clenched harder. "I never said that. I *earned* that internship. Landon didn't know I applied until after I got it."

"Fine. Tell me, what is your grand postcollege business plan?" Joe leaned back and crossed his arms over his chest.

Blake should've waited. He was nowhere near ready to tell anyone but Farrah about his plans. With her encouragement, he'd put together a to-do list of everything he needed to make the sports bar a reality. It was…a lot. The estimated cost alone made his eyes swim.

However, the condescending smirk on his father's face pulled the words out before he could stop them. "I'm opening a sports bar."

A beat of silence followed by loud guffaws as Joe burst into laughter. "Get serious."

"I am serious," Blake said through gritted teeth.

"You know nothing about running a business. A sports bar? C'mon. There are a million sports bars out there. Take it from someone who's been around a lot longer than you have, Son: stick to what you're good at. You're good at football. That's it."

Anger ate away at Blake's stomach. "I'm not going back to football. An NFL career is your dream, not mine."

"Yeah? You sure as hell didn't turn down those Heismans. You have talent and prospects other boys your age would kill for, and you're throwing it all away!" Joe pounded the table. "Do you know how much money you can make in the NFL? Think of the sponsorships. The name recognition. If you're smart, you can take that to the bank even after you retire."

"It's not about the money!" Blake yelled.

"It's not until you're jobless and broke!" Joe yelled back. "If you think your mother and I will bankroll your pipe dream, think again!"

"I don't need you to bankroll me. I'll do it myself!"

"Ha, I'd like to see that happen."

"It will happen, and it'll be no thanks to you." Blake hung up without another word. Pressing the "end call" button wasn't as satisfying as slamming down a phone, but it did the trick.

His heart zipped through his chest like a race car driver intent on winning the Indy 500.

Screw his father. Blake was going to own the most successful fucking sports bar in the world, and when he did, he was going to rub it in Joe Ryan's face.

In the meantime, he needed to calm down before he punched a hole in the wall. Nothing ruined his day like a conversation with his father.

Once the red haze dissipated from his vision, Blake texted Farrah. She was the only person who could make him feel better.

Are you busy? I miss you.

She responded not a minute later. Be right there.

Blake's heart rate slowed. He took a deep breath and tried to clear his mind. He had a lot of shit to do if he wanted his business venture to be a success.

First on the list: figure out where he wanted to open the bar.

He heard a knock.

"I come bearing gifts," Farrah said when Blake opened the door. She unwrapped a paper towel to reveal a pile of Sammy's legendary chocolate chip cookies. "I passed by the kitchen and nabbed a few before Luke got to them. I swear he's here *more* since he moved into his homestay." She shook her head. "How was your call with your mom?"

Blake popped a cookie in his mouth. "Fine. Until it turned into a call with my dad."

Farrah winced. "Not good?"

"That's one way to put it. I told him about the sports bar idea. He thinks it's dumb."

She walked to his desk and set the cookies down. She turned and said, in the calmest voice possible, "Fuck what he thinks."

Blake had to pick his jaw up from the floor. He'd never heard Farrah be so blunt.

"If he can't see your potential, that's his problem. Don't let his limitations run your life. You can do this." Farrah cupped his face in her hands. "I know you can."

His heart ached. The person he saw reflected in her eyes was the person he always wanted to be: brave, smart, passionate. Someone who chased his dreams and believed in himself. Someone worthy of love and respect.

"What would I do without you?"

"Oh, you'd probably be checking yourself out in the mirror and calculating how many push-ups you need to maintain your physique."

Farrah squealed as Blake lifted her up and tossed her on the bed with a playful growl. "Who says I don't do that anyway?"

Her eyes shone with laughter. "I admire your self-awareness."

"Admire, huh? Keep going." Blake nipped her bottom lip, enjoying her sharp inhale.

Yeah, he had a lot of shit to figure out, but he'd do that later. Right now, there were more enjoyable things on the agenda.

"You wish. I'm not here to"—her breath turned shallow as he trailed kisses down her neck, licking and sucking until he reached the pulse fluttering wildly at her throat—"boost your ego."

"What are you here for?" Blake brushed his lips over her

collarbone. Her orange-blossom-and-vanilla scent caused his blood to rush south.

"For this." Farrah brought his head up to hers and captured his mouth in a searing kiss.

Coherent thought slipped away. Their tongues tangled in a sultry duel that left Blake breathless. He lost himself in the taste of her, the heat of their embrace, the heady sensation of being in the arms of the girl he loved.

Farrah tugged on the hem of his shirt. He took her cue and pulled the pesky piece of fabric over his head, eager to be rid of one less barrier between them. She tracked every movement, her eyes molten with desire.

"Blake." Her breathy whisper almost did him in.

"Yes, baby?" Blake lifted her shirt and pressed a hot kiss to her stomach. He inched his way up until he reached the lacy edge of her bra.

"I'm ready."

CHAPTER 19

"I'M READY."

Blake froze.

Farrah's heart slammed against her rib cage. This was it.

Bye-bye, nineteen years of virginity.

"Are you sure?" Blake's brow crinkled with...concern? Not the reaction she'd expected or been hoping for.

"Yes." Farrah maneuvered them so Blake lay on his back and she hovered over him. She trailed kisses over his neck, shoulders, chest, and stomach until the agonizingly slow journey brought her to the top of his jeans. She stroked him through the denim. He was so huge and hard, it sent spikes of fear and anticipation through her.

Blake's stomach muscles contracted; a low growl ripped from his throat. He gripped her arms and yanked her up. "Don't."

"Why not?" She shrugged free and started unbuckling his belt.

He covered her hand with his, forcing her to still. "I don't know if I'll—we don't have to do this now. We can wait." She noticed beads of sweat forming on his forehead.

"I don't want to wait. I'm ready." Farrah had waited nineteen years. She was tired of waiting.

The clock ticked in the corner, reminding her that every second brought them closer to the end. She'd waited her entire life to find someone who made her feel the way Blake did. To experience what her friends always gushed about. She wasn't going to let it slip through her fingers. "I want you now."

Farrah eased her hand out from beneath Blake's. She tugged his jeans and boxers down and sucked in a breath at the sight of his arousal. Her body ached to feel him inside her, while her mind wondered how in the world he'd fit. He was larger than anyone she'd been with, and while she hadn't had actual intercourse with her previous partners, they were manageable. Blake, on the other hand...

"I don't want to scare you." Blake's voice was so rough it was barely recognizable.

"I'm not scared." To prove her point, Farrah kneeled and took him in her mouth. Blake shuddered as she luxuriated in the taste and feel of his warm, velvet-covered steel length. Some of her girlfriends thought blow jobs were degrading, but Farrah disagreed. There was nothing more empowering than having total control over another's pleasure.

Besides, when you're a nineteen-year-old virgin who's done everything but, you get pretty darn good at "everything but."

Farrah swirled her tongue over the swollen head and stroked her hands down his heated shaft. Her mouth followed her fingers from the base to the tip and back again. Blake hissed out a breath and fisted her hair with one hand when she increased her pace. Farrah moaned at the gentle tug on her scalp. The fire in her belly grew; arousal dampened her thighs. She sucked on him greedily while her hands roamed, stroking and caressing until they were both ready to explode with desire.

Blake's body tightened. "I'm going to come," he warned. His breath came out in short pants; a faint sheen of sweat glistened on his skin.

In response, Farrah took him deeper in her throat. She wanted to taste him, devour him, love him. She wanted all of him.

Blake's back arched and his grip tightened as he came in her mouth. Farrah lapped up every drop, milking him dry until he collapsed back onto the bed.

She couldn't hold back a smug smile as she slid up his body and pressed a kiss to his neck.

"Holy shit," he groaned. He ran his fingers through her hair and stared at her with so much love, it made Farrah's heart ache. No one had ever looked at her like that before. It scared the shit out of her, but the thought of losing him scared her more. Farrah snuggled closer to him, comforted by the solid feel of his body against hers. "You're going to be the death of me."

"In French, they use the term *la petite mort*, 'the little death,' as a euphemism for orgasm, so you're technically correct."

Blake's laugh reverberated through her, making her smile. Farrah loved his laugh. It was rich and comforting, like a cup of hot chocolate on a snowy winter day.

She trailed her fingers over his chest and the hard ridges of his abdomen. To her surprise, Blake stirred against her. "How is that possible?"

He didn't bother hiding his cocky grin. "Stamina, baby. I got lots of it."

Farrah's arousal spiked again. She remembered how he felt in her mouth. Now she wanted to feel him inside her, filling her until she lost all sense of time and space.

"Do you have a condom?" She reached for him, her heart pounding with excitement. Finally. She was going to—

Blake grasped her wrist and flipped her over so she was the one lying on her back again. "Not yet. I have a favor to return."

Unease unfurled in her stomach. "It's ok. You don't have to."

"Any guy who doesn't is a dick. Do I look like a dick to you?"

"Well." Farrah flicked her gaze down.

His chest rumbled with more laughter. "We'll get to that later. In the meantime..." He skimmed his lips over her mouth, her cheeks, her jaw, her neck, her shoulders, and her breasts, leaving a trail of fire in their wake.

Farrah closed her eyes and gave herself up to the heat of his touch. Still, a corner of her mind remained alert, anxious, worrying and wondering whether this time would be any different.

Blake's mouth closed around her nipple, tonguing it, while he rolled the other between his fingers. Farrah gasped at the sensation. The ache between her legs intensified, and she dug her nails into his shoulders, leaving crescent-shaped indentations in his skin.

If it hurt, Blake didn't show it. He sucked hard on her nipple, then released it with an audible pop. He blew on the sensitive, swollen tip, which hardened even more from the cool air. He repeated this process on the other side, alternating between her breasts until Farrah squirmed with need.

"Blake, please," she begged.

"Please what?" He eased her shorts and underwear down her legs and slid a finger between her slick folds. He groaned. "Jesus, you're dripping."

She was. Farrah had never been more turned on in her life. Her thighs were slick with her juices; her sex clenched as if she needed something—someone—buried deep inside her.

"Please. I need you." Her whimper turned into a moan when Blake rubbed his thumb over her clit. Her hips bucked, seeking relief.

"You have me." Blake replaced his hand with his mouth.

Farrah's head fell back. Every scrape of his tongue against her sensitive flesh caused a bolt of sensation to sizzle through her. It was enough to turn her body into one giant nerve ending, raw and pulsing with need; it wasn't enough to quiet the voices. They whispered in her mind, raising doubts about her body, about whether Blake enjoyed what he was doing or if he was doing it because he thought he had to. About why she teetered on the edge but couldn't bring herself to step over.

She clutched the sheets so hard, her knuckles turned white. She didn't have this issue when she was alone. Farrah could bring herself to orgasm every time, so she knew it was possible. It just wasn't possible with a guy.

Maybe it'll be different with Blake. She felt more connected to him than with any guy in her past, and Lord knew he was talented. The things he was doing with his mouth...

Farrah cried out when he sucked on her clit and flicked his tongue over the most sensitive spot on her bundle of nerves.

It. Was. Incredible. But it wasn't enough.

She tried to will her body past the finish line. It shouldn't be hard. She was so aroused, she might explode—except she didn't. She remained on the razor's edge, held back by some force that didn't want her to fall. Her body craved relief yet wouldn't give it to her.

It was the world's cruelest joke.

Goddammit.

Tears of frustration leaked from the corners of her eyes. A sob escaped her throat.

Blake stopped. The bed shifted as he moved up to face her. "Are you ok? Did I hurt you?" He sounded panicked.

Farrah shook her head. She kept her eyes closed, too mortified to look at him. Not only couldn't she come, she was crying (and not from joy) in the middle of what was otherwise incredible oral sex. What was wrong with her?

"Farrah, look at me. Tell me what's wrong."

She opened her eyes reluctantly. Concern etched Blake's features, and his brows drew together into a deep V.

"Nothing's wrong," she hiccuped. She swiped her tears away. "I'm sorry. This is so embarrassing."

The mood was ruined. There was no use denying it.

"Don't be sorry." Blake lay next to her and wrapped her in his arms. "Shh. It's ok."

"It's not you. It's really not. I just—" Farrah sniffled. "I can't, you know."

He looked puzzled. "You can't what?"

"I can't...come." She whispered the last word.

A pause, then Blake laughed. "Is that what you're worried about? Farrah, I know it takes girls longer. It's ok, we can—"

"No, I can't come, period." She kept her gaze lowered, afraid of his reaction. "I mean, I can by myself, but I've never been able to orgasm with a guy. Ever."

This time the pause was more prolonged. "Well, you haven't met anyone as talented as I am," Blake joked in an obvious attempt to lighten the mood.

Farrah managed a watery smile. "True." The tears slowed, thank god. "Maybe it's just oral. If we had sex, it might be different," she said hopefully.

You hit different spots during intercourse, right? That could be it.

"We are not having sex like it's a science experiment," Blake said. "Not yet. Though I would love to see you in a lab coat getup one day."

This time he got a weak laugh out of her.

"You know that saying: try, try again. We'll keep trying till we get there. Once we do, we'll move to the next base."

Farrah frowned. Great. She was going to be a virgin for the rest of her life.

"Look on the bright side." Blake kissed her forehead. "You'll have me, Blake Ryan, at your full disposal. I'm basically your willing sex slave. No other girl can say that."

"They better not." Farrah bit her lip. "What if it's me? What if there's something wrong with me?"

Old fears resurfaced, threatening to drown her in their turbulent waters.

"There is nothing wrong with you." Blake's gaze turned fierce. "You're perfect."

"No one's perfect."

"You are. To me."

Farrah buried her face in Blake's chest, afraid he'd see how much his words affected her. She could feel his heart beating, a steady *thump-thump-thump* that forced those old fears to retreat.

But in their place came new ones that were even more insidious because they were grounded in reality.

They weren't fears; they were inevitabilities.

And Farrah knew if she wasn't careful, they could break her heart.

CHAPTER 20

YOU CAN DO THIS. YOU'RE BLAKE RYAN. GIRLS DO NOT scare you.

Blake paced his room, his pulse thrumming with anticipation. His stomach churned, and he couldn't tell whether he was excited or about to be sick.

Probably a bit of both.

Blake had done a lot of scary shit in his life. He'd gotten up in front of a hundred cameras and told the world he was quitting football. He'd flown halfway across the world to spend a year in a country where he didn't know the language or the culture. He was preparing to open his own sports bar even though he had zero experience running anything resembling a business (thank god for Google). In fact, he finished his first real-life business plan the other day. Market analysis, marketing plan, operating plan, financial plan, management plan...all done.

But he'd never once told a girl he loved her—and meant it. He'd said it to Cleo, more out of obligation than anything else, and the words tasted like cardboard. Empty and meaningless. Now, those same words burned inside him, screaming to get out.

Blake almost said it to Farrah the night she told him she was ready to lose her virginity. But then, well, *that* happened. Blake wasn't upset—though he'd be lying if he said his ego didn't take a hit—but the timing was off. He hadn't worked up the courage to tell her to her face again.

In his mind? Yes, a million times. Every time he looked at her, saw her smile, heard her voice, felt the heat of her skin against his, he wondered how he'd survived without her. Twenty-one years of not knowing she existed only to have her turn his world upside down in three months. Yet in those three months, he'd lived more and loved harder than he had in the years preceding them.

There was an entire world outside Texas, and Blake was only now getting a taste of it.

"Don't be a coward." Blake continued to pace, giving himself a pep talk like a crazy person. Thank god he didn't have a roommate. If someone walked in on him like this, they'd have him committed. "There's only three weeks left in the semester. After that, you won't see Farrah again until late next January."

He stared at the elephant figurine Farrah had gifted him after she returned from Thailand. Blake Jr. stared back, positively dripping judgment. *Tell her already, you idiot,* it screamed.

Great. Now Blake was hearing voices from inanimate objects. He needed to get out of here before he really *did* go crazy.

"You got this," he muttered under his breath as he barreled down the hall, nearly bowling Nardo over in the process.

"Where's the fire?" Nardo yelled.

Blake ignored him. He stopped in front of Farrah's room. He couldn't breathe.

Was this a good idea? *Probably not. But what the hell. As Drake said, YO fucking LO.*

After a final moment of hesitation, Blake rapped his knuckles on the door.

Thump. Thump. Thump.

Farrah opened the door. She was wearing her adorable sheep pajamas and one of those goopy white masks that made girls look like horror movie extras.

"Hey." Surprise flared in her eyes. "Is everything all right?"

Blake's mind blanked. The speech he'd rehearsed, gone. His ability to speak, gone.

All he could do was stare at Farrah, wishing the floor would swallow him whole.

Concern replaced surprise. "Do you need to—"

"I love you." The words rolled off his tongue, sweet and rich like honey. It wasn't how he pictured this going. He had a whole flowery speech lined up (thanks to those rom-coms Farrah forced him to watch) before he dropped the *L* bomb. But heck, it was already out there. There was no going back now.

The rest of Blake's confession tumbled off his lips, like it was scared it wouldn't get the chance to see the light of day if it waited too long. "I didn't expect it or even want it, but it happened. If I'm being honest, it happened a while ago, and I'm only now getting the courage to tell you. You said once every second counts, and I don't want another second to go by without you knowing that I am totally, completely, one hundred percent in love with you."

Farrah stilled.

The next minute stretched on for eternity.

Silence wasn't rejection, but he was going to be sick if Farrah didn't say something soon.

Someone cleared their throat.

A girl with green-streaked hair appeared behind Farrah's shoulder. It took Blake a second to identify her as Farrah's roommate, Janice—and to realize she'd heard every word he said.

Fuck.

"Er, I'm going to the library." Janice looked like she was trying not to laugh. "I won't be back for a while, so, yeah."

She was definitely trying not to laugh.

Good luck, she mouthed as she slipped past Farrah into the hall.

Blake's cheeks burned with embarrassment. Luckily (or not), he didn't have to dwell on this humiliating turn of events long.

"Um."

Not the first word Blake wanted to hear after his confession.

"I'm sorry. I need to…" Farrah stepped aside. "Come in."

He did, even though he wanted to run away. He had a feeling he wasn't going to like what Farrah had to say.

You idiot. You stupid, stupid idiot. He should've kept his mouth shut. At least then, he could've held on to the hope that Farrah felt the same way about him as he did her.

Ignorance, as they say, is bliss.

"I need to take this off." Farrah peeled off her mask and tossed it in the trash. Her skin gleamed beneath the lights. "I don't know what to say."

His chest went hollow. "You don't have to say anything." Blake forced a smile and tried to convince himself he wasn't dying inside.

"No. I want to." Farrah fiddled with her necklace. "When I met you, I told myself I wasn't going to fall for you."

Jesus. Her words cut like a surgical knife through Blake's heart.

"I understand." He needed to get out of here. "I'm supposed to meet Luke for dinner so I'll—"

"But I did."

He couldn't stay here a minute longer. He needed to go— *wait, what?*

Blake's head snapped up. "What did you say?"

"I did fall in love with you." Farrah's eyes glowed with emotion. She clutched her necklace until her knuckles turned white.

"That place you're at now? I'm right there with you. It scares the crap out of me, which is funny because I've always considered myself a romantic. You know, I love reading and watching romances, and when I was in middle school, I read all these bridal magazines and dreamt about falling in love and getting married one day. *Not* that I'm expecting us to get married, because obviously it's way too soon—I mean, if it happens at all—but this is the first time I've been in love and I didn't expect to feel this way and—"

"Farrah." Blake closed the gap between them until he could count every lash rimming those beautiful eyes.

"I'm not sure if this is normal and sorry I'm rambling, I don't even know what I'm—"

"Farrah, shut up so I can kiss you."

She shut up.

Blake gently pried her hand off her necklace and tangled his fingers with hers before he captured her mouth with his. What started as an innocent kiss, an exploration of this new stage in their relationship, quickly heated up until Blake's entire body was on fire. His nerve endings thrummed as Farrah swept her tongue between his lips, tasting and teasing.

He was so lost in the heat and taste of her, he didn't notice they'd moved until Farrah pushed him onto her bed and straddled him.

Blake's jeans constricted painfully.

Her hair brushed his chest as she hovered over him, cheeks flushed, mouth swollen, looking for all the world like she'd stepped out of a dream. His dream.

"I love you," she said. Each word came out slowly and carefully, like she was testing them out.

Blake brushed his thumb over Farrah's cheek. Her skin was soft and warm against his. His gaze caressed her face, lingering on the delicate curve of her jaw, the gentle slope of her nose, the tiny mole above her right eyebrow, and the sweep of black lashes framing her deep chocolate eyes.

"I love you too."

He flipped them over until he was the one hovering over her. "Let's try an experiment."

Farrah's brow furrowed. "What kind of experiment?"

"This." Blake brushed his lips over hers and reached down to caress her, reveling in her sharp intake of breath as he explored her most intimate folds.

They'd tried multiple times to bring Farrah over the finish line, to no avail. She got close during their last attempt, but no dice. It was a blow (no pun intended) to Blake's pride. When a girl RSVPed yes, he made sure they came. Always. It was a Blake Ryan hallmark. The fact he couldn't do that for Farrah galled him to no end.

But for once, his pride wasn't the most important thing.

Blake kept his gaze on Farrah's face, taking his cues from her reactions—the way her eyelids fluttered and lips parted when he rubbed his thumb over her clit, the way she arched when he slipped a finger inside her warmth until his fingers were slick with her juices.

Then he guided Farrah's hand down to replace his own. He sat back.

Her eyes flew open. "Wha—"

"Touch yourself for me."

Farrah's cheeks turned the color of ripe tomatoes. "I can't."

"You can. You said you can come when you do it on your own." Blake ran his thumb over the soft skin of Farrah's inner thigh. "Show me."

In his football days, Blake followed a simple learning method: (1) Watch how the pros do it (2) Do it yourself (3) Keep going until you do it well (4) Add your own flair until you do it better.

The method won him two Heismans and three national championships. A girl's body was more complicated than a football play, but the principle was the same. He couldn't believe he hadn't made the connection earlier.

Farrah shook her head. "I need to be alone when I do it."

"Why?"

"Because." She faltered. "I guess I'm more relaxed when I'm alone."

"Do you trust me?"

Farrah swallowed, her eyes bright. "Yes." It came out as a whisper.

Blake released the air from his lungs. "Close your eyes."

Another swallow. Her eyes fluttered closed.

Farrah's initial touch was hesitant. She stroked herself like it was the first time, but eventually, her body arched and her breath came out in sexy little pants as she brought herself to the brink of orgasm.

Lust poured through his veins, burning him with its intensity. Blake curled his hands into fists and willed his body to stay in control.

Farrah groaned and tore her hands away from her body. She opened her eyes. "I can't." Frustration wracked her voice. "I can't do it with you watching. It's embarrassing."

"Embarrassing?" Blake was stunned. "That was the hottest thing I've ever seen, and I look at myself in the mirror every day."

Farrah choked out a laugh. "What a compliment."

"It's not a compliment. It's the truth. I could watch you forever." *Because I want to be with you forever.* The words were on the tip of his tongue, but he swallowed them. "You don't have to be embarrassed around me. Ever. Not even if you're, I dunno, listening to Nickelback."

"I like Nickelback."

Blake tried to conceal his horror.

Farrah giggled. "Kidding. You should've seen the look on your face."

"Thank god. See? If I don't judge you for that, I won't judge you for anything."

"I know." She blew out a breath. "I don't know why this is so hard. I have no problem when I'm alone."

"Would it help if I went first?"

Her eyes grew to the size of saucers. "What?"

"You're embarrassed to touch yourself in front of me. What if I did it first?" Blake reached down and grasped his shaft. He kept his gaze on hers as he slid his hand over his length, rock-hard and throbbing from Farrah's show.

Farrah's lips parted. Her eyes darted down, up, and down again. They stayed there.

Meanwhile, Blake ran his gaze over her face and body. It glistened with a faint sheen of sweat from her earlier exertions. Her hair was tousled and her lips swollen. He remembered how he felt between those lips, remembered the warmth of her breath against his skin and the way her soft curves molded against his.

His breath quickened. He increased his pace until his head fell back, and he came with a roar. Then Farrah was there, enveloping him in the warmth of her mouth, and he came harder, gripping her hair for dear life as she milked every last drop from him.

Once they finished, he collapsed against the wall, ears ringing from the intensity of his orgasm.

Farrah licked her lips. Her eyes were bright with arousal. "That was amazing."

"Not embarrassing?"

She shook her head.

"That's how I feel when I'm watching you. Except more so because guys are horny bastards."

Case in point: Blake hardened again. When it came to Farrah, he was insatiable.

"Good." Farrah eased herself back into her previous position. "Let's try this again."

CHAPTER 21

FARRAH'S PULSE RACED WITH NERVES AND AROUSAL.
She'd seen guys touch themselves before—in porn. It didn't do
much for her. But watching Blake? It felt even more intimate than
she imagined sex would feel.

Flames of lust curled around her, making her breasts ache
and her core weep with need. It didn't help that Blake was
sitting there, looking more gorgeous than any human had the
right to look. His eyes, dark and hooded with desire, watched
her slide her hands over her body for the second time that
night.

"It's okay if we don't get there this time." His voice rolled
over her, hoarse but reassuring. "We'll have next time and the
time after that. We have all the time in the world."

They didn't. They knew that, which was why Farrah refused
to look away as she touched herself. She refused to retreat to the
corner of her mind that taunted her with its doubts. Instead, she
focused on the way her body hummed when she brought it to
life, and when those doubts reached out to drag her to the place
where she alone was allowed, she focused on Blake and the way

he looked at her—like he never wanted to blink. Like he'd never desired anyone the way he desired her.

In that moment, she believed everything he'd ever told her.

Her breath hitched. Images of Blake stroking himself flooded her mind. Her movements grew faster, jerkier.

So close.

Her lashes fluttered. The corner in her mind beckoned. Farrah grit her teeth and ordered her thoughts to shut up. To her surprise, they obeyed.

However, that didn't compare to her surprise when her orgasm slammed through her less than a minute later. The tidal wave of pleasure was so sudden and unexpected she didn't register what was happening until she was already coming down—

"Oh my god," she gasped. Farrah was so caught up in the throes of climax, she didn't realize Blake had moved.

His mouth replaced her hand. His tongue swirled around her tight bud, licking and teasing, before he drew it deep into his mouth and suckled hard.

Farrah cried out. She tried to scoot away, but Blake's strong hands pinned her in place while he feasted on her most sensitive flesh.

Her breath came out in short pants.

She was burning. Burning so hot and so exquisitely she couldn't stand it, yet she never wanted it to end.

Farrah's body didn't have time to recover from its last high before Blake brought her to the peak again. There she teetered, suspended for an eternity, until she crashed down with a force that shocked her. She'd already fallen, but he was still there, coaxing more and more out of her until she had nothing left to give.

After the throes of her last orgasm subsided, Farrah collapsed, limp and exhausted, into Blake's arms. "Oh my god," she repeated. That was all she could say. She couldn't think straight. She couldn't even remember her name.

He nuzzled her neck. "Good?"

"Really, really good. Wow." Now Farrah understood the hype. No wonder her friends gushed about oral sex. Farrah could do this all day, every day.

Blake's chuckle reverberated against her skin. "Lucky for you, babe, you got the best person for the job." He snaked an arm around her waist and pulled her close so her back nestled against his front. He rested his chin on her shoulder. "Thank you for trusting me."

Farrah turned to look at him. "Thank you for being trustworthy."

They were being so cheesy, she would've cringed had she read it in a book, but this wasn't a book. This was her life. And right now, it was perfect.

Blake and Farrah lay in silence, content with each other's presence. Farrah rubbed an absentminded thumb over her necklace.

Three months.

Three months at CCU had changed nothing beyond the superficial. She had new classes, new friends, and a new living situation, but she'd stayed the same person throughout it all.

Three months in Shanghai had changed her life.

To think, she'd been so close to choosing Paris. In an alternate universe, alternate Farrah was gallivanting around the French capital with a different set of friends, kissing different boys, traveling to different cities, and learning a different language.

This Farrah shivered, her heart breaking for every version of herself that wasn't right here in Blake's arms because this was heaven and every other world was a mere imitation.

"You always do that."

"Do what?" She snuggled closer to him to reassure herself he was still there.

"Play with your necklace when you're deep in thought. Or nervous. Or mad. Or sad." Blake rested his chin on her shoulder and brushed his fingers over the silver pendant. "You're not nervous, mad, or sad—at least, I hope not—so penny for your thoughts."

Farrah curled her hand over Blake's. "My father gave me this necklace." The backs of her eyes burned when she remembered that day.

Her dad picked her up for their weekly lunch date. He took her to In-N-Out, like he always did because neither wanted to sit through a full, multi-course meal. It was too awkward. To Farrah's surprise, he presented her with the necklace after they polished off their double-doubles and animal-style fries.

"He bought it for my fifteenth birthday. I still had a few weeks to go, but he said he couldn't wait. He wanted me to have it early. This was before I walked in on my mom crying and I—" Farrah's lips trembled. Blake tightened his grip and pressed a kiss to her shoulder. "In a weird way, the necklace comforts me. Like as long as I have it on, I have my dad with me, and I can say all the things I didn't say when he was alive."

Blake was silent for a long moment. "So you're saying your dad was watching every time we went down on each other?"

"Blake!"

"Sorry. Sorry." He buried his face in her hair. "I make jokes at the most inappropriate times."

A smile tugged at her mouth. Farrah could always count on Blake to lighten things up. "It's ok. I like your inappropriate jokes. Most of the time."

"Wrong thing to say, babe. Now I'll be unstoppable."

"You're the great Blake Ryan. Shouldn't you already be unstoppable?"

His stomach rumbled with laughter. "You got me. But you

didn't answer my question. What were you thinking about earlier? You only go all quiet when you're deep in thought."

Farrah rolled over so she was face-to-face with Blake. He was so close she could count every eyelash and see the faint smattering of freckles across his nose. "I was thinking about how lucky I am to have met you."

His eyes darkened to sapphires. "Luck had nothing to do with it." He tucked a strand of hair behind her ear. "We're here because we're meant to be here."

"Do you really believe that?" Farrah wanted to believe it. If they were meant to be here, then it was fate. Fate, as grand and omniscient as she was, wouldn't bring two people together, then tear them apart.

Fate was the only thing that trumped time.

"I really do."

Farrah let Blake's faith sweep her away because, at the end of the day, that was all they had.

She kissed him, a long, slow kiss that built in heat and passion until she couldn't take it any longer. Their bodies moved together, skin against skin, and she cried out for him, craving that final connection.

"Are you sure?" Blake panted. She could feel him against her stomach, hot and hard.

The ache intensified.

"Yes." She was going to die if he didn't do it. Die of fiery, exquisite torture. "I have condoms in my drawer. Just in case," she said when she saw the look on his face.

That was good enough.

Farrah heard her drawer open and close, followed by the sound of tearing foil. Blake returned, holding and kissing and caressing her until she growled and raked her nails down his back in impatience.

Every inch of her was on fire, consumed by flames of desire. All she could think about was Blake being inside her.

Then finally, wondrously, he was. He entered her in one fluid stroke, sheathing himself to the hilt. Farrah arched into him with a gasp of pain and pleasure.

Blake stilled. "Are you ok?"

"Yes." She gripped his arms. "Keep going."

Farrah set her jaw as he moved again. Blake's initial thrusts were slow, but he was so large it took her a while to adjust. Eventually, her muscles relaxed and the pain subsided, replaced with a sensation so great it robbed her of breath. He filled her completely until there was no space left for anything else. There was only Blake.

She moved her hips in rhythm with his and hissed when he rubbed his thumb over her swollen clit.

Farrah couldn't believe she was doing it. Sex.

Except it was greater than sex. It was all-consuming. Mind, heart, body, soul. All of it laid bare for the boy in her arms.

The flames intensified, drowning her in their heat.

Blake groaned. His thrusts grew faster, harder. In response, she climbed higher and higher, desperate to reach the peak once more now that she knew she wasn't going to be alone when she got there.

"Farrah."

"Yes?" She wrapped her legs around him, urging him deeper until he hit a spot that caused her to gasp in pleasure.

"I love you."

People say you shouldn't trust a guy's confession during sex. That the hormones muddle their brains and make them say things they don't mean.

Maybe that was true for some guys, but Farrah didn't care about other guys. She cared about Blake, and even if he hadn't confessed earlier, even if he'd never uttered the word *love* aloud until now, she saw it in his eyes. A veil had lifted, allowing her to see all of him and all of her reflected in those blue depths. Every feeling, every decision, every choice—not just theirs but those of everyone who'd come before them. Thousands of years, millions of moving pieces that had to fit, if only for a second, so they could be where they were in that moment.

She saw it all.

And now that she'd walked amongst the stars, how could she not believe in fate? How could she not believe in love?

"I love you too."

Blake's smile could have made the sun hide in shame.

To prove their words, they poured everything they had into each other, urging one another to go higher, faster.

Farrah crashed over the edge first; Blake followed soon after, their cries of ecstasy mingling until neither could form a word and they collapsed into each other's arms.

CHAPTER 22

THE WIND NIPPED AT BLAKE'S CHEEKS, NOSE, AND ears. Did he have ears anymore? He couldn't tell. All sensation had left his body.

He deeply regretted his decision to stroll through Tianzifang one last time before the semester ended. The artsy enclave was one of Blake's favorite spots in the city, and its labyrinth of alley-ways, shops, galleries, and restaurants made it the perfect place to while away an evening...unless it was winter.

They should've gone to laser tag like Luke suggested. At least they would've been warm.

"Let's go inside." Farrah squeezed his hand. "You're freezing."

"I'm fine." Blake's breath steamed in the cold air.

"Told ya we should've done laser tag. Told ya you should've worn a hat." Luke rocked back and forth on the balls of his feet. His own beanie sat snug on his head, that bastard. "I'm always right."

"You didn't tell me I should wear a hat."

"Well, I would've had I known you weren't going to."

"What happened to spoiling the birthday boy?" Blake grumbled.

"You said you wanted something low-key. No presents, no party," Courtney reminded him.

"Doesn't mean I want you guys ganging up on me."

"I'm on your side." Farrah kissed his cheek. "Always."

A surge of love flooded Blake's veins and warmed his cold skin. He turned his head so he could give her a proper kiss.

Their friends groaned and made faux gagging noises.

"You guys are giving me a toothache," Kris said. "First Court and Leo, then Liv and Sammy, and now you two. I'm the only sane one left in the group."

She turned her attention to a rare Visa sign posted on a vendor's stall. Even in a tourist-friendly marketplace like Tianzifang, cash reigned supreme. "Ooh. They accept Visa?" She tossed a navy-blue beanie at Blake, who caught it in midair. "Don't say I never got you anything."

"Uh, thanks."

Kris swiped an armful of jewelry and handed her card to the vendor, who looked like he couldn't believe his luck.

Normally, Kris wouldn't touch fake silver with a ten-foot pole, but Blake suspected she was still trying to get back at her dad for marrying "the Redheaded Monster," as she called her soon-to-be stepmother.

The credit card machine beeped. The vendor's forehead creased. "Your card was declined." He returned the Visa to Kris with noticeably less enthusiasm.

"That's impossible." Kris shoved the Visa back into his hand. "Try again."

He did. Declined.

"Try this one." She fished another card out of her wallet.

Also declined.

"It's ok," Blake said. "I can pay for the hat."

"There's something wrong with the machine," Kris snapped.

"It's fine. I have cash." She dumped the jewelry back into their bins and slapped a fifty kuai note on the counter. "Keep the change."

"Thanks for the gift." Blake pulled the hat over his head. Instant warmth. Amazing what a bit of wool can do.

"Yeah, whatever. Wait until my father hears about this." Kris flipped up the collar of her fur-trimmed coat. "Our accountant is going to be in so much trouble."

Beside her, Olivia let out a huge yawn. Her third of the night.

"Why don't you head back to the dorm?" Blake suggested. "You have an early flight. No need to stay up late for me."

"Are you sure?"

"Yeah. Farrah and I are going to hang out here a little longer." Blake wanted some alone time with Farrah before they left.

"I can take a hint. Happy birthday." Olivia hugged Blake and Farrah. "If I don't see you before we leave, have an amazing Christmas."

"You too." Farrah squeezed her friend tight. "Love you."

The rest of the group said their goodbyes and dispersed, leaving Blake and Farrah alone.

"Finally." Blake wrapped his arms around Farrah's waist. "I thought they'd never leave."

She laughed. "They're our friends."

"Yeah, and they were cramping our style." Blake's stomach growled. "Are you down for a second dinner? I'm getting hungry again."

Walking around in the cold really burned off the calories.

"I'm always down for food."

"Great. There's an amazing Vietnamese place around here somewhere."

It took a few wrong turns, but Blake finally located the tiny restaurant he'd stumbled onto a few months ago when his friends were in Thailand. The unassuming spot was tucked into a side alleyway across from a trinket shop. Leather booths lined the walls; wooden latticework, lush green plants, and amber wall sconces emphasized the intimacy of the small space, which despite the late hour buzzed with activity.

"If I didn't know better, I'd think you were trying to seduce me," Farrah teased. She slipped off her coat and hung it on the wall peg near their table.

Blake's dimples flashed. "Is it working?"

"Oh yeah. Wait till we get back to the dorm." Farrah's smile turned sly. "I have another birthday present for you."

Blake's blood heated. Despite his "no presents" request, Farrah had gifted him a beautiful monogrammed business card holder at dinner, "because every successful business owner needs one," she explained. He loved the card holder, but at the moment, he was far more interested in the carnal possibilities flashing through his mind.

"Forget a second dinner." Blake tossed his napkin on the table and stood up. "Let's skip to dessert."

He had some creative ideas involving whipped cream and chocolate he'd like to put into action.

Farrah's silvery peal of laughter caused the other diners to turn their heads. "Oh, no. Sit down," she said. "You can't tempt me with pho without following through on it."

Blake pouted. *Damn.* "I can't believe you're choosing noodle soup over me."

"To be fair, I'd choose noodle soup over almost anything. Except you." Farrah reached across the table and interlaced their fingers. "You know I'd go anywhere with you."

His heart melted into a pile of goo. It was scary how much power she had over him. "And you know I can't deny you any-thing." He brought her hand to his mouth and brushed a kiss along the back of it. "Especially not food. You're scary when you're hangry."

Farrah grinned. "I've trained you well."

"What am I, a dog?"

She patted his hand with her free one. "A very *hot dog*." She giggled. "See what I did there? Hot. Dog. It's funny," she said when Blake raised his eyebrows.

"Be glad I love you so much. Jokes that bad should be banned."

Farrah stuck out her tongue. "I'm only letting that slide because it's your birthday."

A harried waiter approached their table. They hadn't looked at the menu yet but after a quick scan, Blake and Farrah placed their usual orders for Vietnamese food—pho with brisket and eye of round for her, grilled pork banh mi for him, and two summer rolls to share.

"I'm glad we could celebrate your birthday before we left." Farrah rubbed her thumb over Blake's knuckles. "I hope you enjoyed it."

"Today is the best birthday I've had in ages. Because it's my first birthday with you." A year ago, Blake would've choked on the amount of cheese in those words. Now, he didn't care. It was the truth.

Blake's birthday wasn't until next week—lucky him, his birthday fell two days before Christmas—but Farrah insisted on celebrating before they returned home for the holidays. He'd nixed a big party, much to Courtney's disappointment, and settled for a group dinner at one of Olivia's fancy-schmancy restaurants. Blake would've preferred beer and pizza at a casual joint, but the girls would've killed him.

Farrah sucked in a breath. "Who knew you were such a cornball?"

He smiled, trying not to think about the fact he wouldn't see her in person again until late January. He couldn't believe the semester was over. Three and a half months had passed in the blink of an eye. If his life hadn't changed so much, he would've thought he'd just arrived in Shanghai. "Corn with extra cheese, that's me. Do me a favor and don't tell anyone."

Her eyes sparkled with emotion. "Your secret's safe with me."

The waiter returned with their food. One bite told Blake it was as good as he remembered.

"Nine out of ten on food recommendations." Farrah slurped the broth from her spoon. "I'm impressed."

"Nine out of ten?" Blake was insulted. "What's the bad one?"

"That pizza place you took us to."

"Which—oh." Blake grimaced when he remembered the stale pizza crust and funky toppings from a few weeks ago. "Fine. I dropped the ball on that one. But this should be good enough to make up for it."

"Mm-hmm."

They ate the rest of their meal in comfortable silence. This was one of Blake's favorite things about his relationship with Farrah. With his past girlfriends, he had to put on a show and be as lively and charming as everyone expected him to be. This was true even with Cleo, whom he grew up with. With Farrah, he could breathe.

It took them less than twenty minutes to polish off all their food. By the time they finished, Blake's stomach strained against his pants. He was so full, he couldn't move.

Maybe a second dinner was a bad idea.

"I'm going to freshen up." Farrah scooted out of the booth. "I spilled soup on my shirt."

"It's ok. We'll get you out of that shirt soon enough." Blake laughed as Farrah whacked him on the arm.

While she used the restroom, Blake paid the bill. No tipping culture in China, which took some getting used to but which he now appreciated.

After weeks of struggling to adjust to China's unfamiliar customs and way of life at the beginning of the semester, Blake had finally settled into a comfortable Shanghai routine. The noise and pollution didn't bother him so much anymore, and he even liked some of the foods he swore he'd never try. Turned out stinky tofu was quite delicious, once you got past the stinky part.

It was going to be weird going back to the States. Blake was already bracing himself for reverse culture shock, though it would be nice not to have to deal with squat toilets for a while.

After Farrah came back from the restroom, they shrugged on their coats and walked to the nearest metro station. It was so cold their breaths fogged around their face every time they breathed.

"Our last night." Farrah sounded wistful. "It's been a wild ride."

"Our last night in Shanghai this semester," Blake corrected. "We have next semester."

He couldn't wait. He missed his mom and his sister, but he wasn't looking forward to seeing his father. He liked his old man best when he was more than seven thousand miles away. Besides, a month without seeing Farrah was going to be torture.

Sure, they had Skype, but it wasn't the same.

On the other hand, Blake had always wanted to try cybersex...

"You're right." Farrah shook her head. "I didn't mean to get all maudlin on your birthday. Let's talk about something else."

"Like what we're going to do once we're back in the dorm?" Blake wiggled his eyebrows. Fantasies of all the dirty things he and Farrah could do over video transitioned into fantasies of all the dirty things they were going to do in person.

Fuck cybersex. Nothing beat actual sex. Skin against skin. Mouth against mouth. Mouth against...other parts of the body.

Blake hardened until it was almost painful as a surge of lust rocketed through his veins. He eyed the overhead map telling them how many stops they had left before they reach SFSU.

Four.

Fuck. That was four stops too long.

Meanwhile, his arousal didn't go unnoticed. Farrah's eyes darkened with desire, and she stepped closer until her chest grazed his. Even though there were several layers of clothing between them, Blake's body reacted like she'd stripped naked.

If they didn't get off this damn train soon, he was going to lose it. Literally.

It didn't help that Farrah started whispering things in his ear—things that had him ready to throw her on the floor of the train and take her, right then and there, onlookers be damned.

Fortunately, they arrived at their stop before he did something that'd have them arrested for public indecency.

Farrah laughed as Blake grabbed her hand and pushed his way off the crowded train with the urgency of a man on his way to the emergency room for a life-threatening situation.

In his case, the situation was blue balls.

"You think this is funny?" Blake growled.

Farrah's eyes sparkled with lust and amusement. "It's pretty funny."

The dorm came into view.

"Let's see about that."

They made it to his room in record time. Blake kicked the door shut behind him and threw Farrah on the bed, eliciting a small cry of surprise. He didn't waste any time shedding both their clothes.

She watched, eyes bright with excitement, as he rolled on a condom and then...he was inside her, driving deep with one hard stroke.

Jesus. She was so damn tight and wet, it drove him out of his mind. Control became a distant memory. Blake pounded into her, driven by mindless need and insatiable lust.

Their first time had been long, sweet, and gentle. It was making love. This? This was fucking. Fast, rough, carnal. There was nothing gentle about it.

Farrah gave as good as she got, her hips slamming up to meet his, her nails raking down his back until they left red marks in his skin.

Blake hissed in pleasure. He thrust harder, driven by lust and a desire to bury himself so deep, nothing could ever tear them apart.

White-hot lashes of sensation whipped through his body, burning him, enveloping him in their heat, until he felt her muscles tighten around him. He slowed his thrusts and chuckled at Farrah's frustrated growl.

Blake lowered his head to nip at her bottom lip. She whimpered in response. "This is for laughing at me earlier."

Farrah grabbed his hair and yanked his head back up so they were eye to eye. Pain and pleasure washed through him. "Blake Ryan, if you don't fuck me as hard you can *right now*, I will never give you a blow job again."

Blake didn't think it was possible, but he hardened even more. Normal Farrah was sexy. Aggressive Farrah was a whole other level.

Blake braced himself on the bed and resumed his thrusts. Partly because he liked having blow jobs in his future, partly because he was going to come from her words alone.

He increased his pace and force until he slammed into her so hard the headboard banged against the wall. Farrah stiffened. Her nails dug deeper and she cried out, a long, keening wail, as she exploded around him. Pain and pleasure mingled until Blake, too, came with so much force stars speckled his vision.

When they were finally sated, they collapsed, boneless, in each other's arms.

"Happy birthday," Farrah gasped.

He muffled his laugh against her neck. "I think I lost a few brain cells, I came so hard." Blake mustered the energy to remove and dispose of his condom before sinking back into his admittedly lumpy bed. But with Farrah beside him, it felt like heaven.

"You—"

"I know." Blake shook his head. "I set myself up for that one."

Farrah grinned and flipped over to straddle him. He was exhausted, but he perked up all the same. "Out of respect for your twenty-second year on earth, I won't make the joke. I do, however, think we should have one more session. Since it's your birthday and all."

"That's the best idea I've ever heard."

Farrah's hair spilled over her shoulders like black silk. Her sweat-slick skin glowed in the moonlight filtering through his curtains. She was the most beautiful thing he'd ever seen.

Blake rested his hands on her hips. "I'm going to miss you so fucking much."

"The break is only a few weeks." The tips of her hair brushed his chest as she took his mouth in a sweet kiss. "Like you said, we have next semester. It'll be like we never left." She sounded like she was trying to convince herself as much as Blake.

"You're right." He rubbed his thumb over her warm satin skin, trying to imprint the sensation in his mind.

"I'm always right." Farrah fished a fresh condom out of his drawer and rolled it on before slowly guiding him inside her. Blake hissed out a breath. "Now, where were we?"

She started moving, and Blake forgot all about tomorrow, yesterday, or how the hell he got here. The only thing that mattered was that he was here, right now, with her.

Spring Semester

CHAPTER 23

"OH MY GOD. YOUR HAIR!" FARRAH'S MOUTH DROPPED when she saw Olivia.

The other girl touched her locks with a self-conscious hand. "Does it look stupid?"

"No, it looks amazing!" Olivia's once waist-length hair swung around her shoulders in a clean, simple bob. The new style enhanced her cheekbones and made her eyes pop. "I love it."

"Thanks." Olivia beamed. "I thought it would be more professional."

The girls stared at each other for a moment before they closed the remaining distance between them and hugged.

"It's so good to see you!" Olivia squealed. "It's been forever."

"It feels that way." The LA suburbs seemed so mundane after the excitement of Shanghai. Farrah enjoyed the warm weather and catching up with her family and friends, but she missed FEA and Blake. "Have you seen Kris?"

"Not yet. You?"

"Not yet." Farrah helped Olivia haul her luggage up the

stairs. Her arms strained with the effort. *FEA needs to invest in an elevator.* "You think she's ok?"

"She's fine." Olivia sounded unsure. "It's Kris."

The girls' hall was a mess of noise and bags. The dulcet tones of the latest pop hit drifted from Flo and Janet's room into the corridor. Charlotte tromped past, dragging a massive comforter behind her. All around, girls laughed and hugged and reminisced about their winter breaks, so excited they tripped over their words.

FEA was back.

Farrah unpacked Olivia's toiletry bag while her friend tossed her clothing on her bed. "Where's Sammy? I can't wait to see him." Farrah missed his infectious laugh and good-natured jokes. He was the closest to a brother she'd ever had.

"He just landed. He'll be here soon." Olivia's eyes gleamed. She pointed her chin at something behind Farrah. "In the meantime, someone's here to see you."

Farrah spun around. She sensed who it was before her eyes confirmed her hunch.

"Hey, girls." Blake flashed his devastating dimples. "Miss me?"

After six weeks of talking to him through a computer screen, Blake appeared larger than life. His lean, muscular body filled the doorframe. His pale blue shirt stretched across his broad shoulders and matched the color of his eyes—the same eyes that drank Farrah in like a man dying of thirst in the desert.

"Hey, Blake." Olivia nudged Farrah, who remained stock-still while her heart melted faster than Italian gelato during the summer.

Olivia upgraded her nudge to a gentle shove. "It's Blake," she hissed.

That did the trick.

Farrah regained control of her limbs and flew across the room into his arms. Blake caught her, his grip sure and strong.

She buried her face in his neck and breathed in his crisp, familiar scent. "I missed you," she said, too overcome with emotion for banter. "I missed you so much."

"I missed you too." His warm breath tickled her skin. His mouth crashed against hers, their tongues tangling while her fingers dug into his arms. He tasted of hunger and desire. Of longing. Of love. He kissed her like his life depended on it.

Farrah sank into Blake's embrace. After weeks of waiting and wanting, this was better than she'd imagined. She raked her fingers through his hair, desperate to—

"Ahem."

Desperate to get—

"Ahem!"

Blake and Farrah groaned in unison. They tore themselves apart and peered at Olivia, who had unpacked in record time and was now color coordinating her closet.

"Get a room." Olivia draped a strapless cobalt dress over a hanger. "Your *own* room."

"Are you kicking us out?" Blake demanded.

"Yes. I love you guys, but I don't want to watch you have sex."

"Maybe you'll learn a thing or two."

Olivia gasped.

Farrah tried not to laugh. "Don't be rude."

"I'm not." Blake's grin was pure devilishness. "I was merely posing a hypothetical."

"Out!" Olivia pointed at the door. "Farrah, dump this rascal."

"She would never."

"If she had to choose between you and me, who do you think she'd choose?"

Blake looked at Farrah, who shrugged. He raised his hands in surrender. "I'm out, I'm out. I can tell when I'm not wanted."

"I always want you." Farrah entwined her arms around his neck. She could float off the ground, she was so happy.

Blake's eyes darkened to sapphires. "Keep going."

"Ugh." Olivia hung her blue jumpsuit next to her blue dress. "Disgusting."

"Sounds like someone needs a visit from Sammy."

This time Farrah couldn't hold back her laughter. She dragged Blake into the hall and closed the door before Olivia hurled a shoe at his head.

"Don't provoke her! You came this close to getting impaled by a stiletto."

"Nah. I have good reflexes. It's one of my many talents."

"New year, same Blake."

"You can't improve perfection." This time, Blake was the one who pulled her down the hall.

"Your room is the other way."

"Let's go to your room. Janice isn't back yet, is she?"

"Nope." Janice was never in the dorm.

Farrah opened her door and flipped on the lights. It was clear which side was hers and which was Janice's. Janice's half of the space was standard dorm fare—no decorations, no personal touches except for a Billie Eilish poster above her bed.

Meanwhile, Farrah treated her space as a mini interior design project, albeit one on an extreme budget. In addition to her new comforter and bedsheets, she'd snagged a gold throw pillow that jazzed up the décor and matched the picture frames she brought from home. The various-sized frames showcased some of her favorite memories—Farrah and her friends clutching their high school diplomas, Farrah and her mom on her first day of college, Farrah standing in the middle of the first room she ever designed (a pro bono project for her neighbor's preteen daughter), Farrah and her friend Maggie eating pizza in Rome and cheesing for the camera.

Blake picked up the pizza photo and chuckled. "This is a great picture."

"It was a great day." Spring break last year. While their friends partied it up in Cancun and Panama City, Farrah and Maggie escaped to Italy. It was Maggie's idea—she was a classics major and obsessed with all things Greek and Italian. It turned out to be the best decision Farrah ever made.

Well, second best.

It was weird. Italy felt like a lifetime ago. Farrah kept in touch with Maggie, but the Greek life drama and campus shenanigans Maggie had complained about might as well have been from another world.

After a year abroad, junior year was going to be a major adjustment.

Farrah pushed the thought out of her mind. She wasn't going to think about next year, not when she had Blake here and an entire semester of FEA left.

"Come here." Blake sat on the edge of her bed and patted his lap.

She curled up in his embrace, soaking up the familiarity like it was a breath of fresh air after being stuck in a windowless room for weeks.

"Tell me about your break." The deep timbre of his voice caused her to shiver with happiness.

"It was good. I ate a lot. Caught up with friends. The usual. I told you everything exciting that happened." Skype wasn't the same as seeing each other in person, but it was better than nothing. "Except for one thing."

"Really?" Blake's eyes sparkled with intrigue. "What is it?"

"I'll show you." Farrah fished her sketchbook from her nightstand drawer. She flipped it open to her final design concept for the IDAA contest. "I finished this over winter break and submitted my portfolio last week." Her pulse raced with nerves. "That's it. It's out of my hands."

"Holy shit," Blake breathed. He brushed his fingers over the sketch. "Farrah, this is *incredible.*"

After agonizing over the third design for months, Farrah woke up in the middle of the night with a crystal-clear vision of what she wanted to do. She started sketching and didn't stop until she finished the entire thing, afraid to pause lest the inspiration leave her.

"Thanks." Farrah struggled to contain her grin. "I'm really proud of it."

She didn't bother trying to be humble because she *was* proud of her work. It was one of her favorite designs, bar none.

Farrah scrapped her earlier traditional hotel suite idea and shifted to an island villa theme that leaned on natural colors, flowy fabrics, and open spaces: soft, billowing curtains around the bed and draped across the ceiling, an open-air living room with an organic-shaped wood coffee table and natural fiber furniture, indigenous artwork and aqua accents that picked up on the pale blues of the sea.

Interior design wasn't about how a space looks; it was about how it made someone feel. Farrah's villa might not have existed in real life, but just looking at the sketch evoked a sense of freedom, adventure, and happiness.

Hopefully, the NIDA judges would agree.

"I wish we were there right now." Blake brushed his fingers over the sketch. "Just the two of us on a secluded island, where nothing can touch us."

"Maybe one day." Farrah's stomach fluttered. "Do you think I can win?"

"Are you kidding?" Blake brushed his lips over hers. "I'm no design expert, but I can tell this is something special. You will win. It's not a question."

She smiled at his confidence. "You should've been a cheer-leader instead of a football player."

Blake broke into laughter. "You're right. I messed up."

"Anyway, enough about me. How was Austin?"

"Fine." He hesitated. "I have news too. I found an investor for the bar."

Farrah's jaw dropped. "What? That's amazing! Who? How? Tell me everything!"

He chuckled at her giddiness. "Don't get too excited. It's my buddy Landon, so it's not like I convinced a big-time businessman I don't know to invest. His family is huge in the hospitality world, and he came into half his trust when he turned twenty-one. He's trying to show his mom he knows what he's doing, so we're going halves on the bar." Blake grinned. "Plus he's a great friend."

"That's still incredible." Farrah couldn't contain her excite-ment. She'd witnessed firsthand how hard Blake had worked these past few months. She'd read his business plan. She saw the way his eyes lit up when he talked about the bar. His venture was going to be a success. She was sure of it. "I'm so proud of you. Your family must be too."

"I guess. My sister is. My mom's coming around. My dad is skeptical. He thinks the only thing I'm good at is football." Despite his casual tone, Farrah detected the hurt beneath his words.

Anger flashed through her. She'd never met Joe Ryan, but she was going to give that man a piece of her mind when she saw him. "Fuck your dad. He's trying to sabotage your dreams before you even get them off the ground, and I am. Not. Here. For. It."

Blake's mouth quirked up into a smile. "You're adorable when you're angry."

"I'm serious!" She pounded the mattress with her fist. "Don't let him do that to you."

"I don't want to complain too much." Blake rubbed his thumb over her locket. "I know I'm lucky my dad is still around."

Her anger melted away, replaced by an ache in her heart. God, she loved this boy. "If you're worried about me, don't be. My relationship with my father was different. I'm not saying you shouldn't try to mend fences with your dad; he is still your dad. But do *not* let him discourage you. You're capable of great things, Blake Ryan. Don't forget that."

Blake's eyes darkened with emotion. "I don't deserve you. You know that?" He pulled her in tight and rested his cheek on top of her head.

Farrah closed her eyes, soaking in the warm strength of his embrace. "I know."

"I love you." There was a strange undercurrent in his voice, a shakiness that was not like Blake.

Old Farrah would've latched on to that minute detail and overanalyzed the heck out of it, but New Farrah convinced herself it was her imagination.

FEA was in session again, the group was reunited, and she and Blake were back together. It was going to be an amazing semester, and she wasn't going to waste it worrying about demons that didn't exist.

"I love you too."

Their lips met in a tender promise. Blake felt the same, smelled the same, and tasted the same—like rich dark chocolate. Like sin and desire. Like the stars and dreams. He tasted like Blake.

Her Blake.

CHAPTER 24

BLAKE FELT LIKE SHIT.

He woke up with cotton mouth and a granddaddy of a hang-over. Gatorade and a carb-filled breakfast helped with the physical symptoms, but he still felt like shit, and it had nothing to do with drinking too much yesterday.

The urge to regurgitate that morning's jianbing forced him to clamp his mouth shut until it passed, yet his stomach remained queasy.

"Whose bright idea was it to come here after last night?" Luke flinched when the steel drummers banged their instruments.

The sound pierced through Blake's head like a drill through drywall.

"It's the New Year, Luke! Cheer up." Courtney swung Leo's hand back and forth, giddy as a schoolgirl.

"New Year's was weeks ago."

"This is the *Lunar* New Year. Don't be so American."

Luke became grumpier. "I am American. A hungover American."

"You're free to go back to the dorm anytime you want."

He fell silent.

The group wandered through the crowded pathways of Yuyuan Garden. Everyone and their mother (and father and grandparents and siblings) were out in full force for the garden's annual Spring Lantern Festival.

Lanterns of various sizes, colors, and shapes hung from every imaginable perch—roofs, ceilings, doorways, balconies. Massive pig-themed installations served as an ode to the Year of the Pig and dazzled viewers with their sheer size and intricacy. There were activities for all kinds of attendees—lion and dragon dances for the entertainment-minded, lantern riddles for the intellectually oriented, and traditional New Year sweets for the culinary obsessed.

Blake tightened his grip on Farrah's hand. It was his rock, the only thing keeping him from collapsing into a puddle of regret on the ground.

God, I'm an asshole.

"How are you feeling?" Farrah sidestepped an adorable toddler who was staring up at one of the pig installations in awe. Her mouth curved into a small smile before she turned to Blake and her brow wrinkled with concern. "We can go back to FEA if this is too much."

"No, it's New Year's. Besides, you want to see the fireworks."

"I've seen fireworks before."

"Really, I'm ok. I feel much better." Blake squeezed her hand again, this time in reassurance.

"Ok. But if you don't feel well, tell me."

"Yes, Mom."

She scrunched up her nose. "Don't call me that. It's creepy."

He laughed. Some tension eased. The rest remained—a lead ball of worry, self-loathing, and guilt that had plagued him for weeks.

His mind flashed back to Landon's New Year's party over winter break. It did that a lot these days.

Blake should've known better than to drink that much when Cleo was there. Granted, Blake could usually hold his alcohol. Until last month, he'd blacked out only once, when he was a college freshman trying to keep up with his older teammates at his first frat party. The morning after the party, he woke up in the bathtub with penises drawn all over his face in black Sharpie. It was embarrassing and a bitch to get the marker off but harmless.

Waking up naked in a hotel bedroom with no recollection of the previous night while Cleo waltzed out of the shower? Far less harmless.

The urge to throw up rose again. Blake drew in a deep, shaky breath. He couldn't think with all the noise and commotion around him.

That was probably a good thing.

The group paused to watch one of the lion dances. The massive costumes were decorated in bright red and gold, the luckiest colors in the Chinese culture. Red for joy and good fortune, gold for fulfillment and good luck. There were two performers per lion—one to manipulate the head and one the tail. Their agility and coordination would make Blake's old football coach drool.

Despite their heavy costumes, the dancers twisted and turned and jumped from pole to pole with nary a stumble. The audience's gasps and applause drowned out the drums and cymbals in the background when the performers somersaulted off the twenty-foot poles and nailed a rock-solid landing.

Blake watched without watching. Any other time he'd be right there with his friends, cheering the dancers on, but he couldn't shake what happened on New Year's—the American New Year's—out of his mind.

Blake downed his drink and took in his surroundings. The Zinterhofers' duplex occupied the top two floors of their flagship hotel in downtown Austin. Blake had been here more times than he could count, but its magnificence never failed to impress. With its polished wood floors, floor-to-ceiling windows, and panoramic views of the city skyline, the penthouse was a far cry from the Ryans' comfortable but modest home in the Austin suburbs.

Blake swept his gaze over the attendees. It was an eclectic mix of their high school friends and the Zinterhofers' rich associates. Landon was in the corner, speaking with an older woman in a tight gown that showed off an abundance of cleavage. She touched his arm and laughed too loudly at something he said.

Cougar central.

Blake set his empty glass on the bar and moved to rescue Landon from the cougar's grasp. He made it two steps when a familiar voice stopped him in his tracks.

"Hey, Blake."

His throat went dry. He turned. "Hey, Cleo."

The two childhood friends stared at each other. It was their first time speaking since their breakup. He'd avoided her all night—damn Joy for bringing her—but seeing her there right in front of him made Blake's chest hurt. Their romantic relationship may not have worked out, but Cleo was a huge part of his life. They'd been friends since they could walk.

He hadn't realized how much he missed her as a friend until now.

"It's good to see you." Blake ran a nervous hand over the back of his neck. "You look great."

Cleo's green dress matched the color of her eyes. Her skin gleamed beneath the lights and her hair fell in glossy dark curls past her shoulders. In fact, he noticed several guys checking her out from the corner of his eye.

"Thanks. So do you."

There was an awkward pause.

Cleo cleared her throat. "How's Shanghai?"

"It's great!" Blake winced. That came out more enthusiastic than he'd intended. "Different but..."

"Yeah."

Another pause.

He couldn't take it anymore. If he had to dance around the elephant in the room one more time, he'd scream.

It was time to man up and look that damn elephant in the eye.

"I'm sorry about the way I handled things before I left," Blake said. *"And for being MIA since then."*

"You've been busy." Cleo fiddled with her clutch. "I hear you're dating someone in Shanghai."

His jaw tightened. I am going to kill Joy.

"I am." This conversation was getting worse by the minute. "Cleo, I care about you. You're one of my oldest friends. But we never worked as a couple. We both know that."

Cleo's cheeks paled. Her eyes swirled with a mix of sadness, resignation, and...panic? No. That didn't make sense.

"I know." Her smile looked forced. "I don't blame you. You're a good person, Blake, and it was good while it lasted."

Relief fizzled through him. "Yeah, it was."

"Why don't we start over? Put everything behind us and toast to our friendship." Cleo waved down the bartender. "Two shots of tequila," she ordered.

Blake's eyebrows shot up. Cleo rarely drank, and she hated tequila.

Nevertheless, his relief outweighed his surprise. He could tell Cleo wasn't one hundred percent over their breakup, but at least she was willing to try. She could have her pick of guys. She'd eventually move on, which meant his family would have to move on.

A two-ton boulder eased off his shoulders.

"Here's to friendship." Cleo raised her shot glass.

"To friendship." Blake clinked his glass against hers and knocked back the drink. He laughed at Cleo's grimace. "We could've had something other than tequila."

"It's fine." She wiped her mouth with the back of her hand. "Let's do another one. For old times' sake."

"Maybe we should pace ourselves." His suggestion was as much for his own benefit as it was for Cleo's. He should've eaten dinner before the party, but he'd lost track of time Skyping with Farrah. Now, his stomach turned at the thought of another shot.

Cleo clucked her tongue. "Shanghai has made you soft."

Oh, hell no.

"Soft?" Blake narrowed his eyes. Yeah, his head was starting to spin, but his reputation was at stake here. "Soft, my ass." He turned to the bartender. "Another round of shots. Make 'em double."

The lion dance ended to enthusiastic applause from the crowd.

"That was cool." Luke yawned. "Let's get food. I'm hungry."

"We literally ate like half an hour ago," Kris snapped.

"We don't have to get a full meal, just snacks," Luke said in a conciliatory voice.

Blake expected the rest of the group to walk on eggshells around Kris, but Luke? That was a shocker.

They pushed their way through the crowd, toward the vendors selling Spring Festival snacks such as steamed nian gao cakes, glutinous rice dumplings wrapped in bamboo leaves, and various sweets.

Blake followed Farrah through the crowds, too lost in his thoughts to navigate on his own.

Blake cracked his eyes open.

That was a mistake.

The sunlight pierced his retinas like lasers and intensified the pounding in his head. He slammed his eyes shut.

A raspy groan filled the room. It took him a minute to realize it came from him.

Where the hell was he? What day was it?

Blake tried to piece together the events of last night, but all he could remember was arriving at Landon's party, drinking, arguing with Joy, drinking, talking to Cleo, drinking, and...that was it. He couldn't remember the fireworks or what he did when the clock struck midnight.

Blake groaned again. He turned on his side so he faced away from the windows and tried opening his eyes again. Better. Sort of.

"I am never drinking alcohol again," he muttered.

"That's what you always say."

Blake jerked his head up and looked over his shoulder. The bright light hit him in full force, but it was nothing compared to the dread that slammed into his body when his eyes confirmed what his brain knew.

"Good morning, sleepyhead." Cleo stepped out of the bathroom in a cloud of steam. Her damp hair fell past her shoulders in tight curls. A towel wrapped around her body, barely large enough to cover the necessary bits.

"What are you doing here?" Blake's eyes adjusted to the light, and he realized he was in one of the Zinterhofers' suites. They always set aside a few rooms for guests who were too intoxicated to drive home after one of their New Year's parties.

"Showering, silly." Cleo dropped her towel. He averted his gaze.

She laughed at his reaction. "Come on. It's not anything you haven't seen before." He heard rather than saw her get dressed. "You can look now."

"What happened last night?" The pounding in his head intensi-fied. Blake rubbed his temple. "We didn't—did we—" He couldn't bring himself to say it.

There was a pause. "You don't remember?"

If I did, I wouldn't be asking you.

Blake bit his tongue. Hangovers made him moody as shit. "I don't remember anything after our third"—fourth?—"shot."

Cleo blinked. Her eyes glowed bright green in the sunlight. A thousand emotions flickered over her face, too fast for him to discern a single one of them.

"We're friends. Right?"

"Right." Blake tried to smile. The jackhammers in his head multiplied. "Think of all the friendship toasts we had yesterday."

She half laughed, half snorted. "Yeah. So you really don't remember what happened last night?"

Unease unfurled in his stomach. "No..."

"That's too bad." Cleo took a deep breath and looked down. The seconds ticked by. When she looked up again, her expression was almost apologetic. "Blake, we slept together."

"Earth to Blake." Farrah waved her free hand in front of Blake's face. "Hellooo? Anyone home?"

He snapped back to the present, but the guilt and nausea from that morning continued to churn in his stomach.

"Sorry." He had to shout to be heard over the noise. It was close to fireworks time, and anticipation rippled through the crowd. "I was thinking."

"It's ok." Farrah patted his hand. "I support you trying new things in the new year."

Blake side-eyed her. "Do you have to be a smart-ass all the time?"

"It's better than being a dumbass all the time."

He couldn't help but laugh. When he was around Farrah, it

was easy to forget anything else existed. Easy to pretend everything was fine when he wanted to fall to his knees and beg her forgiveness.

He wanted to tell her what happened over New Year's their first night back, but she looked at him with so much love and trust, he knew he couldn't tell her. Not yet.

Maybe not ever.

What happened with Cleo was a one-time thing. There was no use destroying Farrah and himself over a stupid mistake he didn't remember. Right?

The lead weight in his stomach grew heavier.

"The fireworks are about to start." Courtney rubbed her palms together. Her eyes sparkled with excitement. "We need to find a good spot."

"Good luck." Leo scooted closer to her to allow a young couple to pass. "This place is a zoo."

"That's negative thinking and I will not stand for it. We'll find a spot."

True to her word, Courtney shouldered her way through the crowd and squeezed them into a corner on the garden's Zigzag Bridge. She earned them plenty of dirty looks, but they were going to have a fantastic view of the fireworks.

"Damn, Court." Sammy looked impressed. "I could've used you during my holiday shopping."

"Come to Seattle and I'm all yours." Courtney leaned into Leo, who draped an arm over her shoulders. "I missed you guys."

"I'm so glad I'm here instead of back home." Kris twisted her ring around and around her finger. "My dad and the stepmonster-to-be can suck a giant bag of balls."

The rest of the group exchanged glances.

Farrah had filled Blake in on the drama. Kris's dad's fiancée convinced him to cut Kris off for "irresponsible spending." It seemed their extravagant trip to Macau for Courtney's birthday was the last straw. He dropped the bombshell on Kris the day she returned home.

Kris with a black Amex was grumpy enough. Kris without a black Amex? Nuclear territory.

"He'll cave. He always does," Courtney reassured her.

"You're his only daughter," Olivia added. "Obviously, you take priority over his girlfriend."

"Ha. Tell that to *him*. She has him totally brainwashed. Like she's that responsible with money! She owns like twenty Birkins." Kris's lip trembled. She set her jaw and tossed her hair over her shoulder. "It's fine. When I'm home for the summer, I'm going to make my dad see what a pathetic gold digger she is. Their wedding won't happen. Not on my watch."

"Let us know if we can help," Luke said. "We can, I dunno, dig up dirt on her online."

Judging by the expressions on his friends' faces, Blake wasn't the only one who was surprised. Kris and Luke usually bickered more than an old married couple.

Kris choked out a laugh. "Thanks, but I got it."

"Did we enter the Twilight Zone?" Sammy clutched his heart. "You guys are acting like friends."

"Yeah right!"

"As if!"

Kris and Luke spoke at the same time. They stared at each other sheepishly while everyone else laughed.

"We've always been friends. All of us. No matter how much some of us bicker." Courtney squeezed Kris's and Luke's hands. "Actually, we're more than that. We're family. And there's no one else I'd rather celebrate the Lunar New Year with."

The group looked around at each other. Nine college students from all over the U.S., brought together by fate or circumstance.

They couldn't be more different. Some of them would've never been friends had they met anywhere else but Shanghai. Yet here they were.

A family.

In a place as crazy and ever-changing as Shanghai, they were each other's constants. The ones who had each other's backs. From overcoming culture shock to crazy nights on the town, they grew into this city together, and that was a bond only they could share.

Despite the chilly air, Blake's skin warmed. It was almost enough to make him forget about the shitshow that was the rest of his life.

A screeching whistle quieted the crowds. Every head swiveled up. A few seconds later, the night sky exploded in a dazzling display of lights. The fireworks showered the dark canvas with sprays of brilliant color—bright gold, pale green, deep red, and every hue in between. Each time one closed, another bloomed, creating an endless, intricate dance that left the viewers on earth breathless.

Blake tore his gaze away from the spectacle to look at Farrah. Ribbons of light flickered across her features as she gazed up at the show, her eyes bright with excitement and a smile of awe on her face.

If he could have one wish for the rest of his life, it would be for Farrah to be as happy as she was at this moment. Always.

Blake's arms circled her waist from behind. He pressed his cheek against hers. "Happy Lunar New Year, baby."

Farrah snuggled deeper into his embrace. "Happy Lunar New Year, Blake."

No one in the group said anything after that. They took comfort in each other's presence and watched the lights fire up the heavens, so bright they turned night into day.

The dawn of a new year.

CHAPTER 25

FEBRUARY IN SHANGHAI WAS MISERABLE. THE EXCITE-
ment of Lunar New Year soon faded, leaving behind rain, cold,
and humidity. Classes were twice as hard and the workload twice
as heavy as the previous semester. Kris slipped further into a funk
about her dad and losing her credit cards, and Blake was acting
weird.

There were days he seemed like his regular self—cocky,
charming, ready with a smile and a quick quip. Other days he
was moody and distant, like his mind was a million miles away.
Every time Farrah tried to figure out what was wrong, he changed
the subject or distracted her with sex.

Ok, so she let herself get distracted. But not today. Today, she
was going to find out what was going on once and for all.

Step one: bribe Blake with food. Sammy's freshly baked blue-
berry muffins smelled so good, Farrah was tempted to eat them
all herself.

No. I can't. She had to save them for Blake. Like they say,
the fastest way to a guy's secrets was through his stomach. Or
something like that.

Before going to Blake's room, Farrah swung by the girls' hall to change into something more enticing than leggings and a T-shirt.

As Farrah passed by Courtney's room, Leo's raised voice stopped her in her tracks.

"I can't believe you kept that from me this whole time!"

Her eyes widened. She'd never heard Leo yell before, not even when Luke spilled soy sauce on his favorite scarf.

Farrah clutched the muffins tighter. Blake's Modern Chinese History class was going to end any minute now, but morbid curiosity compelled her to step closer to Courtney's door. She heard everything her friends said through the thin walls.

"It's not a big deal." Courtney sounded defiant. "We kissed once, but Nardo and I are friends. That's it."

It took Farrah a moment to register what Courtney said. When she did, she gasped. Did Courtney hook up with *Nardo*?

What. The. Fuck.

Who would hook up with Nardo when they had Leo?

Courtney and Leo must've heard her gasp because they fell silent.

Shit.

Before Farrah could leave, the door swung open, revealing a pissed-off Leo.

Behind him, Courtney stared at her with huge eyes.

"Hi," Farrah said weakly. She held up her bag of treats. "I brought muffins."

"I was just leaving." Leo brushed past her. "Enjoy the muffins."

Courtney crossed her arms over her chest. She didn't stop him.

"What the hell happened?" Farrah asked once Leo was out of earshot. Her mind spun. Leo and Courtney were the bedrock of the group. The first couple, even if they insisted they weren't dating. Their relationship was part of the fabric of FEA.

"We got into a fight."

"No! Really?"

Courtney glared at her. "Can we lay off the snark?"

"Sorry." Farrah stepped into the room and closed the door. "So I, uh, heard something about Nardo?"

To her credit, Courtney didn't bat an eye at the realization that Farrah had been eavesdropping. She looked down and scuffed her shoes on the floor. "We made out at the Full Moon Party."

Farrah gasped again. Holy shit.

Her mind's eye rewound to that night. It was a blur of music and alcohol and dancing beneath the stars, but she remembered Courtney and Nardo being gone for a while. Back then, it didn't seem like a big deal, but now...

"I *thought* you guys were in the bathroom for a long time!"

"There was a long line! And it's not like we had sex. We only kissed."

Farrah pinched her temple. She had so many questions she didn't know where to start. "Why did you kiss him in the first place?"

Out of all the guys in the program, Nardo was the last person she'd expected Courtney to cheat on Leo with (not that she expected Courtney to cheat at all). Nardo was pretentious, insufferable, and not even that cute unless you're into the preppy-hipster type. Meanwhile, Leo was smart and kind and beautiful and, well, better in every way.

"I dunno."

"Court."

Courtney sighed. "I was drunk and pissed at Leo about our fight earlier that day, and Nardo was looking at me like...like he would never say the things Leo said to me. The kiss just happened. It's a shitty excuse, but that's the truth." She looked down again. "It was a one-time thing. It's not like we were having an affair this entire time. Nardo and I don't like each other like that. The kiss confirmed it."

Farrah was torn. A part of her knew Courtney was wrong for cheating on Leo. That was the one thing she'd never tolerate in a relationship—cheating. It wasn't about the physical act. It was about the trust. Once broken, it was hard, if not impossible, to mend.

Still, Courtney was one of her closest friends. She brought Farrah chicken soup when she was sick, held her hair when she had too much to drink, and was always a call or text away when shit went south. Sure, she could be bossy and entitled, but she had a good heart. She was also the core of the group.

If Farrah had to choose between Courtney and Leo, she knew who she'd choose. One hundred percent.

"So why'd you tell Leo now?" she asked. She tried to keep her tone as nonjudgmental as possible. "Thailand was a long time ago."

"I wasn't going to, but my aunt said something—" Courtney gnawed on her lip. "It's not important. Anyway, I couldn't keep the secret any longer and I thought enough time passed that he'd hear me out. I was wrong."

Farrah's head spun, trying to figure out what this meant. "So are you and Leo...over?"

"Most likely." Courtney smiled weakly. "We were never really together anyway. Not the same way you and Blake or Sammy and Liv are. Leo and I both knew whatever we had wasn't going to last after FEA."

"That's not true," Farrah argued. Except, in hindsight, it *was* true. She'd inflated Courtney and Leo's relationship in her mind when she had a crush on him because even the slightest interest from one of her friends in a guy she was interested in was a huge obstacle in her mind. But now that she was no longer interested in Leo, she realized how casual Courtney and Leo's relationship had been, at least compared to the others in the group. "He's still pissed about you and Nardo. That counts for something."

"I suspect that's his ego talking more than anything else." Courtney sighed. "Don't get me wrong. I like Leo a lot, but we're not endgame. He'll cool off, and we'll go back to being friends. I hope." She bit her lip. "That's what I'm worried about most. I don't want the group to fall apart when we only have three months left."

Three months.

Panic inundated Farrah's system. She'd repressed thoughts of what might happen after this semester, but Courtney's words brought all her fears to the surface.

Once FEA ended, that was it. The group would scatter to their respective home bases in the U.S. and see each other...when? Once a year if they were lucky, until enough time passed and study abroad was nothing more than a faint memory.

Farrah's chest heaved at the thought of never seeing her friends again. Sure, there was social media and Skype, but it wasn't the same as hanging out in person. Would the group remain as close as they were now if they didn't see each other every day? Doubtful.

There was also Blake. She lived in California; he lived in Texas. Over a thousand miles separated them back home, and while Farrah knew people who'd been in long-distance relationships, she couldn't think of any that lasted.

She didn't realize she'd reached for her necklace until the metal dug a groove into her palm.

"We're not going to fall apart," Farrah said.

We can't.

"I hope not." Courtney's lip wobbled. "I just wanted us to be a family. I can't stand the thought of ruining things again."

Again?

That didn't make sense. The group hadn't had any major

issues so far. But the sight of a teary-eyed Courtney was so strange, like seeing a lion run wild in the streets of Manhattan, that Farrah didn't have a chance to dwell on her friend's choice of words. She also didn't dwell on why Courtney seemed more upset about the group breaking apart than she did about her breakup with Leo.

It was strange. Courtney was the bubbliest, most outgoing person in the group, but she was also the least forthcoming about her personal life. Even Kris shared more than she did. It wasn't something you noticed until you really thought about it because Courtney did such a good job of glossing over ugly realities and papering them with bright shiny wallpaper.

"You won't. Like you said, Leo will cool off and things will go back to normal," Farrah said. She didn't push Courtney for clarification on what she meant by "again." She knew, better than anyone, that some secrets weren't meant to be shared. "In the meantime, I have muffins from Sammy." She raised the bag as proof. "Guaranteed to make you feel better or your money back, no questions asked."

Courtney laughed. She dabbed a tear from her cheek and tossed her hair over her shoulder. "Give me those."

Farrah did.

She and Courtney spent the night eating and binge-watching K-dramas, and it felt so nice and comforting that Farrah almost forgot about Blake's strange behavior. She still needed to talk to him, but that could wait.

Courtney needed her now.

CHAPTER 26

"MICHELLE KWAN, EAT YOUR HEART OUT!" FARRAH glided so gracefully around the rink, one would think she'd been ice-skating her whole life—if she wasn't holding on to the hockey barrier the entire time.

Blake laughed at the triumphant glint in her eyes. Two hours ago, Farrah had never set foot on an ice rink. Now she swanned about like she was a world champion. The smallest achievement—a simple spin, a tiny jump—caused her face to light up with excitement.

It was fucking adorable.

"I'm sure Michelle Kwan's Olympic medals are trembling in fear," he teased.

"They should." Farrah released the barrier and reached for Blake with her other hand. He slowed his pace, waiting for her to hit her stride before he led them to the middle of the rink.

The place was all decked out for Valentine's Day—twinkling lights and strings of pink, red, and white pennants crisscrossing overhead. A special concession stand sold hot cocoa, chocolates, and other assorted sweets on the sidelines, while a vendor wandered through the arena, hawking red roses to unsuspecting couples. An eclectic playlist of love songs that included everyone from Luther Vandross to Ariana Grande blasted through the loudspeakers.

"I'm a fast learner." Farrah entwined her arms around Blake's neck. "If I tried, I could have *three* Olympic medals."

"Of course. You can do anything." Blake brushed his lips over hers. She tasted like wine and chocolate and something that was quintessentially Farrah. If heaven had a taste, this would be it.

"You're trying to suck up to me for sex tonight, aren't you?"

"Hmm. I had something else in mind for sucking."

Farrah's cheeks turned the color of ripe tomatoes.

Blake chuckled. Farrah was a wildcat in bed, especially now that they'd done it a few (ok, dozens of) times, but she still got so flustered whenever he made jokes like that, he couldn't help but tease her from time to time.

"Shhh! Someone might hear you."

"Let 'em. We have an awesome sex life. Maybe we'll inspire them."

Farrah shook her head. "What am I going to do with you?"

"I can think of a few things."

"Hmm." She stepped closer until her body was flush against Blake's. All his blood rushed south, leaving him so hard, he thought he might shatter. "So can I."

"Careful," Blake growled. His pulse pounded with desire. "Don't start something you can't finish."

"I think we've established that I *can* finish." Farrah hooked her fingers through his belt loops and pressed their hips together until his arousal nestled in the cleft between her thighs. His breath rushed in and out; his skin was so sensitive, the slightest breeze caused him to jerk uncomfortably. "Me and you."

The student had become the teacher.

Their lips touched in a sweet, warm kiss that didn't match the dirty, *un*sweet thoughts racing through Blake's mind. He tangled his hands in Farrah's hair and deepened the embrace, letting himself get lost in the taste and touch of her. It was only the two of them—no worries, no guilt, no decisions to make about the future.

"Happy Valentine's Day." Farrah's lips brushed against his as she spoke.

"Happy Valentine's Day." Blake rubbed his thumb over the smoothness of her cheek. "I hope you're enjoying it."

"This is the best Valentine's Day I've ever had. Granted, it's the only Valentine's Day I've celebrated as part of a couple, but still. It's amazing." Farrah's eyes twinkled. "You did good, Blake Ryan."

"I aim to please." Blake smiled, but an all-too-familiar guilt wormed its way into his stomach at the love in her eyes. With help from Sammy—who got his intel from Olivia—he'd crafted the perfect Valentine's Day celebration. By pure luck, the holiday landed on a Friday this year, so they didn't have to worry about classes tomorrow.

Their date started with a couple's massage after their Friday test to help them unwind from the week, followed by a chocolate-tasting and truffle-making class, a leisurely stroll in the surrounding neighborhood, and a sunset dinner at a rooftop restaurant overlooking the Bund. Now, they were at their final stop of the night: the ice-skating rink. Farrah mentioned wanting to learn how to skate every time they watched an ice-skating scene in a rom-com—turns out, there are a *lot* of those types of scenes—so it seemed like a fitting end to the night.

Yes, it was over-the-top (and Blake didn't even want to check his bank account), but this could be the last Valentine's Day they spent together in person for a while. He wanted to make it count.

If he was honest, he was also trying to make up for what happened on New Year's with Cleo—not that he'd told Farrah yet.

The guilt expanded into a lead balloon. He should tell her. The secret was killing him inside, and she deserved to know.

It was a stupid one-time mistake—one he didn't even remember. Maybe she'd understand. Valentine's Day wasn't the best time to bring it up, though. He'd wait a week, give it enough time between today and her birthday so—

"It's the perfect day. I'm glad things are back to normal, at least with us."

Blake frowned. "I didn't realize they were not normal."

"Well." Farrah hesitated. "You've been acting kind of strange recently. Like you're here but your mind is a thousand miles away. I thought...I don't know. That something was up." Her eyes searched his face. "You'd tell me if something was wrong, right?"

The lead balloon grew heavier. "Yeah. I'm stressed about the bar, but it's a bunch of technical stuff I didn't want to bore you with. Leases, liquor licenses, permits. That sort of thing." Blake forced a smile. "Lots to do before I go home."

It wasn't a total lie. He had a shit ton on his plate. Fortunately, Landon was on the ground in Austin, which made it a lot easier to scope out potential rental spaces and deal with contractors. That didn't mean Blake was going to sit back and let his best friend do all the work.

It was his idea to open a sports bar; he needed to take ownership.

"I can imagine." Farrah's face cleared. "Let me know if I can help."

"Thank you." Blake kissed her on the forehead. "I will."

"I was overthinking, as usual." Farrah rested her cheek against his chest. "Now if Leo and Courtney would just make up, everything would be perfect."

"They're still not speaking to each other, huh?" Farrah had filled him in on what happened. Blake wasn't surprised. Courtney didn't take well to pushback and things not going her way.

Then again, he'd done something far worse, so he wasn't one to talk.

"More like Leo isn't speaking to her. I think he needs space. Not that I blame him." Farrah snuggled closer to Blake. "If someone cheated on me, I'd never speak to them again."

His heart stopped, then raced double time. "Really?"

"Yeah. It's a huge violation of trust. If someone cheats once, they'll cheat again."

Blake had the sudden urge to throw up. Maybe ice-skating wasn't the best idea right now. He needed to sit down and breathe. "That's not always true."

"It is ninety-nine percent of the time." Farrah lifted her head to look at him. "I mean, in Court's case, it was only a kiss. Which isn't great, but at least she didn't sleep with Nardo. That would be unforgivable."

"Yeah. Unforgivable," Blake choked out.

Fuck. Fuck fuck fuckity fuck.

"I'm sorry. I didn't mean to bring up such a depressing topic, especially on Valentine's Day." Farrah laced their fingers together. "Let's focus on something else. Like what we're going to do when we get back to the dorm." She wiggled her eyebrows. "I have a long to-do list. Pun intended."

Blake forced a smile as his stomach heaved. All traces of arousal had disappeared, replaced by panic.

Forget telling Farrah about what happened with Cleo over New Year's.

She couldn't find out.

Ever.

CHAPTER 27

"TELL ME ABOUT THIS BLAKE." FARRAH'S MOM appraised her daughter with a hawk's eye. "Who is he? Where is he from? What is he studying? How does he treat you?"

"Mom, stop." Farrah crossed her legs and adjusted her laptop to minimize the screen glare. "We're not playing Twenty Questions."

"Those are valid questions. I've never heard you sound as giddy as when you're talking about this boy," Cheryl teased. "I'm your mother. You should tell me these things."

"You'd like him." Farrah grinned at the thought of Blake meeting her mother. He was tough, but Cheryl would destroy him in a second if he stepped over the line. "He's from Austin. He's a senior at Texas Southeastern. He used to be the quarterback of their football team."

"Used to be?"

"He…" Farrah hesitated. "He decided he doesn't want a career in football."

"He's right. Sports are dangerous. One wrong hit and you're out. At least he has common sense." Cheryl nodded in approval. "So what does he want to do?"

"He's studying business."

"What kind of business? Is he planning on getting an MBA? Did he get into any MBA programs? Is he going to Wharton?" Cheryl lit up. "That's a great program. Graduate from there, and you're set for life."

Farrah was used to her mom's endless questions about her love life, but they never made her nervous—until now. "He's opening his own business."

"What kind of business?"

"Er, a restaurant." Her mom wouldn't take kindly to "sports bar." She considered them "low-class" establishments.

"What kind of restaurant?"

"Mom!"

"You can't blame me for being curious. I want to know about the boy my daughter is so infatuated with. What's his GPA?"

Farrah groaned. "How am I supposed to know his GPA?"

"You ask him."

"I am not asking him."

"Why not?"

"Because. It's invasive."

"You're not giving him a colonoscopy. You're asking what his grades are. A good GPA leads to a good job and a good life. Remember that."

"That is so antiquated. There are plenty of successful people who didn't graduate college. Look at Bill Gates and Steve Jobs."

"Oh, I'm sorry." Cheryl raised her eyebrows. "I didn't realize he invented the next Microsoft and Apple. Send me a demo so I can show it off to my friends."

"Har-har." Farrah threw a popcorn kernel at the screen while her mom laughed. "I'm just saying, grades aren't everything. Blake's smart and works hard. And I really like him."

Cheryl's face softened. "I can tell. I'm glad you found someone you like so much. As long as he treats you well and isn't a dum-dum." She shuddered. "Don't marry a stupid guy or spend the rest of your life taking care of him."

"Mom, I'm wayyy too young to think about marriage."

"I'm not saying get married *now*. You're almost twenty. By the time you graduate, get a job, and date for a few years, it'll be time. You don't want to wait too long to have babies. You won't have the energy to run after them. Take me, for example."

"Hey! I was a good baby," Farrah protested. "Besides, you had me when you were twenty-eight."

"Yes, and it would've been easier if I'd had you when I was twenty-five."

Over Farrah's dead body. "I want to enjoy my twenties, thank you very much."

Cheryl shook her head. "You're young. You don't listen to me now, but you'll see."

"How did we get on this subject?" Farrah uncrossed her legs and shook them out. Tingles shot up and down her thighs and shins. "It doesn't matter. Tell me what's going on with you."

"Drama at the association, as usual." Cheryl was a member of a local Chinese dance association that, technically, focused on ball-room dancing but was really an excuse for LA's older Chinese com-munity to gather weekly and gossip. "Elections for the presidency are coming up, and everyone's fighting over it. So stupid."

Cheryl always complained about the other members but refused to take Farrah's advice and quit. Then again, between the dance outings, potlucks, holiday parties, and weekend trips to Canada, she had a better social life than Farrah.

"You should run for president."

"Ha! I go to dance and eat free food. They can fight over the presidency all they want. I have enough to do at my real job."

Valid.

"By the way..." Cheryl's eyes sparkled. "Something came for you in the mail today." She brandished an envelope with a distinctive gold and pale-green logo in the upper-left corner.

Farrah's heart stuttered. The competition. Holy shit.

She'd submitted her application and portfolio in early January and hadn't expected to receive finalist results until March. There was one more round after that, but still, this was a big freakin' deal. She was either moving forward or dead in the water.

"I didn't open it—"

"Open it!" Farrah raised her fist to her mouth. Her heart was this close to leaping out of her chest, reaching through the screen, and ripping that envelope open.

This was it.

Make-it-or-break-it time.

Oh god, what if she didn't make it to the final round? What was she going to do? Farrah had applied to a few other internships just in case, but to be honest, she hadn't tried her hardest on those, and they—

"You're a finalist."

They probably saw right through her application. Some chic New York designer was probably poring over her application right now with a furrowed brow, wondering—*hold up*.

Farrah lowered her fist, unsure whether she heard right. "I'm a finalist?"

"You're a finalist."

Mother and daughter stared at each other before erupting into simultaneous squeals.

"I'm a finalist!" Farrah bounced up and down in excitement. Her MacBook slipped off her lap and would've crashed to the floor had she not grabbed it at the last minute. She held the screen close to her face, eyes wide. "I'm a finalist, I'm a finalist!"

Was this real life?

Maybe she was dreaming. *God, that would* suck.

Farrah pinched herself in the thigh.

Holy—ok. Not dreaming.

Of all the aspiring interior designers in the world (ok, in America), she, Farrah Lin, was a finalist for the most prestigious student competition in the industry. She could work for her idol, Kelly Burke. Hell, if things went well, she could have a job offer at the end of the summer.

This was unreal.

Wild, restless energy raced through her. She needed to do something. Tell someone the good news. Dance. Scream at the top of her lungs. *Something!*

"I'm proud of you." Cheryl beamed. "Good thing I didn't raise a stupid daughter. Although I can't believe they didn't email you. What is this, 1999? Are you sure you want to work for a company that doesn't know how to use email?"

"Mom!" Farrah was in too good of a mood to take offense. "They're traditional like that. It's part of their appeal."

"I guess you know better than me. Now, what are you still doing here?" Cheryl waved her daughter away. "Celebrate with your friends. I'll talk to you later."

"Ok! Talk to you later," Farrah sang.

They didn't say, "I love you." In fact, the thought of saying those words in Cantonese made Farrah cringe. *So awkward.* But some things didn't need to be said.

Farrah waved goodbye, closed her laptop, and ran into the hall.

She hesitated, debating who to tell first. After a split second's indecision, she ran to Olivia's room and knocked on the door.

"Ladies, this is long overdue." Courtney sighed in bliss as the pedicurist massaged her feet.

The spa smelled like lotion and lavender essential oil. Soothing music piped from hidden speakers. Half-empty glasses of bubbly sat next to each girl.

It was heaven.

"Mmm." Farrah couldn't muster enough energy for actual words. Massages always lulled her into a sleepy dream state.

"*So* overdue." Olivia wiggled her toes. "I've been so stressed. Do you know how hard it is to find a good summer sublet in New York?"

"I told you, you can stay at my family's place in the city. We never visit New York in the summer." Kris shuddered. "Heat and tourist central."

"Thanks, but I'm not sure the Upper East Side is my vibe. No offense."

"I don't care." Kris sipped her champagne. "The offer's open if you change your mind."

"Thank you. Love you." Olivia blew her a kiss.

"When do you get the final decision?" Courtney asked Farrah.

"April. Internships start in June." NIDA covered the winner's flights and housing, so the short timeline wasn't a big deal. But now that the high of being a finalist wore off, Farrah went right back to worrying again. She was one step away from the internship of her dreams. If she came so close and didn't get it… Farrah didn't want to think about it.

"So you'll be in New York?" Olivia was so excited she almost kicked her pedicurist in the face. "Oh my god, *dui bu qi!*" *Sorry!*

The pedicurist waved it off. "*Mei shir.*" *It's ok/don't worry.*

"You, me, and Sammy in New York together." Olivia sighed. "It'll be the best summer ever."

"I haven't won yet." Farrah vacillated between excitement and nerves. She didn't want to jinx it, but she could picture it already: shopping in Soho, picnics in Central Park, cocktails in the Meatpacking District. Blake would visit, and they'd go on romantic double dates in the city and take fun hikes upstate on the weekend. "Even if I do, I'm not guaranteed my first-choice location."

"Pssh." Olivia waved off her concern. "Of course you'll win."

"We'll see." Anticipation bubbled in Farrah's stomach. Olivia was right. If everything worked out, it'd be an amazing summer.

"Ugh, major FOMO." Courtney pouted. "You guys will be living it up with your awesome internships, and I'll be stuck babysitting middle schoolers at camp."

"You love being a camp counselor," Kris said. "You can do arts and crafts *and* boss people around all day."

"Hmm. That is true."

Everyone laughed.

Farrah sank deeper into her chair. Her chest glowed with warmth. It had been too long since the girls hung out, just the four of them. It reminded her of the early days of FEA.

"What are your summer plans?" she asked Kris.

"My father says I have to get a job." Kris said *job* like it was a Prada bag from last season. "Which is totally unfair and my evil stepmonster's doing. I've never had a job, and I don't intend to start now. Jobs are for plebeians. No offense."

"Eh."

"None taken."

"Whatever."

"Anyway, he'll cave like he did with my credit card." Kris brandished her Amex Platinum in the air. "I have a two-thousand-dollar monthly limit, but I just have to give him the cold shoulder for a while longer. I *am* his only daughter. I'm irreplaceable."

Sometimes, Farrah marveled at the world Kris lived in. It must've been nice.

"Never change." Olivia patted Kris on the arm.

"I love you guys. I wish we could stay in Shanghai forever," Courtney sighed.

If only. Farrah dreaded the day they had to leave. She'd have to say goodbye to Blake, her friends, her favorite café and jianbing spot and bubble tea place...

Don't think about it. You have two months left. Enjoy it.

"Wait." Courtney shot up in her chair, her eyes sparkling with excitement. "Let's make a pact."

"I'm not making another blood pact. Don't ask," Kris said when Farrah's and Olivia's jaws dropped.

"I'm not." Olivia grimaced. "Some things are better left unsaid."

"It's not a blood pact. It's a wedding pact!"

Farrah wasn't sure she heard right. "Excuse me?"

"We all have to invite each other to our weddings. Because that means we have to stay in touch. For years and years."

"What if I don't want a wedding? What if I elope?" Olivia asked.

The other three stared at her.

"*Kidding!* I would never elope. I already have my wedding Pinterest board." Olivia laughed. "God, me eloping. Can you imagine?"

"No," Kris said. "I can't."

Weddings were the Olympics of planning, organization, and seating charts. It was basically Olivia's wet dream.

"So, ladies? Are we in?" Courtney held out her hand.

"Despite my foresight when it comes to Pinterest boards, I don't plan on getting married until I'm in my thirties with a senior executive position on Wall Street and a weekend cottage in the Hamptons," Olivia warned. "But I'm in." She placed her hand atop Courtney's.

Farrah followed suit. "Me too." She was so not ready to think about marriage, although she and Blake *would* make the cutest babies. One day. She loved the idea of the pact, though. It'd keep their Shanghai legacy alive.

"Kris?" Courtney prompted.

The brunette shrugged. "Sure. Whatever." She put her hand on top of Farrah's, completing the pact.

"Repeat after me: I swear I'll invite you all to my wedding, no matter what."

"Seriously?"

"Just do it, Kris."

"I swear I'll invite you all to my wedding, no matter what," they recited dutifully.

"That's it. The pact is unbreakable." Courtney grinned. "You're all stuck with me at your weddings, bitches."

A wicked glint entered Kris's eyes. "Anyone wanna bet on who gets married first and when?"

"Not against you," Farrah laughed. "Too rich for my blood."

"It doesn't matter. We'll reunite before the first wedding," Olivia said. "Maybe even before we graduate!"

"Duh," Courtney said with the confidence of someone who's seen the future. "Of course we will."

CHAPTER 28

"THANKS FOR YOUR HELP, MAN." BLAKE FIST-BUMPED Sammy. "Appreciate it."

"No problem." Sammy unwrapped his scarf. The heat in the dorm was on full blast, turning the lobby into a scorching desert compared to the chill outdoors. "I'm sure Farrah will love it."

"Yeah." Blake peeked inside his shopping bag to double-check the gift was still there. It'd taken forever to figure out what to buy Farrah for her birthday and longer to track it down. If it weren't for Sammy, he'd have been stuck deciding between cliché jewelry options. "I hope so."

"I'm never wrong."

It was a wildly un-Sammy-like thing to say.

The boys took the stairs two at a time until they reached the second-floor landing. "Olivia's rubbing off on you."

"There's a ninety-nine-percent chance you're right."

"Don't tell her what I got Farrah," Blake warned.

Sammy clutched his heart. "I can't believe you think I'd spill the beans. I—"

"You were going to tell her, weren't you?"

"Well, she already knows."

Blake opened the door to his room and shoved the shopping bag under his bed. "Unbelievable."

"What, you think I came up with that gift idea on my own? Don't worry. Liv won't tell."

"If Farrah finds out before her birthday, I will kill you in the most painful way possible."

Sammy didn't seem concerned. "You are so gone. It's adorable. Really."

"Get out of my room."

"Maybe you should've bought her a diamond instead."

Blake shoved the other boy into the hall and slammed the door in his face.

"You're welcome!" Sammy shouted through the door.

"The most painful way possible!" Blake reminded him. He waited until Sammy's laughter and footsteps faded before he flopped onto his bed and opened his laptop. He had a movie date with Farrah in a few hours, but first things first: email.

The search for a home for the bar was in full swing. There wasn't a lot Blake could do from Shanghai, so Landon was scoping out potential rental spaces while Blake sorted out their business registration.

His stomach fluttered as he looked over the documents. Even after he created his business plan, owning a bar seemed like more of a dream than reality. Now, that dream was becoming more concrete by the day.

Take that, Dad. Blake couldn't wait to see his father's face at the grand opening. It was going to be epic.

A new email notification popped up. Landon. The subject line: *round three.*

Blake opened the dozen or so attached images. Landon had

been busy scouting places. He wished he could've been on the ground with his friend, but for now, photos would have to do.

Blake dove into dissecting the layouts, the lighting, the square footage, and whether it fit what he envisioned for the space. The one with the loft intrigued him. It was the most expensive of the lot, but the upstairs area would make a sick game room. He could deck it out with a pool table, darts, shuffleboard, the works. The beer pong tournaments at Gino's were always popular. Maybe he'd use the space to host weekly bar sports Olympics. People who liked sports were competitive—they would eat that shit up.

Blake was so engrossed in the blueprints, time slipped away. When he checked the clock again, two hours had passed.

"Shit!"

Farrah would kill him if he was late. Movie previews were her favorite part.

He was about to shut his laptop when another notification popped up. This time it was an iMessage from Cleo.

Are you busy?

Blake's heart stopped. He hadn't heard from Cleo since New Year's. He'd thought of reaching out to her a few times—more out of hope she'd change her account of what happened than an actual desire to talk to her—but something stopped him each time.

His fingers hovered over the keyboard. He could ignore the message, but....

No. I'm free, Blake typed.

Morbid curiosity compelled him to stay. What prompted Cleo to contact him after weeks of radio silence?

Great. I'll Skype you.

The unease in Blake's stomach grew as he accepted the Skype call.

Cleo's face filled the screen.

"Long time no see." He attempted to lighten the mood. They were thousands of miles apart, but the air between them crackled with tension.

"That's because you're in Shanghai." Cleo looked paler than usual. She'd tossed her hair into a messy ponytail—a sure sign she wasn't feeling well—and tension lined her mouth.

"I'm well aware."

They fell into silence. Funny. If they hadn't dated and ended things the way they did, they'd be talking as often as Blake did with Joy. Part of him wished they could go back to the way things were. Another part recognized that was impossible, no matter what they'd agreed to over New Year's (before they slept together).

Things change. People change. But they never change back.

"What happened on New Year's—" They spoke at the same time.

"You go first—"

Blake and Cleo looked at each other and laughed in a rare moment of normalcy.

"You go first," Cleo repeated. She fiddled with her sleeve. With her oversize sweatshirt and bare face, she looked like she was fourteen.

That was the year it all changed. Blake was sixteen, caught up in the throes of high school stardom. Meanwhile, Cleo began looking at him the way girls always looked at him.

Blake wished she hadn't. He missed the simple early days of their friendship, before hormones and family and society got in the way.

Regret gnawed at him. "I'm sorry for running out like that," he said. When Cleo told him they'd slept together, he shot out of the room like there was a pack of hellhounds in pursuit. "I remembered I had to be somewhere."

It was a lame lie, and they both knew it.

A strained smile touched Cleo's lips. "It's ok. You always run."

Blake frowned. Before he could ask her what she meant, Cleo added, "I'm sorry too. We agreed to put the past behind us and be just friends, and well, we kinda messed up."

"Yeah. Tequila's a bastard." Blake drummed his fingers on his thigh. Nervous energy zigzagged through his veins. "I've never seen you drink so much."

"I'm not going to drink alcohol for a while, I'll tell you that much." Cleo cleared her throat. "How's…?"

"She's good." Speaking of Farrah, he was running late for their date.

Funny how that was the thing he focused on when there was the bigger issue of him *sleeping with his ex-girlfriend while he and Farrah were together.*

The cramping intensified.

Cleo watched him closely. "You really love her, don't you?"

"I really do."

"I'm so sorry."

"It's not your fault. I'm the one who didn't control myself. I could've stopped drinking. I could've—"

"That's not what I meant." Cleo took a deep breath. Her eyes swam with regret and apology. "I'm sorry for what I'm about to say."

Shit.

That didn't bode well. At all.

Blake gripped the edge of his laptop. The drumbeat of dread mounted in his chest, growing louder and louder until he thought he'd go deaf from the sound.

Cleo bit her lip, which she always did when faced with a

hard decision. He'd seen it when she had to decide between attending TSU or Texas A&M for college, and when she wasn't sure whether to break up with her ninth-grade boyfriend or not.

This time, the stakes were far higher than college and fleeting high school relationships, but Blake didn't know how high until Cleo opened her mouth and upended his entire world.

"Blake, I'm pregnant."

CHAPTER 29

"...HAPPY BIRTHDAY, DEAR FARRAH, HAPPY BIRTHDAY to you!"

Farrah closed her eyes and blew out the candles on her cake while her friends clapped and cheered. Courtney's camera flash lit up the room, so bright Farrah saw it behind her lids.

Twenty years old. She was officially no longer a teenager.

Farrah had been dreading this day for years, but twenty didn't feel so different. She had the same dreams and worries, the same tastes in food and music and clothing. The world didn't come crashing down.

In fact, she was excited. She had a whole new decade to live and explore, and she was starting it off in the best way possible: surrounded by people she loved in one of the greatest cities in the world.

Twenty could be worse.

"What'd ya wish for?" Luke asked.

"Nice try." Farrah sliced into the cake, a massive chocolate affair with cream cheese frosting courtesy of Sammy. Her mouth watered at the sight. Knowing Sammy, it'd be delicious. "If I tell you, it won't come true."

"That's a myth," Luke scoffed. "I tell people my wishes all the time. For example, I wish you'd cut that cake faster."

"Don't be rude." Olivia loaded the slices onto paper plates and passed them around. She saved Luke for last, which earned her a disgruntled glare.

"Maybe what you wished for is in one of those bags." Courtney nodded at the pile of presents on the table. She perched on the arm of the student lounge couch, camera in hand and at the ready. "There's only one way to find out!"

"Subtle." Nardo laughed. "Farrah, Courtney will combust if you don't open your presents soon."

He was acting like a normal human being. It freaked her out.

Leo leaned against the wall on the other side of the room with a smirk. He was on speaking terms with Courtney again, thank god. They weren't dating—that relationship was over for good—but at least things were back to normal with the group. Farrah wouldn't have been able to take another second of tiptoeing around Courtney and Leo, trying to avoid saying the other's name.

"I love presents, even when they're not for me." Courtney shoved a medium rectangular box into Farrah's hands. "Open mine first. Pleeeease."

"Ok, ok." Grinning, Farrah unwrapped the present and opened the box to reveal two framed prints. One was an architectural sketch of Shanghai, the other a photo of the group at the Bund last semester. They were on a postmidterms high and had spent the night eating, drinking, and laughing their way through the city. It must've been four, five in the morning by the time they circled back to the Bund. By then, the lights were off and the city quiet. Farrah didn't remember what they did there, but she remembered how she felt—like she'd never been more in love, with a city or with the people around her.

Like anything was possible.

Like the moment would last forever.

In a sense, it did.

Farrah skimmed her fingers over the frame. There she was with her friends, their grins immortalized for posterity.

"Do you like it?"

"I love it." Farrah hugged Courtney, breathing in her friend's familiar Tommy Girl perfume. "Thank you."

"Anytime, babe." Courtney squeezed her tight.

Farrah pulled herself together and finished unwrapping the rest of her presents, which included a beautiful monogrammed sketchbook from Olivia, delicate gold-and-aquamarine earrings from Kris, a fun tote from Sammy, and a silk scarf from Leo. She saved Blake's for last.

Farrah shook the large box. It rattled in response.

"Ooh. What's this?" Jewelry didn't make that noise. Maybe a book? No, there were definitely multiple objects in there.

"You'll see." Blake's dimples flashed. The sight eased the tension in Farrah's shoulders. He'd been acting off these past few weeks—more so than at the beginning of the semester—but he seemed in a better mood tonight.

Stop overthinking. He's stressed about the bar. That's it.

It was her twentieth birthday. Farrah wasn't going to sabotage her own celebration with her doubts.

"Open it," Blake encouraged. His eyes twinkled with anticipation.

Yep. She was overthinking. Things were *fine*.

Farrah ripped open the wrapping paper, determined to put those pesky voices in her head to bed once and for all. She gasped when she saw what lay beneath the multicolored foil. "Oh my god, where did you find this?!"

"It took a while," Blake admitted. "Sammy helped me track

it down to a little store in the art district. I think it's the only place in the city that sells it."

"Are those"—Kris squinted at the box—"markers?"

"They're not *just* markers. They're limited-edition Pantone dual-ended markers in one hundred and fifty colors, created in collaboration with Kelly Burke, a.k.a. the best interior designer ever. They're only on sale for a month." Farah hugged the box to her chest. "They're *beautiful*!"

She couldn't believe it. She'd wanted the markers since Kelly Burke announced the collaboration last year, and now here they were, in her arms. Imagine all the things she could do with them!

Farrah's mind buzzed with ideas. She was tempted to leave the party right now and start experimenting.

Kris wrinkled her nose. "To each their own."

"Those markers are expensive." Leo eyed Blake. "At least a few hundred bucks."

"Really?" Kris reexamined the set with more respect. "Huh."

In her giddiness, Farrah had forgotten why she didn't buy the set for herself—the markers *were* expensive. Too expensive for her to justify their cost, no matter how much she wanted them.

"It was worth it," Blake said before she could open her mouth. "As long as you like them."

"I adore them." Farrah set the markers on the table and planted a lingering kiss on his lips. "Thank you, babe."

"You're welcome." He skimmed the back of his hand down her cheek. "Happy birthday."

Farrah closed her eyes, reveling in his touch.

Twenty was freakin' awesome.

She stepped away from Blake to hug Sammy. "Thank you for helping. And for the cake."

It didn't take a genius to figure out how Blake found out about the markers. The only person Farrah had told was Olivia, who must've told Sammy, who told Blake.

Still, Farrah was touched Blake and Sammy went to so much trouble to find her present. Finding such a niche product in Shanghai wasn't easy. She couldn't believe they sold the markers here at all.

"It was nothing. Blake did most of the legwork. I merely translated." Sammy kissed her cheek. "Happy birthday."

"Mm-hmm. Thank you anyway." Farrah winked at Olivia. "You've got a good one."

"Right back atcha."

The girls exchanged knowing glances.

"I'm going to bring this"—Farrah gestured at the pile of presents—"up to my room. You guys go ahead. I'll meet you at 808."

"I'll help you." Blake started gathering the crumpled wrapping paper.

"Sure you will." Luke smirked.

Farrah's cheeks reddened. She ignored her friends' suggestive hoots as she swept the gifts up from the table. "C'mon, Blake. Let's go. Maybe when we return, they'll have matured," she said pointedly.

"Maturity is overrated." The opening beats of Jeremih's "Birthday Sex" blasted from Courtney's iPhone. "Have fun," she sang. She dragged the last word out to multiple syllables.

Blake chuckled. Farrah's flush deepened. "I hate you guys."

"Love you too." Olivia blew her a kiss. "Happy birthday, babe."

Farrah softened. "Thanks. For the presents and cake and… everything. You guys are the best, even if you act like thirteen-year-olds." She tried to laugh but got choked up again.

"Oh, no. No crying on your birthday. Go put your presents away and have sex." Courtney waved her off. "You deserve it."

"Let's be honest, they're not making it to 808," Farrah heard Kris say.

Farrah's and Blake's shoes echoed in the stairwell as they made their way to the third floor. The rest of FEA was at 808, but Farrah had wanted to have her cake and gift unwrapping in the dorm. It was easier than going out, hauling the presents back to her room, and going out again.

To her surprise, she opened the door to an empty room. Farrah had invited Janice to the prebirthday celebration, but Janice declined, saying she had work to do. She'd expected to find Janice on her laptop, but her roommate was nowhere in sight.

Farrah wasn't sure whether to be relieved or insulted. It was possible Janice lied about having work to get out of attending her birthday, which sucked. At the same time...

"Looks like we have your room to ourselves. A birthday present from the universe, perhaps?" Blake placed her presents on her desk and winked. Even in a simple white shirt and jeans, he caused her heart to flutter.

"If it is..." Farrah added her haul to the pile and walked over to Blake. She hooked her fingers through his belt loops. "Far be it from me to refuse."

Their lips met in a long, deep kiss that drove every other thought out of her mind. She parted her lips and he swept his tongue inside, increasing the heat until she smoldered with need.

Blake lifted her up. Farrah expected him to carry them to her bed. Instead, he slammed her against the wall, eliciting a gasp of surprise and anticipation from her. He kept one hand on her waist while he used the other to unclasp her dress and bra. His movements were jerky, almost desperate as he eased the material down her body.

Her nipples hardened in the cool air. Blake brushed an open palm over them and she shuddered, an all-too-familiar ache blossoming between her legs. He played with her breasts for a while longer, tugging and twisting so expertly he might as well be in her head. Farrah had always assumed this level of sexual connection and expertise was unrealistic, concocted by romance movies and novels to give the female population hope, when in fact a majority of guys were like the ones Farrah encountered in the past—quick, clumsy, awkward.

Not Blake. He knew exactly what to do, when to do it. By the time he lowered his head to suck on her sensitized nubs, Farrah was ready to fall apart. Her body was a live wire of sensations, crackling and scorching hot. Every nerve ending was sensitive to the touch.

Blake slipped a finger between her slick folds and found *that* spot, and she *did* fall apart. Farrah exploded with pleasure so intense she saw stars. It went on and on, and just as she came down from the high, Blake tossed her on the bed. She heard the rustle of a condom being unwrapped. A second later, he was inside her, filling her to bursting.

Farrah clutched his shoulders and cried out. The heat surged until the flames consumed her once more. She arched up, pressing her chest against Blake's. His hand slipped down between their bodies. His fingertips brushed her clit as he pounded into her, taking her higher and higher to a place where she couldn't breathe, couldn't think. The sensations ran wild through her system, so intense and all-encompassing, she nearly wept. Farrah craved release yet never wanted this to end. All she could do was ride the wave of pleasure until her body detonated and her cries of ecstasy mingled with Blake's as they crashed back to earth together.

After twenty years, she'd found the guy who could take her to heaven and back.

Farrah collapsed on the bed and tried to catch her breath. "Best. Birthday. Present. Ever," she wheezed.

Blake chuckled. He rolled onto his side and smoothed her hair from her face. "Better than the markers?"

"It's close. I really like the markers." Farrah ran her hand up and down his arm. Kris'd been right. They weren't making it to 808. She had zero desire to get dressed and sweat her ass off in a crowded club. She'd much rather stay here with Blake in their own little world. "But I like you more."

She expected him to reply with a smart-ass remark. When he didn't, she looked up to find him gazing at her with such love, it hurt her heart. Not because of the love but because of what hid behind it—a sadness that reawakened her earlier sense of foreboding.

"What's wrong?"

"Nothing's wrong." Blake played with the ends of her hair. "How does twenty feel?"

"It's fine, and don't change the subject. Something's wrong. I can feel it." Farrah propped herself up on her elbow so that they were at eye level. "Is it your dad?"

"No. I'm stressed about the bar, is all. There's so much left to do."

He'd said that the last time she brought up his strange behavior. She'd believed him then. She wasn't sure she believed him now.

"Let's talk about something else. I don't want to be a downer on your birthday."

"You can talk to me about anything, anytime. You know that."

There it was—that melancholy that shouldn't have been there. "Have I told you how much I love you?"

Farrah smiled even as her heart clenched with unease. "You might have mentioned it once or twice, but I wouldn't mind hearing it again."

"Well, I do. I love you so, so much." Blake cupped her cheek. She detected a slight shake in his hand. "Never forget that."

"I won't." She leaned in for a kiss.

"Farrah." The fierceness in his voice startled her. "I mean it. No matter what happens, never forget how much I love you." Blake's eyes darkened with emotion. "I am totally, completely, one hundred percent in love with you. I always will be."

A lump formed in Farrah's throat. "I know," she said softly. "I'm totally, completely, one hundred percent in love with you too." She examined his face, searching for answers to a question she didn't know. "Are you sure everything's ok? Besides the stress over the bar."

Blake laced his fingers through hers with his free hand and squeezed like he was holding on for dear life. "We don't have a lot of time left."

No, they didn't. They had eight weeks.

Eight weeks, fifty-four days, one thousand ninety-six hours before they had to reenter reality.

But they didn't have to do it now.

"We have plenty." Farrah returned his squeeze. "We have tonight."

Blake and Farrah kissed again, a deep, searching, passionate kiss that gave her everything her romantic side wanted.

Farrah lost herself in the embrace, letting it sweep aside her worries and the little voice inside telling her that this kiss, loving and tender though it may be, was also the type of kiss you gave someone right before you said goodbye.

CHAPTER 30

Two weeks later

BLAKE SIGNALED FOR HIS CHECK. THE END ZONE WAS his refuge these days. No one in FEA knew about this place, which meant he could wallow in self-pity in peace.

The bartender brought the bill. It wasn't Mina, who had left Shanghai months ago. She had sent him a short text before she left, and that was that.

Honestly, their short-lived fling seemed like it happened a lifetime ago.

Blake tossed back the rest of his whiskey and scribbled his signature. On the wall, the clock ticked toward six. The group had six thirty dinner reservations at some hot new restaurant Olivia picked out. Farrah had texted him the invite. He hadn't replied.

"See you tomorrow," the bartender said.

Blake nodded. He shouldered his way through the happy-hour crowd and stepped outside. Spring had arrived in Shanghai, and the city burst with color and sunshine. Given Blake's mood, it may as well be gray and storming.

Two weeks.

Two weeks of avoiding Farrah and making excuses about why he couldn't hang out.

Two weeks of not seeing her, touching her, hearing her laugh.

Two weeks of hell.

Blake had to tell her about Cleo. He'd told himself to wait until after her birthday, but every time he tried to get the words out, they stuck in his throat like splintered glass, cutting him open from the inside until he couldn't speak at all.

He tapped his metro card on the reader, so lost in his thoughts he barely registered the rush-hour traffic streaming around him. Office workers, families, and students crowded into the station, their chatter so loud, it sometimes drowned out the PA announcements.

A little girl, around four or five years old, ran past Blake toward the platform. His stomach plunged when he saw the train pulling into the station. He started to run after her when her panicked father caught up and scooped her up in his arms. The girl laughed and threw her arms around her father's neck, oblivious to how close she'd come to danger.

Blake exhaled and followed them onto the train. The relief lasted two seconds before images of all the terrible things that could happen to a child rushed in—kidnapping, bullying, road accidents. Things no parent could control.

His shoulders tensed. More people squeezed onto the train before the doors closed, packing them in like sardines in a can.

Sweat broke out on his forehead.

Blake wasn't ready for any of this. Not to go back to the dorm, not to tell Farrah the truth, and certainly not to be a freaking father. He was twenty-two, for chrissakes! Cleo was twenty. They had no clue what they were doing.

Blake didn't know how to change a diaper or soothe a baby to sleep. What if he messed up and ruined the kid for life? How could he be responsible for another human being when he couldn't get his own life together?

The sweat intensified. Jesus, it was a sauna in here.

The woman next to Blake scooted away from him. No doubt she saw how sick he looked and worried he might throw up on her.

It was a valid fear.

Blake's head pounded, sharp and heavy.

He could ask his mom for help. He'd told her about Cleo's pregnancy a few days after Cleo broke the news. Ripped the Band-Aid off and all that.

Once she got over her shock, Helen had been ecstatic. She wanted grandbabies more than anything and she loved Cleo. She'd never hidden her desire for Blake and Cleo to marry and settle down one day. Now, her dreams had come true, albeit earlier than she'd expected.

Blake's father? Not so happy. If it weren't for Helen, he would've disowned Blake on the spot. In his eyes, this latest bombshell proved once and for all what a fuckup his son was.

He was right.

Ever since Blake quit football, his life had spiraled into a hopeless mess. His relationship with Farrah was the one good thing to come out of it, and he was about to lose that too.

The train rolled to a stop at the SFSU station. Blake shoved his way out, ignoring the other passengers' protests and dirty looks. He took the stairs two at a time until he reached street level and gulped in a lungful of cool, fresh air.

The claustrophobia eased.

The anxiety didn't.

As he walked toward the dorm, Blake ran through scenarios of how to break up with Farrah. Should he tell her about Cleo at all?

It was only a kiss. Which isn't great, but at least she didn't sleep with Nardo. That would be unforgivable.

Farrah's words from Valentine's Day haunted him. It was stupid because he was going to lose her either way, but he didn't want her thinking he'd done the one thing she deemed unforgivable.

So what the hell should he tell her?

Blake entered FEA's lobby and beelined for the stairs. His head pounded with indecision.

He needed one more night to figure out how to end things with Farrah.

He knew he was dragging out the inevitable. He had to let Farrah go. It didn't matter if it happened tomorrow or two months from now. It'd crush him all the same.

But for now, he had one more—

"Hey."

Blake stopped in his tracks. Farrah stood outside his door, arms crossed. She wore a frown and her favorite sheep pajamas.

Blake's lips tugged up into a brief smile before it disappeared.

"We should talk," she said.

So much for one more night.

He swallowed and jerked out a nod. He couldn't put it off any longer.

There was no tomorrow.

Time was up.

CHAPTER 31

GOOSE BUMPS PEPPERED FARRAH'S SKIN. SHE RUBBED her arms and shivered from a combination of cold and dread.

"You didn't go to dinner." Blake unlocked his door, shoulders tense and jaw set.

"No." Farrah followed him inside and sat down on the empty bed opposite his. Normally she would've curled up in Blake's bed and waited for him to join her, but that no longer felt right.

Blake shoved his wallet in a drawer and tidied the books on his desk. He centered his laptop and lined up his pencils until they sat parallel to each other. Only then did he sit across from Farrah, his face shuttered. Only a few feet separated them, but they may as well have been sitting on opposite sides of a canyon.

Farrah's trouble radar inched closer to the danger zone. "We haven't talked in a while."

After her birthday, Blake had dropped off the map. He stopped going out, ate without the group, and answered her texts and invitations with curt excuses. She couldn't find him in his room or, if he was there, he didn't answer the door.

Farrah had tried to wait it out. If Blake needed time alone

to sort out personal issues, she respected that. She would've preferred more communication, but everyone handled problems their own way.

However, they were entering the third week of Incommunicado Blake, and she'd reached the end of her patience. Every second they had left in Shanghai counted, and they'd wasted millions of seconds.

Enough was enough. She wanted answers.

Blake rested his forearms on his knees and clasped his hands together. He stared at the floor like it was the most fascinating thing he'd ever seen. "I've been busy."

Farrah resisted the urge to throw a pillow at him. "With?"

"Classes. Bar plans. That sort of thing."

That old refrain again. He sounded like a broken record.

Anger sharpened Farrah's senses. She was tired of his excuses, of the uncertainty, and of feeling like crap because her boyfriend had gone AWOL. She wanted to know what the *fuck* was going on. "You'll have to do better than that."

Blake's head snapped up. Pain and surprise flickered across his face before his expression shut down.

Despite her irritation, Farrah's heart leapt at the sight of those beautiful blue eyes, then shriveled like a prune at the lack of feeling in them.

"Tell me the truth." She forced the words past the lump in her throat. "You can trust me."

The bigger question was, could she trust him? Farrah hated doubting him, but it was hard not to lose faith when the love of your life avoided you like you had the plague.

Blake's shoulders hunched. Tension rolled off him in waves. He closed his eyes, and when he opened them again, they were as hard and cold as the walls surrounding them.

Farrah's stomach plummeted.

"I'm sorry." His voice was flat and empty. "I didn't want to do it like this, but I don't think we should see each other anymore."

Time stopped. Blake's words swirled around her, threatening to drag her under yet refusing to sink in.

Farrah's body reacted first, her heart slamming against her chest in double time while her brain struggled to process the implications of Blake's statement.

"What?"

"It was fun while it lasted, but the year is almost over and I—I'm not interested anymore. I'm sorry," he repeated.

"You're lying." He had to be. There was no way. No way she could've been so wrong.

The past seven months flashed through Farrah's mind's eye like a movie playing at two times speed. Their first run-in in the stairwell. Their first kiss. Their first time having sex. The first time they said, "I love you." The secrets they shared, the places they explored, the nights they spent in each other's arms.

She struggled to breathe. The air thickened into a dark ugly ooze, making it impossible for oxygen to reach her lungs. There were so many thoughts running through her mind, she couldn't focus, so Farrah grasped at the easiest one to swallow.

Blake was lying. She'd looked into his eyes and seen the love there. She'd felt it. You couldn't fake that kind of emotion.

He stiffened. "I'm not."

"You are." Farrah didn't know who she was trying to convince more, him or herself. "You said you loved me."

"I lied."

Farrah inhaled sharply. True or not, those two words sliced through her like a knife.

Don't cry. Don't cry. Do. Not. Fucking. Cry.

"You're full of shit." Her voice trembled with uncertainty. "Look at you. You're shaking."

Blake clenched his hands into fists. His knuckles turned white. "Farrah." His voice sounded like a bomb going off in the silence. "I got back with my ex-girlfriend over the holidays. I didn't know how to tell you. I love her, and I made a mistake here. With us. But I'm trying to fix it."

A sob escaped. The temperature dropped another twenty degrees, and a strange roaring filled her ears. The fist around her heart squeezed, and right as she was about to explode from the pain, it released its grip and shattered everything in its wake.

I need to get out of here.

Yet Farrah's feet remained glued in place as she tried to comprehend what was happening. The Blake in front of her wasn't the Blake she knew. He was so stoic, so unsympathetic, she wondered whether this was a nightmare or if the past seven months had been a dream.

"I'm sorry."

That broke the spell.

"Stop saying that!" Blake's eyes widened. Farrah gripped her necklace tight with one hand until the metal dug painful grooves into her palm. "It was all a lie then, this past year."

Blake looked away.

"Why? Why did you pretend you cared? Was it some sick joke? You wanted to see whether I'd be gullible enough to fall for you? Well, congratu-fucking-lations." Tears burned her eyes. "You won. Blake Ryan, the champion. Your father was right. You shouldn't have quit. No one plays the game better than you."

A tear slipped out and scalded her cheek. Farrah wiped it away angrily. She'd already given him too much. She wasn't going to give him the satisfaction of seeing her cry too.

Blake may as well have been carved from marble for all the emotion he showed. "I'm sor—"

Her blood bubbled with rage. "If you say, 'I'm sorry,' one

more time," she hissed, "I'll go to the kitchen, come back, and cut your balls off with a rusty knife. In fact, I may do that anyway. You're a fucking asshole. *I'm* sorry I wasted all this time on you, and I'm sorrier for your girlfriend. She deserves better."

Farrah summoned the strength to stand. She walked to the door, praying her legs wouldn't give out before she reached the hallway. She gripped the doorknob and turned around for a last look at Blake.

Other than the slight tremble in his shoulders, he sat there unmoving, face blank.

Blake Ryan. Her first love. Her first lover. Her first heartbreak.

Farrah closed the door with a soft click. Her feet moved. One step, two steps, and so on until she reached her room. The ringing in her ears pounded in sync with her steps.

She prayed Janice wasn't there. She was.

Lady Luck hated her today.

Janice glanced up when Farrah entered before she dove back into her book. A second later, her head popped up again. Her brow furrowed with worry. "Are you ok?"

"Yes." Farrah smiled so hard her cheeks hurt. "I'm fine. I'm great. I'm—I'm—"

The alarm mounted on Janice's face.

"I—" Farrah's anger faded like a flame losing oxygen.

No. Don't you dare fucking leave.

She grabbed at the remaining tendrils of fury with desperate hands. They were the only things left holding her together, but she may as well have tried to grab sand. They slipped through her fingers until there was nothing left.

"I'm—" Pain rushed in to fill the void. Incredible, soul-crushing pain, the kind that forced her to double over, it hurt so much. The dam she'd erected to keep her tears at bay collapsed, sending streams of liquid grief down her cheeks.

That was it.

Farrah curled up into a ball on the floor. She hugged her knees to her chest and sobbed—huge wracking sobs that shook her body but made nary a noise. Her stomach ached. Her sides ached. Her heart ached so much she was sure she was dying.

All the while, her brain tortured her with memories.

"I love you."

"Never forget how much I love you."

It had seemed so real, so sincere. Farrah didn't just love Blake; she *trusted* him. She trusted him enough not only to give him her virginity but her heart. Turns out, he'd been playing her this entire time.

I am such an idiot.

Farrah buried her face in her knees, struggling to breathe between sobs. Her mouth dried and her eyes burned, but she couldn't stop. It was too much.

Everything—the pain, the embarrassment, the shock—it was too much.

Janice sat next to her on the floor and, even though the two girls hadn't spoken more than a dozen words to each other since the year began, she placed her arm around Farrah's shoulders and stayed with her until Farrah ran out of tears to cry.

CHAPTER 32

One month later

THE DAY HAD COME. FEA GRADUATION. THEIR LAST
night in Shanghai.

Blake didn't shed a tear at his high school graduation, but a
lump formed in his throat as Wang *laoshi* ended his speech and
the ceremony segued into the retrospective portion of the evening.
The lights dimmed, a giant projector screen slid down the wall,
and the opening strains of Emil Chau's classic song "Peng You
(Friends)" filled the auditorium.

Images from the past year flashed across the screen. There
were Blake and Luke, sweaty, grinning, and flashing cheesy
thumbs-ups after their orientation-week scavenger hunt. Then a
semicandid shot of FEA's first night at 808—Sammy and Olivia
dancing together, Farrah sticking her tongue out at the camera,
and Courtney onstage, clutching a drink in each hand with her
face screwed up in laughter.

The lump in Blake's throat grew at the joy on Farrah's face.

His gaze drifted to where she sat two rows down and three seats to his right. Was she laughing? Crying? She sat so still, he couldn't tell.

The slideshow continued. The guys playing basketball. Farrah and Olivia on a beach in Thailand. The group on the Great Wall prehike. Courtney and Leo holding scorpions on sticks at a Beijing night market.

There were countless other photos of Blake and his friends in restaurants, taxicabs, rickshaws, bars, and clubs; posing in dressing rooms and dorm rooms and VIP rooms; hosting a mock singing competition in the student lounge; on the street with random people whose names they forgot or never knew to begin with.

Blake couldn't help but laugh when he saw the photo of Farrah passed out on the couch of a karaoke lounge. They'd hiked the Sheshan trail that day, and by the time evening rolled around, they were too tired to go clubbing. They settled for KTV instead. Farrah fell asleep after the second song.

Sammy had ducked his head into the picture frame. He'd had a few drinks, and his face matched the color of his red shirt. Courtney pretended to lick Farrah's cheek while Olivia grabbed a handful of the sleeping girl's hair and did an exaggerated sexy pose behind the couch, her lips pursed into a model pout.

Blake's laugh died when the next picture came up. Blake and Farrah, kissing on a rooftop bar by the Bund, their fingers intertwined by their sides. The skyline glittered behind them, bright and full of promise. He could only see their profiles, but the love radiating from the photo hit him like a punch to the gut.

Blake looked away. The pain had stabilized into a dull ache over the past month, but now the sharp pangs of his heart breaking returned with a vengeance.

Thankfully, the slideshow ended, and Wang *laoshi* started calling students onstage to receive their ceremonial graduation certificates.

"Congratulations." Wang *laoshi* shook Blake's hand. "Good luck with your future endeavors."

"Thanks." He was going to need it.

Between school, the bar, and preparing for life as a father, Blake barely slept these days. He ran on pure adrenaline and fear of what might happen if he slowed down.

So he didn't.

Blake looked out at the crowd before he exited the stage. The lights made it hard to see any details, but he could just make out Farrah in the crowd. She sat stone-faced, like she was watching a comedy that wasn't particularly funny.

They hadn't spoken since their breakup. They'd barely seen each other, even though they lived in the same dorm. That was probably a good thing, because every time Blake so much as thought about Farrah, pain scissored his insides and shredded his heart all over again.

He heard from Luke—the only one of his friends who spoke to him anymore—that Farrah won the design competition. Blake wished he could say something. He knew what the competition meant to her. He remembered the nights they'd spent together in the library—him working on his business plan, her working on her designs—taking breaks to laugh and kiss in between.

Blake's jaw tightened at the memories.

Get it together, man.

He returned to his seat and examined the certificate in his hands. It wasn't his official college diploma, but it may as well be. It signaled the end of the carefree student chapter of his life. The next chapter as an actual adult and father loomed in front of him like a storm cloud. Beautiful, inescapable, somewhat exciting but mostly terrifying.

It didn't matter that he wasn't ready.

The future was coming, whether Blake liked it or not, and that meant he had to leave the past behind.

Onstage, Wang *laoshi* passed out the last certificate and gazed around the auditorium. "It's been a pleasure. Class, you're dismissed."

The room erupted into cheers, although Blake saw more than one person wipe tears from their eyes.

The chatter intensified as everyone stood up and filed out the door. They had an hour before the official end-of-semester dance.

Outside, the scent of an impending storm hung warm and heavy in the air. The humidity clung to Blake's skin like Saran Wrap. He needed to shower before the dance.

A part of him wanted to skip the dance altogether, but FEA deserved a proper goodbye.

"You're in for hell later," Blake said when Luke fell into step with him. "Courtney was already glaring daggers at you for sitting with me."

Luke shrugged. "Tonight's our last night. What's she gonna do, kick me out?"

Blake cracked a smile. "That's brave of you."

"Hey, I'm pissed you didn't tell me about your girl back home but"—Luke clapped him on the shoulder—"you're my best friend here. I got your back."

Another lump formed in Blake's throat. "Thanks, man. That means a lot."

Awkward silence.

"So—" They spoke at the same time.

"This moment never happened," Blake said.

"Never."

"Cool."

"Yep."

When they reached the dorm, they found their friends—or in Blake's case, ex-friends—huddled in the courtyard. Farrah stood in the middle of the group, her hand resting at the base of her throat. Her necklace, the one from her father, was missing.

"Are you sure you didn't leave it in your room?" Olivia asked.

"I had it in the auditorium, but it must've fallen off. I don't know where." Farrah's voice tightened with stress.

A flash of lightning lit up the sky, followed by a crack of thunder that made them all jump.

"We'll find it. It has to be around here somewhere, and the auditorium isn't too far from the dorm." Sammy placed a hand on Farrah's shoulder. "For now, let's go inside. It's going to pour."

Courtney noticed Blake watching. "Can I help you?" she snapped.

"Be nice, Court." It was the first time Blake heard Luke admonish Courtney.

Shock flitted across her face.

"I hope you find your necklace," Blake said to Farrah.

The group fell silent. Seven pairs of eyes darted between the ex-lovers.

Farrah's fingers curled into a fist. Like Courtney, she remained silent.

Another boom of thunder rocked the air.

Huge droplets of water splashed onto the ground and blurred Blake's vision. What started as a drizzle turned into a downpour. Panicked shouts filled the air as everyone ran inside to avoid getting drenched.

"My new Gucci!" Kris wailed.

Blake wiped the water from his eyes and followed the others into the lobby.

"Hey, you mind if I borrow your hair dryer? No way I'm going to make it to my homestay and back for the dance." Luke raked his fingers through his wet locks.

"Yeah. It's in my bottom drawer." Blake tossed his friend his key card. "I'll catch up with you later."

"Cool. See ya."

No one else spoke to Blake on their way to the stairs, though Sammy did throw him an odd look. He hadn't been as hostile as the girls. He even said hi on a few occasions. But he'd clearly chosen a side in the breakup.

Farrah brushed by Blake. The air between them crackled with electricity for a moment, and then she was gone.

Blake waited until the lobby emptied before he placed his soggy certificate on a nearby table and returned outside.

"You are an idiot," Sammy muttered under his breath. He dodged a puddle only to step in another one. Water splashed all over his shoes and pant legs. "Dammit!"

He had to leave his phone in the auditorium tonight of all nights, when the biggest storm of the year rolled into town. He didn't realize he didn't have his trusty electronic sidekick until after he changed for the dance.

Sammy checked his watch. He had half an hour to get to the auditorium, find his phone, return to his room, and change before the buses left for the dance.

FEA paid good money to reserve a hotel ballroom for the semester send-off, and the money-minded Wang *laoshi* made it clear: anyone who missed the bus would have to find their own way to the hotel. On a normal night, he could take a taxi, but trying to find an empty cab on a night like this? *Good luck.*

Olivia's going to kill me.

Sammy had the auditorium in his sights when he noticed a figure lurking in the bushes nearby.

His pace slowed; his heart rate quickened. No one in their

right mind would linger outside in this weather. The figure was either a crazed murderer or just plain crazed. Either way, Sammy had no interest in being that evening's homicide news item.

Lightning streaked the sky and illuminated the figure, who wore a familiar gray T-shirt and jeans. They rifled through the foliage like they were looking for something.

Sammy's pulse returned to normal. "Blake?"

Blake's head snapped up. He didn't have an umbrella or raincoat on, and his shirt was so soaked it looked black. "What are you doing out here?"

"I left my phone in the auditorium." Sammy stepped closer and raised his umbrella so that it covered both of them. "What are *you* doing out here?"

This was their first real conversation since Blake and Farrah's breakup. Sammy had nearly fallen over when he heard about their split. It didn't make sense. He'd seen the way Blake looked at Farrah. There was no faking that kind of emotion.

There had to be more to the story than Blake was telling them. But it didn't matter. If Blake wanted to tell them the truth, he would. Otherwise, it was best to let Farrah grieve and move on instead of trying to fix things and making them worse.

"I'm looking for my contacts."

"I didn't know you wore glasses." Sammy was sure Blake *didn't* wear glasses. The guy could read a menu posted outside a restaurant from twenty feet away.

Blake shrugged.

A sad smile crossed Sammy's face. If only Farrah knew how much Blake still loved her.

CHAPTER 33

THUNDER CRASHED OUTSIDE, FOLLOWED BY THE LOUD pitter-patter of raindrops splattering against the windows. Flashes of lightning illuminated the skies with an eerie light. It was the worst storm they'd experienced in Shanghai, and it matched Farrah's mood to a tee.

She reached for her necklace before she remembered she didn't have it. Hope of finding it before her flight tomorrow morning dwindled by the second.

Farrah should be looking forward to this summer. She won the design competition—the one she'd dreamed of winning since she found out about it years ago. She received the email while waiting to board her flight after FEA's spring semester trip to Chengdu, and her resulting scream nearly got her arrested by airport security.

Yes, she was excited about potentially interning in New York with Kelly Burke (final internship placement pending). But she also mourned what had to end for the next chapter of her life to begin.

Farrah curled her hand into a fist and rested it at the base of her throat as she meandered down the fourth-floor hallway. Group photos of every class since FEA Shanghai's inception in the eighties lined the walls. The groups started small—there'd only been a dozen students in the first class—before expanding to the current size of seventy-plus undergrads.

It was surreal, looking at the photographs and realizing how many people had walked these halls before them. Members of the first class would be in their fifties by now. Yet there they were in their photo, immortalized behind glass, forever nineteen and twenty and twenty-one. Farrah detected a shadow of her friends in all of them—a hint of Sammy's good-natured grin, a trace of Kris's regal haughtiness, a mischievous twinkle in the eye that would make Courtney proud.

The superficial resemblances were there, but she wondered if they'd laughed as hard and loved as deep, if they'd had their hearts broken and if they'd found family here, or if they had just been ships passing in the night. Did they keep in touch decades later? Did Shanghai change them, or was it a mere footnote in the stories of their lives?

Inexplicably, her heart ached for these strangers. She would never know their stories and secrets, but she knew them. She was, after all, walking in their footsteps.

Farrah skimmed her hands over the glass-encased images until she reached the end of the series. This year's class photo, taken yesterday and already mounted on the wall like the dozens before them. They'd arranged the students by height. Farrah stood in the middle row with Olivia and Nardo, while Kris and Courtney sat cross-legged in front of them. Luke, Sammy, and Leo towered in the back.

Farrah's gaze strayed to the blond next to Luke. Blake's dimples were out in full force, but there were shadows beneath his eyes and a furrow in his brow.

She fought the urge to overanalyze the minutiae of his expression. Instead, Farrah tore her eyes away from the photo and focused on the stretch of blank wall following it. Next year, there'd be another picture. Then another, and another, until Farrah's class was just one of FEA's many memories.

The sound of heels clacking against linoleum echoed in the stairwell. Only one person in FEA who wore heels that made that noise.

"Hey." Kris stopped beside Farrah.

"Hey."

The two friends examined the wall in silence. Kris smelled like her usual mix of Chanel perfume and expensive shampoo. Farrah breathed it in, letting the familiar scent comfort her.

"It's crazy, isn't it?" Kris touched their class photo before pulling back like it burned her. "This year flew by."

"Yeah. I can't believe it."

"It won't be the same." Kris looked at Farrah. There were no tears, no overt emotion except for the wistfulness in her voice. "Even if we all come back to Shanghai, it won't be the same."

Farrah dropped her hand from her throat and wrapped an arm around Kris's waist. "I know."

Kris rested her head on Farrah's shoulder in an uncharacteristically vulnerable gesture, but neither girl acknowledged its strangeness.

Instead, they stood there, soaking in their last moments together in this place, while the storm raged outside.

CHAPTER 34

THE LIGHTS DIMMED. THE MUSIC SWELLED. THE AIR filled with giddiness and nostalgia.

Within an hour, the FEAers transformed the program's staid dance into a rave reminiscent of their heady first days in Shanghai, only this time, it was a last hurrah instead of a kickoff.

Blake leaned against the wall and sipped his drink. A few months ago, he would've been right there with them on the dance floor. Now it felt wrong. Were soon-to-be dads allowed to dance like that? The parenting ebooks he downloaded didn't cover party etiquette for parents.

"Did you do it?" He sensed the new presence next to him without having to turn his head.

"Yeah." The disapproval came through loud and clear. "You should've done it yourself."

"I couldn't."

"You have arms and legs. You could've picked up that locket, walked into the dorm and up the stairs to Farrah's room, and handed it to her."

"You know that's not what I meant." Blake tossed back the

rest of his drink and slammed it on a nearby table. His head pounded with tension.

"I don't know shit because you won't tell me shit." Sammy jabbed a finger into Blake's chest. "You better clue me in fast unless you want a punch to the face. Obviously, you still have feelings for Farrah, so why the big breakup?"

"It's complicated."

"Uncomplicate it."

Blake exhaled sharply. He looked around. Everyone was too lost in their own worlds to pay attention to him and Sammy. Luke, Leo, and Nardo gathered at the bar with a few other guys. Courtney and Kris danced like maniacs to the latest Top 40 chart-topper. Farrah and Olivia were nowhere in sight.

"Not here."

Blake led him to the terrace and closed the sliding door behind them, muffling the music and raucous laughter. The rain had cleared, and the moon shone bright in the sky.

Sammy leaned against the railing and crossed his arms over his chest. "Let's hear it, Ryan."

"Who are you, and what have you done with Sammy Yu?" Blake tried to lighten the mood. He'd known Sammy for months. He'd never seen him like this.

Sammy didn't smile at the unintended play on words. "It pisses me off when people hurt my friends, and you hurt one of my best friends. I want to know why."

Sammy might tell Farrah. She was, as he said, one of his best friends.

But this was Sammy. As much of a stranger as he'd been this past month, he would never go back on his word.

Blake's jaw worked as he rifled through his options. "Promise you won't tell anyone. Not even Olivia. *Especially* not Olivia."

"I promise."

Blake hesitated another second before he spilled the beans. New Year's, Cleo, her pregnancy, why he broke up with Farrah. Everything. As he spoke, Sammy's expression morphed from anger to shock to sympathy before settling on a mix of all three.

"Holy shit."

"Yeah."

"You're going to be a father."

"Yeah."

"You're in love with Farrah, and you're having a baby with someone else."

Blake flinched. Sammy's matter-of-fact summary of his mess hit harder than it should have. Blake had had months to reconcile himself with his situation; clearly, he still had work to do.

"You need to tell Farrah."

"No!"

Sammy's eyebrows shot up at Blake's vehement response.

Blake sucked in a deep breath. The mere thought of Farrah finding out the truth had his heart skittering like a panicked rabbit. "She deserves a clean break."

"She thinks you played her."

"And that's the way it'll stay," Blake said grimly. "You promised."

Was it better that Farrah thought he played her instead of cheated her? Probably not. Given his harsh words the night they broke up, cheating was more redeemable—even if she did hate cheaters. After all, Blake didn't even remember his night with Cleo.

But that was the point. Blake didn't want to be redeemable. Farrah deserved a clean break, and she couldn't get one if she thought he still loved her and just made a mistake over New Year's. She had to think he never loved her at all. It was the only way she could move on.

262 | ANA HUANG

A spike hammered into Blake's heart at the thought of Farrah moving on with someone else.

"Jesus." Sammy rubbed a hand over his face. "What are you going to do?"

"The only thing I can do. Go home and be a father."

Sammy's gaze flicked toward the balcony door. He pushed himself off the railing and clapped a hand on Blake's shoulder. "Good luck."

Something in his tone compelled Blake to turn around. His blood ran cold.

Farrah stood in the corner, half-hidden in the shadows. He couldn't see her face, but he knew every curve of her body. Her scent, the way she moved, it was all imprinted into his memory.

"How long have you been standing there?" His pulse pounded with fear. If she'd heard what he said...

"Since right before Sammy left." Farrah stepped out of the shadows, and his heart tripped over itself trying to get to her. Standing there bathed in moonlight, she reminded him of the first time they kissed. The Great Wall, the stars, their kiss...they may as well be a dream from a previous life.

Blake shoved his hands into his pockets and clenched them into fists, stopping his runaway emotions in their tracks. "You found your necklace."

Her pendant rested against her throat, where it belonged. At least one thing went right today.

"Sammy found it." Farrah fiddled with her necklace. "You guys looked like you were having an intense conversation."

"We were reminiscing," Blake lied.

This was their first conversation since she visited his room. Farrah wasn't ignoring or yelling at him, but he would've almost preferred that to her obvious yet civil contempt.

"What time is your flight tomorrow?" Small talk wouldn't

wipe that look off of her face, the one that said she thought he was lower than scum on the bottom of her shoe, but he was desperate to hear her voice.

"Ten in the morning." Farrah glanced over her shoulder toward the ballroom. "You?"

"Eight. At night. I'm one of the last ones out."

There was a beat of silence. "Well." Farrah stepped toward the door. "Have a safe flight."

"Wait." Blake didn't know what made him do it. Maybe it was the fresh air or the fact it was their last night together. Maybe it was a last-ditch attempt to reclaim the magic of a love lost, if only for a moment. Whatever it was, it made him close the gap between them until they were only inches apart. "I need to tell you something."

Farrah stared up at him, her eyes liquid in the moonlight, her face inscrutable.

"I—" Blake reached for her before he thought twice and dropped his arm. "I'm sorry."

"For what?"

"For everything." *For more than you can know.* "I never meant to hurt you. I was a jerk when I broke up with you and I'm sorry."

He was repeating what he said during their breakup, but dammit, he needed her to know.

"You were more of a jerk when you cheated on your girlfriend."

Blake flinched. He deserved that. Didn't mean it didn't hurt like a bitch.

"I have something to tell you too." Farrah's voice was as smooth and cool as glass. "Thank you."

He must've heard her wrong. "Excuse me?"

"You're right. You are an asshole."

"Er, I didn't say I'm an *asshole*—"

"But you taught me some important lessons. One day, I'll find the person I can trust more than anyone else because you showed me everything I shouldn't look for."

Blake's heart wrenched. It'd be so easy. Right then and there, when he and Farrah were the only people in the world, it'd be so easy to tell her the truth. It wouldn't set things right—he cheated on her, even if he didn't remember doing it—but at least she'd know. Everything he did, everything he told her was true. She was the love of his life.

Then he remembered the look on Cleo's face when she told him she was pregnant. His family's reaction. The folder of parenting ebooks on his computer. How his mom was already picking out color swatches for the nursery.

He remembered all the reasons Farrah couldn't know the truth, and so he said the words that scraped his throat raw when he forced them out.

"I hope you find him."

Farrah's nostrils flared. For a split second, her stony mask cracked, and he saw the hurt in her eyes.

His heart wrenched again.

Farrah turned and walked into the ballroom without another word.

All Blake could do was watch her leave. There was nothing left to say except the three words he could never say to her again.

I love you.

CHAPTER 35

THE FEAERS ENDED THEIR NIGHT AT THE ONLY PLACE that made sense: Gino's. Their home away from home. In the past year, they'd spent enough money here to keep the bar in the black for at least another twelve months, which may have been why the owner treated them to a round of free beers on their last night.

Courtney raised her drink and looked around at the dozens of faces staring back at her. "Guys, we've made it this far. This is our last night. Our last chance to make sure we don't leave Shanghai with any regrets. Say what you want to say, do what you want to do, or forever hold your peace."

Farrah flicked her eyes toward the back of the group, where Blake stood still as a statue.

"I hope you find him." His words echoed in her mind, taunting her.

"We go back to our own cities and lives tomorrow, but no matter what happens, I think it's safe to say this is a year we'll cherish forever. So, cheers!" Courtney raised her drink higher. "To FEA, Shanghai, and a night we won't remember with friends we'll never forget!"

"Cheers!"

Farrah lifted her glass as FEA erupted into a cacophony of chatter and glasses clinking.

In her peripheral vision, Farrah saw a tear slip down Janice's cheek. The end of the semester hit everyone harder than expected.

Janice caught Farrah's eye, and the two girls exchanged watery smiles. They were roommates, not friends, but Farrah wouldn't forget the way Janice comforted her the night of her breakup with Blake. Part of her wished she'd gotten to know Janice better this year, but it was too late for that.

"I can't stand this sentimental shit," Kris said.

"Don't lie. You love it." Olivia draped an arm over Kris's shoulders. "I'm going to miss you."

Kris sighed and finished her cranberry vodka. "I'm going to miss you too." She caught Farrah's eye and rolled her eyes jokingly. Farrah smiled. Kris may be prickly, but she would kill for her friends. That type of loyalty was hard to come by.

The music switched to The Wanted's "Glad You Came," one of Farrah's favorite throwback songs. Her heart ached at the lyrics. Of all the cities in all the world, they ended up here. But what if they hadn't? Even if one person chose another city, this whole year would've been different.

In that way, the lyrics couldn't have been more fitting, though she knew the song was about orgasms.

That was fitting too.

Farrah's mouth tilted up at her own inside joke.

She might have loose ends to tie up. She might never forget Blake, and she might not see half the people here again, but she was grateful for everything that happened these past eight months. How lucky was she to have spent a year in Shanghai, to have strangers turn into family, and to have loved so deeply, it left scars on her heart?

Her and Blake's story didn't end in a happily ever after, but he'd showed her that love—that deep, all-consuming love people wrote songs and movies and books about—was real. Farrah experienced it, even if he hadn't. While this story hadn't turned out the way she'd hoped, perhaps the next one would.

Farrah took a deep breath and pushed her sadness aside. It was her last night. Time to enjoy it.

She joined her friends on the dance floor. Sammy's unbuttoned shirt bared his muscular chest, a sure sign he was drunk. Courtney hopped onto Luke's back and fist-pumped the air, even though they weren't playing fist-pumping music. Olivia and Kris took turns spinning each other around until Kris crashed into Nardo, who tried to start a conga line. No one except Flo joined him, but it was nice to see him loosen up for a change.

"Farrah, get your sexy ass over here!" Courtney climbed off Luke's back and corralled Farrah, Kris, and Olivia into a group hug.

"I love you girls," she said, her blue eyes bright with emotion.

"No crying," Kris warned. "It gives me the heebie-jeebies."

Olivia's jaw dropped. "Did Kris Carrera just use the term *heebie-jeebies*?"

"No, I didn't. You can't prove it. If you tell anyone, I'll kill you."

They cracked up at the same time. Farrah took a mental snapshot and tucked it away in her box of cherished memories. She hoped she never forgot the love she felt in that moment.

"This is it, guys." She squeezed her friends tighter. "Let's make it count."

And for the rest of the night, they did. Farrah and her friends soaked up the magic of their last hours together, surrendering themselves to the music, the lights, and the pulsing neon energy that coursed through Shanghai.

Tomorrow seemed like ages away.

CHAPTER 36

MIDNIGHT CAME AND WENT. BLAKE DIDN'T JOIN FEA'S revelry, afraid of the secrets that might spill out should he drink too much. Nevertheless, he couldn't bring himself to return to the dorm.

After Courtney's toast, Blake went outside for some fresh air. He ended up staying on the bench by Gino's entrance, watching the comings and goings of after-hours Shanghai: the street vendors hawking meat skewers to drunken revelers, the cabdriver chain-smoking out his open window, the group of hip teens drinking by the curb, even though it was a school night and they couldn't be older than sixteen.

Blake tried to square the scene in front of him with his life back home: neighborhood barbecues, white picket fences, and minivans in the Texas suburbs. He couldn't.

He remembered arriving in Shanghai and being overwhelmed by the noise, the people, the strange foods and sounds and sights. He'd never visited Asia before. Hadn't even thought about it until he quit the team and the ensuing chaos forced him to run as far away as possible.

Blake hadn't expected to love this city so much. It had its flaws, but this year it became his home away from home. Here, he was free to be who wanted to be—and he liked who he was in Shanghai.

It had opened his eyes to a world beyond Texas, and now that he'd seen it, he didn't want to go back.

His son or daughter would grow up, and if the bar was successful, he'd expand. If not, he'd try a different market. Either way, Blake wasn't meant to stay in his hometown for the rest of his life. That, he knew for sure.

As the wee morning hours wore on, FEAers trickled out of Gino's in waves. Some had early flights; some had other activities in mind.

Luke and Janice were the first to leave. He winked at Blake on his way past while Janice nuzzled his neck. As far as Blake knew, they'd spoken less than ten words to each other before tonight.

Ending the semester with a bang—literally. Good for them.

Courtney, Kris, Leo, and Olivia left next. They all ignored Blake except Leo, who acknowledged him with a slight chin tilt.

By the time the clock struck two, most of FEA had left.

Except Farrah.

Worry niggled at Blake. He was about to check on her when the door swung open and a sobered-up Sammy stumbled out holding Farrah. Her eyes were half-closed; her head lolled forward on her chest.

"Is she ok?" Unsure of what to do, Blake stood, sat, and stood again.

"Yeah. She should be fine after some rest and water. She fell asleep in there, and Gino's is about to close." Sammy propped Farrah up against the railing. "Can you take her back to the dorm? I have to get Nardo. Last I saw, he was hurling his guts out in the bathroom."

Blake hesitated. "Sure." He draped Farrah's arm over his shoulder and wrapped his free arm around her waist. "Go take care of Nardo."

"You're not leaving till tomorrow night, right?"

"Yep."

"Cool. See you later."

Sammy disappeared inside while Blake struggled to guide Farrah to a cab. She didn't weigh much, but it wasn't easy dragging 115 pounds of deadweight down the stairs and across the street without killing either of them.

Blake finally corralled them into a taxi. The minute they sat down, Farrah dropped her head onto his shoulder. Her soft snores filled the back seat, drowning out the maudlin eighties ballad on the radio.

Blake's mouth edged up into a smile when he remembered how Farrah used to deny she snored.

Outside, the streets of Shanghai whizzed by in a blur of lights. Blake tried to focus on the passing cityscape instead of the girl next to him. How many times had Farrah rested her head on his shoulder while he held her? It was such a familiar sensation, he almost tricked himself into believing they were still a couple.

He didn't touch her. He was too afraid to even look at her, lest his heart break all over again. Still, he felt like he was taking advantage by stealing these private moments when she wanted nothing to do with him when she was awake.

The cab rolled to a stop in front of the dorm. Blake paid the driver and picked Farrah up bridal-style. He'd learned his lesson; dragging was not the way to go.

Once they arrived at her room, Blake set Farrah on her feet and held her up with one arm while he searched for her key with the other. Fortunately, she carried a small bag instead of one of those cavernous totes girls loved. Blake found the key in no time.

The door clicked open. Janice must've gone to Luke's homestay because her bed was empty.

Blake laid Farrah on her bed and went to work taking off her shoes, setting the garbage can beside her bed, and moving a half-empty water bottle from her desk to her nightstand.

All set.

He allowed himself the luxury of lingering an extra minute. His chest constricted as he looked down at Farrah's sleeping form. In the past, Farrah always wore a small smile while she slept, like she was so happy, the joy followed her into her dreams. Now, her brow furrowed and her mouth turned down at the corners.

Before he could stop himself, Blake smoothed his fingers over her temple, like that would somehow wipe her sadness away.

Farrah's face relaxed. She sighed and shifted positions.

Blake froze. He needed to leave before she woke up and saw him there.

He turned off the light and—

"Blake," she murmured.

Shit.

"You promised you wouldn't leave." She shifted again. Blake's eyes adjusted to the darkness enough to see hers were still closed, and he realized she was talking in her sleep.

That Farrah was asking for him in her sleep proved she wasn't as over him as she pretended to be. It should've made Blake feel better; it didn't. It made him want to cry because he understood firsthand how much she must be hurting.

"I know, baby," he whispered. He tucked a strand of hair behind her ears. "I won't. You'll always have a piece of me with you."

Farrah sighed.

The tightness in his chest intensified. Blake pulled his hand away, but Farrah whimpered and grasped his sleeve. "No. Stay with me..." Her voice trailed off sleepily.

A tear slipped down his cheek, and Blake had to hold his breath so his sob didn't disturb the silence.

He eased into the bed next to Farrah and held her in his arms. He kept his touch light, lest he wake her. "Ok. I'll stay with you." Another tear escaped and landed on her forehead. Blake kissed it away. "I love you, Farrah," he whispered.

Farrah heaved another, more contented sigh. "Thanks for staying." She buried her face in his chest, muffling her words. "I love you, Blake."

By now, the tears were falling too fast for him to wipe away, so he lay there and let them fall. Blake couldn't stay with Farrah the entire night. It was too risky. But he stayed until her chest rose and fell in a steady rhythm, and she dozed off with a small smile on her face, the way she always did when they were together.

CHAPTER 37

"THIS IS IT."

Farrah and Olivia stared at the dorm, the place where they lived, laughed, and loved for a year and where Farrah had some of the best—and most heartbreaking—moments of her life.

She was the first of her friends to leave. She'd spent the entire morning saying goodbye—to her friends, to FEA, to everything and everyone she'd loved this past year.

All except one.

Farrah's chest squeezed.

"We'll see each other soon," Olivia said. "We'll be in New York together this summer."

"Hopefully." Farrah hadn't received her summer assignment yet, but the thought of New York was the only thing keeping her going today.

Farrah, Olivia, and Sammy together in New York—it would be a dream. She didn't even mind playing third wheel to her friends' nauseatingly sweet relationship—the only one in their group that lasted the whole year.

But as much as Farrah loved Olivia and Sammy, it wasn't

about the three of them. It was about the collective, and she didn't have the heart to tell her friend that even if they all somehow met up again, it wouldn't be the same. They would never be as young and carefree as they were now. They would never live in the same dorm, knowing the others were just a few rooms or a floor down. They couldn't hop into a cab and grab dinner in the French Concession, or dance the night away in 808, or take spontaneous day trips to a neighboring water town. The magic of the group only existed in this place and moment in time.

What scared Farrah the most was not leaving Shanghai; it was the possibility they'd forget what FEA meant to them. For a year, maybe two or three, they'd reminisce and stay in touch, but what would happen after five years, ten years? Shanghai would be just another memory, relegated to the sandbox of time.

Her cabdriver, who'd been busy cursing his future son-in-law on the phone, hung up. He got into the driver's seat and turned on the engine, a clear signal it was time to leave.

Panic and regret washed over Farrah. She'd resisted going to Blake's room to say goodbye. She had no reason to. They didn't stay friends after their breakup, but it felt wrong to leave without seeing him one last time. She didn't need to speak to him; she just wanted to see him. To remind herself that, despite how it ended, what they had was real.

Tears prickled Farrah's eyes. She sniffled and wiped them away with the back of her hand. "Sorry. I'm a mess."

Olivia wasn't paying attention. She stared over Farrah's shoulder with a strange expression on her face.

Farrah turned. Her heart burst out of her chest when she saw Blake standing there. She may as well have conjured him with her thoughts. Dressed in a warm-up suit with earbuds embedded in his ears, he was clearly en route to the gym.

They stared at each other, both at a loss for words.

Farrah couldn't breathe. She'd dreamed about him last night, a dream so vivid she could've sworn it was real. She even woke up to what she thought was his signature crisp, citrusy scent lingering in her sheets. Sometimes, her wild imagination sucked.

Olivia cleared her throat. "I'm saying, 'See you later,' since this isn't goodbye." She squeezed Farrah tight and whispered, "Do what you need to do."

"I love you so much." Olivia had been her confidante, partner-in-crime, and the best friend she could've asked for in Shanghai. Farrah would never forget that.

Olivia looked sadder than Farrah had ever seen her. "I love you too."

Their hug lingered for a few more moments until Olivia released her. She flicked her gaze to Blake before disappearing into the lobby.

Farrah took a deep breath and turned around again. Blake was still standing there, but he'd taken his earbuds out. His jaw tensed. He closed the distance between them and opened his arms without a word.

That one simple gesture caused Farrah to forget everything, from the impatient cabdriver to the way Blake broke her heart to all the nights she'd spent crying over him. Instead, she acted on instinct and went into his arms, pressing her cheek so tight against his chest she heard his heart beat.

His strong arms enveloped her in a familiar embrace. Farrah squeezed her eyes shut and tried to savor every millisecond, knowing each one could be the last.

They weren't friends. They weren't enemies, either. Whatever they were, this felt like a proper goodbye. For better or worse, Shanghai wouldn't have been the same without him.

"Have a safe flight." The deep rumble of Blake's voice startled her from her trance.

Farrah allowed herself one more second before pulling out of Blake's grasp. His hands dropped to his sides.

"Thanks." Farrah held back a fresh wave of tears. *Not now. Not yet.*

"I guess this is goodbye."

"Yes." Her voice came out hoarser than she would've liked. She cleared her throat. "I guess it is."

Blake looked down. His Adam's apple bobbed. "Farrah, I—"

That slight hesitation caused her heart to gallop like a racehorse upon hearing the starting pistol.

"I—" Blake's jaw clenched. "Goodbye."

Farrah deflated. What did she expect? That he was doing to drop to his knees and say how much he loved her and what a huge mistake he'd made? Life wasn't a book or a movie. It was silly to think otherwise.

She climbed into the cab, unable to look at Blake any longer. She was about to close the door when he spoke again.

"Do you hate me?"

Her head jerked up in surprise. Blake's jaw remained tense as he waited for her response.

Did she hate him? She had reason to. He broke her heart, made her believe they'd be together forever when she was just another notch in his belt, and ruined her last few months in Shanghai. At the same time...

"No."

His eyes flared with surprise. "No?"

"No."

Blake had caused her more pain than she could've imagined, but he'd also made her happier than she'd thought possible. He confirmed True Love did exist, even if it was unrequited, and that made all the heartbreak worthwhile.

One day Farrah would find someone who'd make what she

had with Blake pale in comparison, and maybe then she'd forget about the blue-eyed boy in front of her. But Blake would always be her first love, and for that, she could never hate him, no matter how much she wanted to.

"I'm sorry." Blake's stony expression cracked. His eyes shone with regret, sadness, and something Farrah couldn't identify. "For everything."

"I know."

They stared at each other for the last time. The air between them was heavy with broken promises and unspoken words, but their time had run out. Not everyone gets a happy ending, and not all loose ends get tied up in real life. The only things they could take with them were the memories.

"Do they actually work for you?"

"Excuse me?"

"Your cheesy pickup lines. Do they actually work for you?"

"Thank you for trusting me."

"I think you drive me crazier than any person ought to. And I think I might die if I can't be with you."

Farrah smiled a sad smile. It had been good while it lasted. "Goodbye."

She closed the cab door and settled into her seat. She kept her eyes forward as the driver pulled out of the courtyard.

They didn't make it to the main street before the skies opened up and droplets of water spattered against the windows like crystal tears.

Farrah leaned her head against the glass. She could just make out the buildings that defined Shanghai's skyline through the rain: the Pearl Tower, the Jin Mao Tower, the World Financial Tower.

It had been a morning of heart-wrenching farewells, but now she had to say the hardest goodbyes of all: to Shanghai and to the person she was here, in this place and time, knowing she'd never be this way again.

Goodbye, Shanghai. Until we meet again.

CHAPTER 38

THE CAB PEELED OUT OF THE COURTYARD, TAKING with it the tattered remains of Blake's heart.

His jaw clenched so tight, he thought his teeth would crack. It took all his willpower not to fall to his knees in front of Farrah and beg her forgiveness. The hug was bad enough—he shouldn't have done it, but what choice did he have? He couldn't let her leave Shanghai without…something.

Blake wished he could take back everything that had happened since winter break. He wished he could give Farrah promises of future visits and emails and phone calls, of more tangible ways to stay connected beyond shared memories and regrets. He couldn't, so he gave her the only thing in his power to give: apologies and a last embrace.

Blake ducked his head, plugged in his earbuds, and resumed his walk to the gym. The farther he walked from the dorm, the easier it was to tuck the past year's memories in a safe drawer near his heart. He didn't have the luxury of dwelling on the past. He had a family and an ex(?)-girlfriend he needed to face in less than forty-eight hours. He had a baby on the way and a lot of shit he needed to figure out. But the memories would always be there for him to draw upon when he needed them.

The last image—that of Farrah's face right before she left—slipped inside, and Blake closed the drawer with a firm push.

It broke his heart, but he couldn't deny it any longer.

This chapter of their lives was over.

What happens when Blake and Farrah run into each other again? Read *If the Sun Never Sets* for the conclusion to their sweeping romance.

BONUS: Read the Macau bar scene from (a very jealous) Blake's POV: anahuang.com/bonus-scenes

Continue on for a sneak peek at the next If Love installment

CHAPTER 1

THIS WAS IT. THE MOMENT SHE'D WAITED THREE years for.

Twenty-five-year-old Farrah Lin smoothed a hand over her skirt as she walked toward her manager's office. Sweat dampened her underarms—thank god she'd worn black today. Sweat stains were the last thing she needed during a promotion meeting.

"Nice top." Matt fell into step with Farrah, *GQ*-ready in a black Helmut Lang blazer and Diesel jeans with a smirk pasted on his handsome face.

Farrah flashed a tight smile. "Thanks."

Like Farrah, Matt worked as a design associate at Kelly Burke Interiors. Unlike Farrah, he'd bypassed the junior grunt years and sailed straight into a midlevel role. All thanks to his godmother, Kelly Burke herself.

Farrah wouldn't mind so much if Matt worked hard. He had talent, but he treated his job like it was a hobby he could pick up whenever boredom hit. Given the size of his trust fund, it was possible his job *was* a hobby.

Case in point: KBI had a *one-hour lunch break* rule, which

Matt obliterated by skipping out for two or more hours in the afternoon on a regular basis. No one said anything, because he was Kelly's best friend's son and the apple of their boss's eye, but his blatant disregard for the rules infuriated Farrah.

Then again, part of growing up was knowing when to keep your mouth shut. So she did.

They reached their supervisor's office. Farrah knocked and held her breath, both out of nerves and in an attempt not to inhale Matt's overwhelming cologne. The man smelled like an ` store on steroids.

"Come in." The thick oak door muffled Jane Sanchez's summons.

Farrah opened the door, and Jane gestured to the two brass-framed, ivory leather chairs across the desk from her. "Take a seat."

As Kelly's right-hand woman, Jane ran a tight ship. She oversaw the nuts and bolts of all projects, managed client relationships and the firm's twelve employees, and brought donuts to the office every Friday to celebrate that week's wins. As far as managers went, she was great.

Nevertheless, Farrah's sweat intensified. Nothing wracked her nerves like a Friday afternoon meeting with a higher-up.

"First, I want to thank both of you for how hard you worked on the Zinterhofer project. It was a tough one, and we all had to pull long hours to complete it on time. But I'm pleased to say Z Hotels is *thrilled* with the outcome." Jane beamed.

Farrah and Matt smiled back. For the past ten months, they'd worked nonstop on the Z Hotels flagship property overlooking Central Park. Landon Zinterhofer, heir to the Z luxury hotel empire, had taken over the brand's mid-Atlantic portfolio last year. His first order of business: modernizing the NYC outpost and broadening its appeal to wealthy young travelers instead of just the Old Guard of high society.

KBI rarely assigned two associates to a project—not when Kelly was the principal designer—but Z Hotels was their biggest client.

"That's great!" Farrah's skin tingled with pride. She may not have led the project, but she'd put a ton of time, sweat, and creative energy into it. Redesigning an entire hotel—including 253 rooms and dozens of public spaces—in ten months was no cakewalk.

Good thing Farrah thrived on challenges. Besides, Z Hotels looked fantastic on her résumé, and the project was a straight shot to a senior associate position at KBI, five years ahead of schedule.

Well, almost a straight shot.

"However, we all know why we're here." Jane's eyes turned serious behind her red-framed glasses. "Last year, I mentioned one of you will be promoted to senior associate pending exemplary performance on the Z Hotels project. Even though senior associates usually have at least eight years of experience, Kelly and I agreed you're both talented enough to take on the increased responsibilities, and we'd much rather promote internally than hire externally. Z Hotels was your test."

Farrah resisted the urge to grip her necklace. Instead, she clamped down on her chair's armrests until her knuckles turned white. Beside her, Matt slouched in his chair, dripping confidence.

"You both did an excellent job and impressed us with your diligence, creativity, and commitment. I wish we could promote both of you, but we're a small firm and we don't have the capability right now."

Get on with it already. Farrah appreciated the praise, but she was going to pass out if Jane didn't get to the point soon.

"That being said, I want to congratulate—"

Oh my god, this is it. Farrah was finally going to get what she'd been working so hard for these past few years. She was going to be—

"Matt. You're the newest senior design associate at Kelly Burke Interiors. Congratulations." Jane adjusted her glasses, sounding unenthused.

A senior associate at the tender young age of—what?

Ice water replaced the blood in Farrah's veins. She must've heard wrong.

There was no way Matt—who couldn't keep the names of their vendors straight and who complained that reading blueprints gave him a "headache"—got promoted over Farrah.

No freaking way.

"Wow, thanks so much." Matt grinned, not appearing at all surprised by the news. "This is such an honor."

Jane smiled tersely. "It was Kelly's decision. Matt, can you give me and Farrah some privacy? I need to speak to her alone."

"Of course." Matt patted Farrah's shoulder on the way out. "Better luck next time." He oozed condescension.

Farrah flip-flopped between the urge to throw up and the desire to clock Matt in the face.

No. You are not a violent person. Take a deep breath. In one, two, three. Out one—aaaargh!

Jane examined Farrah with a worried frown. "How are you feeling?"

How do you think I'm feeling? Farrah bit back her caustic reply and forced a smile instead. "I'm fine. I'm happy for Matt."

Her manager sighed. "Farrah, you and I both know you're supremely talented. That's why we promoted you to a midlevel role so quickly after you joined the firm. You did exceptional work on the Z Hotels project. *Exceptional.*" She shook her head. "Please do not take this as a negative reflection of your work or your role here at KBI. You're a valued member of the team."

"But not valued enough to receive the promotion."

Jane hesitated. "The final decision wasn't mine to make."

"I know. It was Kelly's." Farrah met the other woman's gaze. "Tell me the truth. Did the fact that Matt is Kelly's godson play a role in her decision?"

Jane didn't answer, but the look on her face said it all.

Disappointment snaked through Farrah. She'd idolized Kelly since she was a teenager and had been over the moon about interning at KBI after she won the National Interior Design Association's student competition in college. Sure, Kelly as a person was more aloof, competitive, and demanding than she'd expected—not exactly mentor material—but Kelly was also one of the top interior designers in America. She *had* to be demanding.

But Farrah thought Kelly valued talent. Hard work. Meritocracy. It was one thing for her to push up Matt's promotion to a midlevel role. There were no limits on those. It was another for Kelly to promote Matt over someone who'd given the company everything she had these past three years.

Matt hadn't given a shit about the Z Hotels project. He'd seen it as an opportunity to schmooze with a hotel heir and add a line to his résumé without doing any of the hard work. Farrah was the one who'd burned the midnight oil every night, scrambling to pull things together. She was the one who'd spent hours on the phone with contractors, smoothing over issues and misunderstandings. She was the one who'd ensured they delivered great results on time, even if Kelly received all the glory.

Farrah didn't think she was entitled to a promotion, but dammit, she'd *earned* it.

"There'll be another promotion opportunity in two years," Jane said. "Be patient. Your time will come. I promise."

Maybe that was true, but Farrah knew she'd never win in a game where nepotism ruled. Still, she wasn't a risk-taker by nature, which was why the next words out of her mouth surprised her as much as they did the woman sitting across from her.

"I quit."

CHAPTER 2

"THIS PLACE IS SICK." BLAKE RYAN TOOK IN THE MATTE hardwood floors, high ceilings, and wall of windows offering spectacular views of the Hudson River and city skyline. "Thanks for hooking me up."

"Anytime. Glad to have you in the city for good." His oldest and best friend, Landon Zinterhofer, clapped him on the back. "Besides, I'm not the one who paid for it."

Blake laughed. His new two-bedroom waterfront West Village condo cost an arm and a leg, but it was worth it. He'd been flitting around the world for too long, never staying in a city for more than a few months at a time. It'd been fun at first, but now he craved stability, and there was no place he'd rather settle down than in one of his favorite cities in the world: New York.

"How'd the hotel turn out?" he asked.

Landon had fought his mother tooth and nail on the revamping of her precious New York flagship hotel, but he'd worn her down and spent the past year running around like a crazy person. Between his project and Blake's constant travels, this was the first time they'd seen each other face-to-face in half a year.

290 | ANA HUANG

"Great." Landon raked a hand through his black hair. "We got fantastic press and the new interiors are amazing. Even better than I'd imagined. I could refer you. The design firm did a top-notch job."

"The bar design is set," Blake reminded his friend. Besides buying his apartment and ending his nomadic lifestyle, he had another reason for coming to New York: Manhattan was getting its very own Legends.

Since Blake's original Legends sports bar took off in Austin four years ago, he'd expanded the brand into a renowned international chain at a breakneck pace. From London to LA, Legends was the place to go on game days. Even on nongame days, it buzzed with activity, thanks to its bar Olympics, theme and trivia nights, and celebrity guest bartenders. It was a rite of passage for NFL, NBA, and MLB players to do at least one stint behind the bar of their local Legends. Blake had even bought back Landon's share of the company last year.

They'd been equal partners, and the Zinterhofer name and connections in the hospitality industry had played a role in Legends' rapid ascent to the top, but Landon had given Blake the startup capital as a friend helping a friend. The more Landon became enmeshed in his mother's business, the less time he had for Legends, so splitting as business partners had been a mutually beneficial decision.

Yes, the Legends empire was alive and well, but Blake's vision for the New York branch wasn't just a regular ol' sports bar. It was going to be different. Elevated. And he couldn't wait to unveil it to the world this October.

T-minus six months.

Blake was successful enough now to have a team that dealt with the details and grunt work he'd shouldered in the early years, but he liked to be present and oversee things before any grand opening.

New York was going to the biggest opening in Legends history, and he sure as hell was going to be here every step of the way.

"I'm not talking about the bar." Landon opened the fridge and handed Blake a beer like he was in his own apartment. He'd connected Blake with the seller—a famous fashion designer who'd moved to the South of France after tiring of city life—so Blake couldn't complain too much. "I'm talking about this apartment."

"What's wrong with the apartment?"

"Nothing. The apartment is great. The decor sucks."

Blake cracked open his beer with a frown. "Give me a break. I bought this place a week ago."

Landon raised a skeptical brow. "So you're planning to decorate it all by yourself?"

Blake grimaced. While he appreciated a nice home, he had no desire, patience, or time to tackle a design project. Besides, you don't *need* anything other than a couch, coffee table, and TV in your living room. Right?

"Bro, let me set you up with the interior designers I used for the hotel. They do residential work too. There was one who was particularly good, and she's much nicer than the other two."

An ache spread through Blake's chest at the words *interior designers*. It was sad, how the slightest thing could still remind him of her after half a decade.

Blake wondered how she was doing. They weren't friends on social media, and her accounts were private, but he managed to squeeze an update out of Sammy every now and then. Last he heard, she was living in New York.

His stomach did a dumb little flip when he realized they were within fifteen miles of each other. He hadn't reached out to Farrah after he ended things with Cleo—partly because he'd been in such a dark place the first few years and partly because he didn't think he deserved her forgiveness or sympathy.

But now that they were in the same city...

Blake's mouth dried. He shouldn't. He didn't want to barge in and upend her life after five years, but he missed her so damn much. It was selfish, but he wanted to see her again. Maybe, after all the time that had passed, she didn't hate him as much.

"Blake?" Landon prompted. "What do you think about hiring a designer?"

"Fine." Blake was too flustered by memories of warm chocolate eyes and golden skin to argue with Landon. "I'll hire a damn designer."

Note to self: Text Sammy and get Farrah's number.

"Excellent." Landon grinned. "I'll set up a meeting. They'll have this place feeling like home in no time."

Home.

It'd been so long since Blake had a home, he'd forgotten what it felt like. He didn't visit Austin enough for it to count.

After they finished their beers, he and Landon moseyed over to the balcony to watch the sunset with fresh drinks in hand. The proud lines and towering heights of New York City beckoned in the distance—the grays and browns of hundreds of buildings softened by the soft glow of sunset, the lights in the windows twinkling like tiny beacons of hope, and the sharp, iconic spire of the Empire State Building piercing the sky with an arrogance that was unapologetically New York.

Blake soaked in the sight while another pang wrung his heart. Manhattan's forest of skyscrapers, pulsing energy, and glittering lights reminded him of another city he loved long ago and far away.

Acknowledgments

This book has been, literally, ten years in the making. I wrote the first draft when I was nineteen, fresh off my study abroad program in China. Although the characters and events in *If We Ever Meet Again* are fictional, they are loosely inspired by the many amazing people I met and the adventures I had in Shanghai.

It's been a long journey to rewrite the story in a way that captures the emotions of falling in love abroad for the first time, and I want to thank everyone who's made crossing the finish line possible:

My beta readers Jennifer, Lasairiona, Georgina, Kristina, and Anca for whipping the manuscript into shape.

My editor April Jones and proofreader Krista Burdine, for your feedback and attention to detail.

To all the bloggers and reviewers who helped with social media promotion and posted reviews—you are incredible.

And, of course, to all my readers for your endless support and enthusiasm. This book is for you.

xo, Ana

Keep in Touch with

Ana Huang

Reader Group: facebook.com/groups/anastwistedsquad
Website: anahuang.com
BookBub: bookbub.com/profile/ana-huang
Instagram: instagram.com/authoranahuang
TikTok: tiktok.com/@authoranahuang
Goodreads: goodreads.com/authoranahuang

About the Author

Ana Huang is a #1 *New York Times, Sunday Times, Wall Street Journal, USA Today,* and #1 Amazon bestselling author. Best known for her Twisted series, she writes New Adult and contemporary romance with deliciously alpha heroes, strong heroines, and plenty of steam, angst, and swoon.

Her books have been translated in over two dozen languages and featured in outlets such as NPR, *Cosmopolitan, Financial Times,* and *Glamour UK.*

A self-professed travel enthusiast, she loves incorporating beautiful destinations into her stories and will never say no to a good chai latte.

Also by Ana Huang

KINGS OF SIN SERIES
A SERIES OF INTERCONNECTED STANDALONES

King of Wrath

King of Pride

King of Greed

King of Sloth

TWISTED SERIES
A SERIES OF INTERCONNECTED STANDALONES

Twisted Love

Twisted Games

Twisted Hate

Twisted Lies

IF LOVE SERIES

If We Ever Meet Again **(DUET BOOK 1)**

If the Sun Never Sets **(DUET BOOK 2)**

If Love Had a Price **(STANDALONE)**

If We Were Perfect **(STANDALONE)**